the silence before

a savannah shadows psychological thriller
book two

L.T. Ryan

with
Laura Chase

LIQUID MIND MEDIA

savannah shadows series

Echoes of Guilt
The Silence Before
Dead Air

chapter
one

BY MID-MARCH, Savannah was already shedding winter's cool embrace for a tentative warmth that hinted at the sultry days ahead. The breeze carried the faint perfume of early-blooming jasmine, mingling with the earthy scent of brick-lined streets still damp from last night's rain. Fiona Stevens stepped into the newsroom of The Savannah Chronicle, her heels clicking on the scuffed linoleum.

The Chronicle was a relic of Savannah's past, steeped in the charm and scandal of its genteel society. Its glossy front page often featured vibrant photographs of garden parties, debutante balls, and ribbon cuttings, with headlines hinting at social intrigue just scandalous enough to sell papers but polite enough not to offend its upper-crust readership.

Fiona had grown weary of covering stories about who wore what to the Azalea Gala or whose feud had erupted during a garden club luncheon. She craved meatier stories, the kind that unearthed secrets and peeled back the layers of Savannah's polished veneer. But at the Chronicle, the priority was keeping readers entertained with gossip and fluff pieces. It paid the bills, she reminded herself, even if it didn't nourish her ambitions.

She glanced at the clock: 9:15 a.m. Just enough time for coffee before her meeting with Jacobs.

"Stevens," Denise quipped from her cubicle, her head popping up like a meerkat's. The features writer held a mug with a faded *I'd Rather Be at Tybee* slogan and a pen tucked behind one ear. "On a mission, I see."

"Mission's an understatement," Fiona replied, tugging at her blazer to smooth the wrinkles from her walk. "Jacobs is going to need convincing, and I'm ready."

"Ah, the famous Jacobs' gauntlet. What's the pitch this time?"

Fiona hesitated. Sharing her idea now felt like bad luck. "You'll hear soon enough," she said with a grin. "Assuming I survive."

Denise laughed, leaning back as Fiona continued toward the break room. The coffee pot sat on the hallway counter, predictably empty. She sighed, abandoning caffeine and instead bracing herself for what she hoped would be a productive morning. As much as she loved pitching stories, the stakes felt higher today. This wasn't just another society profile or feature on Savannah's latest garden craze. This was her chance to elevate her work beyond the Chronicle's usual fare.

Jacobs' office held the faint scent of tobacco and leather, mixing with the sharper notes of aftershave and cheap cologne. Fiona knocked twice on the half-open door and waited.

Jacobs didn't look up from his desk when he said, "Come in, Stevens."

She entered, clutching her leather-bound notebook. "Good morning, Jacobs."

"Whether it's good depends on what you've got for me." He whipped the glasses off his nose, his weathered face betraying years of missed deadlines and red-inked documents. "What's this earth-shattering idea you're so eager about?"

Fiona crossed the room and placed her notebook on his desk, flipping it open to her carefully refined notes. "The Savannah Tour of Homes and Gardens," she began, watching his expression. "It's next month, and Dolores Bates is participating. I want to do a feature on her estate."

Jacobs raised an eyebrow. "The same Bates family whose serial killer son was murdered last year?"

"He was framed for those crimes, but yes. And that's exactly why this could work. The estate has a fascinating history—centuries of intrigue, old Savannah money, and connections to the Wesley fortune. Plus, it'll draw attention to the Tour itself, which hasn't had great press recently."

Jacobs leaned back, rubbing his chin. "Dolores isn't exactly known for her charm. How are you planning to convince her to talk? Or are you hoping for one of those 'exclusive exposés' everyone's obsessed with?"

"Neither. I plan to pitch it as a profile." Fiona allowed herself a small smile when Jacobs' eyebrows rose. "It's not about prying into her personal life—at least not initially. The goal is to let her control the narrative, focus on her house's grandeur. Once she's comfortable, we might dig deeper."

Jacobs snorted. "You're not just dealing with a guarded socialite. Mrs. Bates is outright hostile."

"If I position this as an opportunity to highlight her estate's history, to frame her as a cornerstone of Savannah's elite, I think she'll bite."

Jacobs tapped his pen on the desk, fixing his gaze on her. "This is risky. If she shuts you out, it's dead in the water."

"But if it works, it'll sell papers. People love glimpses behind the curtain of high society. And if I can frame Mrs. Bates as more than just the tragic widow or the woman whose family legacy has been tainted ... it could be a game-changer."

"This still feels like a long shot."

"Let me sweeten the deal. My sister is on a first-name basis with Dolores."

"Oh, that's right. The sister who defended her serial killer son."

Fiona deadpanned. "For a news editor, you sure don't pay attention to the news. I told you; he was falsely accused."

Jacobs waved dismissively. "So what? You think your sister will secure this story for you?"

"I wouldn't go that far. But worst case, if Dolores shuts me out, Claire might pull a few strings to at least get me in the door."

"Ah, nepotism. Journalism's old reliable."

"It's not nepotism if it gets the story."

Jacobs let out a long breath, nodding slowly. "Fine. Go for it. But don't waste time if she won't play ball. The second she shuts you down, move on."

Fiona's shoulders relaxed. "Thank you. I won't let you down."

"Make sure you don't," Jacobs said, already returning to his stack of proofs. "And Stevens? Get a fresh angle. Don't recycle last year's fluff about the Tour."

Back at her desk, Fiona felt the first pangs of nerves. The Savannah Tour of Homes and Gardens was a springtime staple, drawing locals and tourists alike to the grand antebellum houses lining the historic district. The Bates estate, a sprawling mansion with pristine white columns and lush gardens, was this year's crown jewel.

It was also a place steeped in shadows—rumors of affairs, a mysterious death, and the tangled legacy of family fortune. Fiona had no doubt Mrs. Bates would be challenging, but the thought of peeling back the layers of that carefully curated facade made her pulse quicken.

Denise appeared at her cubicle's edge, holding a bag of bagels. "You look like you just scaled Everest."

"He signed off," Fiona replied with a smile. "Now the real work begins."

"Well, enjoy your climb. Want a bagel?"

Fiona laughed, reaching for one. "Thanks. I'll need all the carbs I can get for this."

As Denise returned to her desk, Fiona opened her laptop and began drafting her email to Mrs. Bates. Her fingers hovered over the keys before she typed:

Dear Mrs. Bates,

My name is Fiona Stevens, and I'm a journalist with the Savannah Chronicle.

She paused, her mind drifting to stories whispered over coffee and cocktails—about the missing woman, the almost-divorce, the whispers that Mrs. Bates' temper concealed more than just disdain for the press.

Fiona refocused on her task. First, she had to get Mrs. Bates to agree. Then she'd see where the story led.

As the newsroom's hum faded into the background, Fiona felt a flicker of excitement. If this story turned out as she imagined, it would be the kind of piece that defined careers.

chapter
two

THE CAFÉ on Forsyth Park was already filling with its midday crowd when Fiona arrived. She spotted Claire sitting at a small table near the window, her hair tugged into a practical ponytail, a steaming cup of tea in her hands.

Fiona slid into the chair across from her sister, placing her bag on the floor. "Thanks for meeting me. I figured I'd need backup."

Claire smirked, her eyes glinting with amusement. "Backup for lunch? Or for whatever you've gotten yourself into now?"

"Both," Fiona admitted with a grin. She flagged down a server and ordered an iced coffee and chicken wrap before turning back to Claire. "I pitched a new article to Jacobs today."

"Let me guess. Another piece about Savannah's most eligible bachelors or the latest rooftop bar trend?"

"Not even close." Fiona leaned forward, excitement in her voice. "It's a feature on Dolores Bates and her estate, tied to the Savannah Tour of Homes and Gardens."

Claire's reaction was immediate—a sharp intake of breath followed by a wary shake of her head. "Are you serious?"

"Completely. Her estate is a centerpiece of the Tour this year. It's the perfect opportunity to delve into the history of the house—and maybe even her family." Fiona toyed with her napkin. "I think she might actually agree to it."

"Agree to what? You interrogating her in print?" Claire's tone was skeptical, with an undercurrent of concern. "You realize she's notoriously private, right? And after everything she's been through ..."

"Okay, fine," Fiona said quickly, pulling her laptop from her bag. "Maybe it's a longshot, but I've already drafted an email to her. I figured it was worth a try."

Claire stared at her sister, incredulous. "How did you even get an email address for Dolores Bates?"

"It's listed on the website for the Tour tickets." Fiona spun the laptop to face Claire. "Look, it's straightforward and professional. No pressure. Just an invitation to tell her story on her terms."

Claire squinted at the screen. "'Dear Mrs. Bates ... highlight your estate ... celebrate your contributions ...' This reads fine if she actually uses email. Which she doesn't."

Fiona frowned. "How can you know that?"

"I only worked with her during the few months I put together Anthony's appeal. She only ever called me. And because she's Dolores Bates," Claire said, as if that explained everything. "Even if she did use email, do you think she'd monitor a random address tied to a public website? It's probably managed by some assistant—or just sitting in an inbox no one checks."

Fiona deflated slightly. "Well, it's better than nothing."

Claire sighed, softening. "I'll make a call on your behalf. It's been a while since we spoke, but maybe she'll still pick up the phone for me."

Fiona's eyes lit up. "You'd do that for me?"

"Of course." Claire's expression softened. "You're my sister. And if you're determined to take on Dolores Bates, you'll need all the help you can get."

Fiona leaned on her elbows. "What have you been up to since the Bates' case? Still taking time to figure things out?"

"I guess you could say that. I've been—" Claire paused, her tea midway to her lips. "Selective about the cases I take. It's not like before, where I'd take anything that came my way."

"That makes sense. After what happened with Anthony, I wouldn't blame you for being cautious."

Claire set her cup down, her fingers tracing the rim. "It's not just caution. It's—" She paused again, searching for words. "I want to make sure I'm doing something meaningful. Something I can handle. I don't want to dive into something overwhelming and end up right back where I was."

Fiona nodded, understanding. The weight of Anthony Bates' case had left its mark on her sister, both professionally and personally. His death after his release from prison, the truth about the real culprit. All of it was enough to haunt anyone.

"Detective Lawson keeps asking me to come work with her," Claire added, breaking Fiona's train of thought.

Fiona's eyebrows shot up. "That's big. Are you considering it?"

"Maybe?" Claire sighed, uncertainty in her voice. "She means well, but working with her would mean diving into the kind of cases I'm trying to avoid. She keeps saying I'd bring something new to the team, but I don't know if I'm ready."

"You'd be great," Fiona said earnestly, smiling as the waitress set her lunch before her. "But if it's not what you want, don't let anyone pressure you."

Claire offered a small smile as Fiona took a bite of her wrap. "Thanks. For now, I'm happy taking things one step at a time. The world of high-stakes legal drama can survive without me for a while."

Fiona chuckled, but her mind was spinning with possibilities. If Claire still had connections to Detective Lawson, that might come in handy—especially if Dolores Bates proved as difficult as everyone warned.

"Aren't you going to order something?" Fiona asked.

Claire shook her head. "I'm good with just tea for now."

Fiona shrugged, spearing the last piece of chicken from her wrap. "Any big plans this weekend? Or are you still pretending to be a hermit?"

Claire smirked, setting her teacup down with a delicate clink. "I'm not pretending to be anything. But I was thinking about heading to Tybee for a week. Maybe rent a kayak, read a book by the water. Decompress."

"Tybee is so close. It's almost like why bother leaving? What about that road trip we talked about? The one to Shenandoah?"

"I thought you were joking about that."

"No, I wasn't! A cabin in the mountains, some hiking, maybe a wine tour—doesn't that sound perfect?" Fiona leaned forward, a playful glint in her eyes. "You could use the break, and I could use a partner who won't judge me for trying to mix work and relaxation."

Claire raised an eyebrow. "Work? On a vacation?"

"The Shenandoah's got history. There's bound to be a story hiding in one of those old estates or tucked into a quirky art gallery."

"Of course you'd find a way to turn a vacation into research," Claire said, laughing. "But honestly, I'm not up for a grand adventure. After Anthony's case and everything that came with it, I've been trying to keep things ... simple. Staying near Savannah makes that easier."

Fiona's smile softened. "That's fair. You've been through a lot. But don't stay stuck. You deserve to get out there—just maybe not straight into another high-stakes situation."

Claire nodded, contemplative. "I'll admit, the idea of a quiet cabin in the mountains does sound tempting."

"I'll take that as a maybe," Fiona said with mock solemnity, raising her hands. "Whenever you're ready, I'll be here. In the meantime, if you hear anything from your network, especially about Dolores, let me know. I feel like this is my big chance to prove myself. To break out of the Chronicle's fluff mold."

Claire tilted her head, studying her sister. "I get it. Just don't forget —Dolores Bates isn't just some society matriarch. You might be walking into something bigger than you realize."

"Bigger stories sell papers," Fiona said, her grin sharp. "But I'll be careful, I promise."

Claire sighed, affection in her exasperation. "You better be. And don't overthink the email. I'll make the call, and we'll see where it goes. Just ... be ready for the possibility that she might slam the door in your face."

"Or throw me out on the lawn," Fiona added with dramatic flair. "Still, thanks for the help. I owe you one."

"You owe me about ten."

As they gathered their things and headed out, the conversation settled into comfortable silence, and Fiona's mind raced ahead, spinning with possibilities. Dolores Bates might be a fortress, but Fiona had always been good at finding cracks in the walls.

chapter
three

THE RINGTONE jarred Fiona awake from her half-daze, her coffee cooling untouched on her desk. She grabbed her phone, heart leaping at Claire's name.

"Hey," Fiona said, tucking the phone between her ear and shoulder. "What's up?"

"Drop whatever you're doing," Claire said without preamble. "I just got off the phone with Dolores Bates. She agreed to meet with you—but she wants to do it now."

"Now?" Fiona bolted upright, pulse quickening. "Like, right now?"

"Yes. Her exact words were, 'If this woman wants to waste my time, she'd better be punctual.' She waits for no one, Fiona. You're welcome, by the way."

"Claire, I could kiss you!" Fiona grabbed her bag and keys in one motion. "Thank you."

"Save it. Just don't blow this."

Fiona hung up, mind racing as she scrambled to leave her cubicle. Halfway to the door Denise appeared, coffee mug in hand and curiosity etched on her face.

"Where's the fire?"

"I'm meeting Dolores Bates." Fiona tried to keep the tremor from her voice as she checked her phone for directions. "Claire just called—

she got me a last-minute meeting, and apparently Mrs. Bates waits for no one."

Denise's eyebrows shot up. "You're kidding."

"Wish I was," Fiona muttered, slinging her laptop bag over her shoulder. "I don't even have time to prep. I just have to show up and hope I don't blow it."

"Good luck with that." Denise sipped her coffee, more amused than concerned. "What's the angle? Please tell me it's something juicier than flower arrangements and antique armoires."

Fiona paused, glancing back. "It's a feature on her estate for the Tour of Homes and Gardens, but it could become more. Her story, her family ..."

Denise gave her a sly grin. "You and your 'under the surface' missions. Just don't come back in pieces. I've heard rumors about her temper."

"Noted," Fiona said, her nerves tightening. "If I'm not back by tomorrow, send someone to look for my remains."

Denise laughed, waving her off. "Go get your scoop, Stevens. And hey, if she does throw a vase at you, take notes. That's the kind of gossip our readers love."

"Thanks for the vote of confidence," Fiona shot back, but she couldn't help smiling as she hurried out.

The drive to Dolores Bates' estate was a blur, thoughts bouncing between potential talking points and worst-case scenarios. By the time she pulled up to the sprawling mansion, her nerves were taut as piano strings.

The house loomed ahead, its white columns and manicured gardens an ostentatious display of old Savannah wealth. As Fiona stepped from her car, she adjusted her bag and approached the grand entrance. The house was as impressive as she'd imagined, but small details caught her eye—uneven paint on the doorframe and cracks in the brick pathway.

The heavy door opened before Fiona could knock. Dolores Bates stood in the doorway, her presence as commanding as the house itself.

Tall and angular, with silver hair swept into a chignon, her piercing blue eyes pinned Fiona in place.

"You're late," Dolores said, even though Fiona was at least five minutes early.

"Thank you for seeing me on such short notice, Mrs. Bates," Fiona said, stepping forward with a polite smile. "I appreciate the opportunity."

Dolores waved her inside without a smile, turning sharply on her heel. Fiona followed, eyes darting around the grand foyer.

The house was impressive, with its gleaming hardwood floors and antique furnishings. But there were oddities—scratches on the baseboards, a faint crack in one windowpane. And then the personal touches: a framed photo of a younger Dolores at the helm of a sailboat, her face alight with determination, and another of a boy with sandy hair, his grin wide and carefree. Anthony, Fiona guessed. Her chest tightened.

Dolores moved with brisk precision toward a sitting room. Before they could settle, the sound of a vacuum hummed to life down the hall.

"Karen!" Dolores snapped; her voice sharp enough to make Fiona flinch. A moment later, a woman in a crisp cleaning uniform appeared, looking sheepish.

"I'm sorry, ma'am," Karen murmured, clutching the vacuum.

"Not now. We'll finish later."

Karen disappeared, and Dolores turned back to Fiona, expression unreadable. "Where were we?"

"You were about to sit," Fiona offered lightly, hoping to ease the tension. Dolores didn't smile, but she took a seat on the edge of an armchair, back ramrod straight.

Fiona sat across from her, pulling out her notebook. "Thank you again for meeting with me. I wanted to discuss a potential feature for the Savannah Chronicle ahead of the Tour of Homes and Gardens. Your estate is such a centerpiece of the event, and I think our readers would love to know more about its history—and you."

Dolores tilted her head, eyes narrowing. She brushed imaginary dust off her skirt before folding her hands tightly. "There are plenty of other decent homes on the Tour. Why single me out?"

Fiona hesitated, choosing her words carefully. "Your home is one of the most iconic in Savannah. It's a reflection of the city's history, its elegance and resilience. And honestly, people are curious about you."

"I've seen what curiosity does." Dolores' lips pressed into a thin line. "It turns into speculation, gossip."

"That's not my goal," Fiona said. "This isn't about prying into your personal life. It's about celebrating your contributions to Savannah's history and culture. The Tour is a perfect opportunity to showcase that."

Dolores was silent for a long moment, gaze flicking to the window. Outside, garden staff tended to flower beds with mechanical precision. Finally, she turned back.

"And what happens when people ask questions about ... other events?" Her voice was low, almost a whisper.

Fiona swallowed, careful not to meet the woman's sharp gaze too directly. "I'm hoping this piece will refocus the narrative. It's a chance to remind people who you are beyond recent events."

"And you think writing about my home is going to do that?"

"I think your home is a starting point. A way to tell a story about legacy and resilience, not tragedy. And I think people want to see that side of you."

Another interruption came as a housekeeper reappeared with a dust cloth, hesitating at the doorway. Dolores waved her off, irritation flickering across her face.

"Forgive the disruption," Dolores said. "It seems the entire household is in disarray today."

"It's fine," Fiona said, though she couldn't help but notice the nervous energy radiating from Dolores.

As they moved to the next room to discuss scheduling, Dolores began plucking at small imperfections—a vase slightly out of place, a corner of a rug that had folded under.

Fiona followed, taking mental notes. More photos lined the hallway walls—Dolores at various sailing competitions, a framed newspaper clipping about her late husband's business ventures and, tucked almost out of sight, a small painting of Anthony as a child. There was warmth in the images, but distant, memories held at arm's length.

They stopped in a study that smelled of lemon polish. "Let's schedule a formal interview next week," Dolores said, "but I'll need to review your questions beforehand. My lawyer will be in touch with whatever documents you need to sign."

"Of course. And, what's his name?"

"Henry Caldwell."

"Got it. Thank you again, Mrs. Bates. I really think this will be a great opportunity to showcase your home."

Dolores gave a curt nod, gaze drifting to the doorway. "We'll see."

As Karen passed by with a mop, Fiona caught the way Dolores' hands twitched, fingers gripping the back of a chair as if anchoring herself. It struck Fiona that the house, with all its grandeur and imperfections, mirrored its owner—meticulously maintained on the surface, but with cracks hidden just beneath.

chapter
four

THE CALL CAME JUST as Fiona was finishing her notes from the meeting with Dolores Bates. Her phone buzzed across the desk, and she caught it before it tumbled off the edge. The number wasn't familiar, but the area code was local.

"Hello, this is Fiona Stevens," she answered, trying to mask the fatigue in her voice.

"Ms. Stevens, good afternoon," came a deep, smooth voice. "This is Henry Caldwell. I'm Mrs. Bates' attorney."

Fiona straightened in her chair, caught off guard by how pleasant and warm he sounded. She'd imagined someone gruff and world-weary, a lawyer with decades of Savannah's secrets etched into his face. This man sounded younger, more relaxed, as though he had just walked out of an expensive golf lesson.

"Mr. Caldwell," Fiona said, recovering quickly. "Thank you for calling. I assume Mrs. Bates mentioned the article I'm working on?"

"She did," Henry replied. "And while she doesn't exactly love the press, she's agreed to this feature. My job is to ensure all the administrative details are handled and that the interview process stays respectful of her privacy."

"Of course," Fiona said, keeping her tone professional even as her thoughts churned. *Respectful of her privacy?* That had to be the lawyer's way of saying, *I'm here to keep you in line.*

"I was hoping we could meet to go over some preliminary items," Henry continued. "I'll also need to clarify a few things about the article —where it will appear, how you'll be framing it, and so on."

"Absolutely," Fiona said. "I'm free this afternoon, if that works for you."

"Perfect. How about we meet at Cornerstone Coffee on Bull Street? Say, three o'clock?"

Fiona glanced at her watch. That gave her an hour. "Three works. I'll see you there."

Ending the call, she leaned back in her chair, the thrill of a meeting with Henry Caldwell mingling with the nerves fluttering in her stomach. She needed a minute to clear her head before diving into preparation. Standing, she grabbed her water bottle and headed toward the breakroom, but halfway there, someone familiar stepped out of the restroom.

"Hey, Fiona!" The voice belonged to Mia Parker, a reporter from the Chronicle's lifestyle section. She was petite but carried herself with a confidence that made her seem taller, her short curls bouncing with each step.

"Mia," Fiona said, stopping in the hallway. "What's up?"

"I just ran into Denise. She told me you're working on some big feature about Dolores Bates. Is that true?"

Fiona blinked, momentarily caught off guard. Denise's tendency to gossip was no secret, but she hadn't expected word to spread so quickly. "It's still early days. I'm on my way to a meeting with her lawyer to iron out some details."

"Dolores Bates," Mia mused, crossing her arms and leaning against the wall. "Now there's a name that stirs up a mix of awe and suspicion. Half the city thinks she's a misunderstood relic of old Savannah, and the other half thinks she's hiding a dozen skeletons in that mansion of hers."

"I'm not looking to stir up gossip—this is a feature tied to the Tour of Homes and Gardens. It's about the house and the history, not ... whatever skeletons people think are in there."

Mia raised an eyebrow. "Sure. But you wouldn't be you if you didn't find a way to dig a little deeper."

"Guilty," Fiona admitted with a smirk. "But Dolores isn't exactly known for her patience with journalists."

Mia grinned, pushing off the wall. "Well, if anyone can crack her, it's you. Just don't let her chew you up and spit you out in the process. And if you find anything juicy, we're going to lunch, 'cause I want to hear about it."

"Deal," Fiona said, shaking her head as Mia disappeared down the hall.

She filled her water bottle in the breakroom and headed back to her desk. Her mind wandered to the tightrope she'd have to walk with Dolores Bates. If she could get past the walls, the house might reveal more than just history.

Cornerstone Coffee was bustling when Fiona arrived, its cozy interior filled with the hum of conversation and the aroma of freshly brewed espresso. She scanned the room, unsure who she was looking for. She reached for her phone to double-check the time just as a man stood from a corner table and gave her a small wave.

"Ms. Stevens?" he asked, his voice carrying easily over the café noise.

"That's me," Fiona replied, stepping closer. He extended a hand, and she shook it, noting the firm grip and the easy smile that followed. "Call me Fiona."

"Henry Caldwell," he said, motioning to the chair across from him. "Thanks for meeting on short notice."

"Thanks for reaching out. I wasn't sure what to expect, honestly."

"Neither was I," he said with a chuckle, sitting back down. "But here we are."

He was younger than she'd expected, maybe mid-thirties, with thick dark hair that looked like it had just been combed back but was already defying gravity at the edges. His tailored navy blazer and crisp white shirt gave him the polished look of someone who had spent years perfecting the art of first impressions. And then there was the charm—subtle but undeniable—radiating from his easy smile as he stood to greet her.

"Can I get you something? Coffee? Tea?"

"I'm fine, thanks," Fiona said. Setting her notebook on the table, she studied him briefly and feeling just a little off-balance. "I'll admit, you're not what I expected."

Henry raised an eyebrow, his grin amused. "Oh?"

She gestured loosely with her hand. "I figured Mrs. Bates' lawyer would be, well ... older. Maybe a little more intimidating. You know, someone straight out of a legal drama."

Henry laughed, leaning back in his chair. "I'll take that as a compliment. Though you're not wrong—most people expect my father when they hear the name Caldwell. He worked for the Bates family for over three decades. Handled everything for them—estate planning, contracts, even some personal matters. When he retired a few years ago, I took over his practice. Mrs. Bates has been one of my most significant clients since then."

"That's quite the legacy," Fiona said, jotting down a note. "Did you always plan to follow in his footsteps?"

Henry chuckled, leaning back slightly. "Not exactly. Growing up, I swore I'd never go into law. But here we are."

He was disarming, she realized, in a way that made her lower her guard almost instinctively. She chastised herself—he was a lawyer, after all. A professional at making people feel at ease.

Henry gestured to her notebook. "I understand you're focusing on the estate for the article. That's a smart approach. Mrs. Bates is proud of her home, even if she'd never admit it outright."

Fiona tilted her head. "What do you mean?"

Henry hesitated for a fraction of a second. "She's particular about how the house is perceived. She likes it to be seen as a symbol of resilience and tradition, even if—" He shook his head, frowning. "I shouldn't have said that. Forget I mentioned it."

Fiona's pen paused mid-note, her journalist instincts flaring. *Even if what?* She didn't press him, not yet. Instead, she smiled and nodded. "Got it. The house as a symbol. I can work with that."

Henry visibly relaxed, sipping his latte. "Good. Mrs. Bates can be challenging, but she appreciates people who respect the story she wants to tell. As long as you keep things focused on the estate and the Tour, I think she'll be cooperative."

"And if she's not?" Fiona asked lightly, though the question carried more weight than she let on.

Henry smiled wryly. "Then I'll help smooth things over. That's part of the job."

Fiona leaned back, studying him. His friendliness was out of place, considering who he worked for.

"I appreciate that," she said. "It sounds like you have a good relationship with Mrs. Bates."

Henry shrugged. "It's professional. She respected my father, and I think that respect has extended to me, though I'm still earning it."

The way he said that—'earning it'—made Fiona wonder just how difficult Dolores could be behind closed doors.

"What about the rest of the family?" Fiona asked, keeping her tone casual. "Did you ever work with Anthony?"

Henry's expression flickered, just for a moment, before he recovered. "Not directly. By the time I took over, he was ... no longer involved in family matters."

Henry's carefully measured response made Fiona's pulse quicken. " No longer involved" was lawyer-speak for any number of things, but given what she knew about Anthony Bates, it was a glaring understatement. Acquitted of seven murders only to be murdered himself shortly after. It wasn't just messy—it was a scandal that still lingered over the family like a storm cloud.

Instead, she shifted gears, her tone light. "So, what do I need to know to make this process as smooth as possible?"

Henry brightened, grateful for the shift. "I'll send over a confidentiality agreement for you to sign—standard stuff, just to ensure certain aspects of Mrs. Bates' personal life remain private. And if there are specific questions you want to ask, I recommend running them by me first."

"Understood," Fiona said, scribbling it down. "Anything else?"

"Just keep in mind that Mrs. Bates has been through a lot," Henry said, his tone softening. "She doesn't always show it, but you probably noticed."

Fiona nodded, thinking back to Dolores' restless movements during their meeting, the way she'd straightened objects and picked at imaginary dust. "I did."

Henry hesitated again, then smiled. "She's not as intimidating as she seems. At least, not all the time."

Fiona allowed herself a small laugh. "I'll take your word for it."

As they wrapped up, Fiona couldn't shake the feeling that Henry was more than just a gatekeeper to Dolores Bates. He was young, charming, and perhaps a little too willing to let things slip. If she played her cards right, she might be able to coax out the pieces of the story Dolores wouldn't want her to have.

chapter
five

THE BAR Over Yonder was a favorite among the staff at The Savannah Chronicle, tucked into a narrow street just far enough from the tourist traps. Its dark wooden interior and low lighting offered a reprieve from the newsroom's bright fluorescents. The clinking of glasses and hum of conversation filled the space with an easy energy.

Fiona slid into a booth where Denise and Mia were already waiting, a pitcher of margaritas between them. "We started without you," Denise said with a grin, pouring a drink into Fiona's glass before she could protest.

Mia stirred her drink with a cocktail straw. "Long day?"

"Something like that." Fiona dropped her bag onto the seat beside her and took a sip. The sweet, tart flavor hit her tongue, and tequila tingled the back of her throat. "I just met with Dolores Bates' lawyer."

Denise perked up, her dark eyes gleaming with interest. "What's he like? Old and cranky, or boring and buttoned-up?"

"Neither, actually. Henry Caldwell. He's young. And not what I expected at all."

Mia raised an eyebrow. "How young are we talking?"

"Early thirties, maybe? And he's polished. Confident. Charming, even."

"Charming," Denise said, leaning forward with a devilish grin. "Do go on."

Fiona rolled her eyes. "He's a lawyer, Denise. It's literally his job to be charming. But I'll admit, I thought Dolores' lawyer would be this old-school grizzled guy. Turns out, it's his dad who fits that description. Henry took over the practice a few years ago."

Mia exchanged a look with Denise. "So, let me get this straight. You've got this young, attractive lawyer involved, and you're working with Dolores Bates, who's basically Savannah's resident soap opera? Fiona, this isn't just a story for the Chronicle—this is a romance novel waiting to happen."

"Absolutely not. The guy's professional, and I'm not about to mix business with ... whatever it is you're imagining."

Denise waggled her eyebrows. "So, you're saying he's not your type?"

"I'm saying this is work," Fiona replied, her tone firm but amused. "And if I don't stay focused, Dolores Bates will chew me up and spit me out, as everyone keeps telling me."

"Fair point," Mia said, leaning back in her seat. "Still, if he's as charming as you say ..."

"Focus, people." Fiona raised her glass. "This is a story about an estate and a family, not a matchmaking service."

Denise smirked as she poured the last of the margarita pitcher into their glasses. "Sure, sure. A story about an estate. And a family. With a charming lawyer thrown into the mix."

Mia laughed, nudging Fiona. "You can't blame us for wanting to spice things up a little."

Fiona rolled her eyes, taking a sip of her drink. "You two are impossible."

"We're realistic," Denise countered, leaning forward. "But seriously, since you're focusing on Dolores, tell us the goods. What's she like? What's the house like?"

Mia nodded, her eyes sparkling with interest. "Yeah, spill. Is she as intimidating as everyone says?"

Fiona considered the question, swirling her drink. "She's intense. Very controlled, particular. Like she's always a step ahead of you, even if she's not saying much."

"Sounds delightful," Denise said with a smirk. "What about the house? Is it as perfect as it looks in the brochures?"

"Mostly. It's grand, for sure, but there are these little things—like peeling paint on the doorframe, cracks in the brick walkway. Nothing huge, but for a place that's supposed to be flawless, it felt ... off."

"Like a metaphor for her life," Mia quipped, earning a laugh from Denise.

"Maybe," Fiona said. "She seemed uncomfortable, though. Kept fussing over things, straightening vases, picking at imaginary dust. It was like she needed to keep moving."

"So she's controlling and maybe a little unhinged," Denise summarized, leaning back in her seat. "Not shocking, considering her reputation."

Fiona raised an eyebrow. "What reputation?"

"You know, the real story."

Fiona frowned, the teasing tone fading as her curiosity piqued. "What do you mean?"

"You seriously don't know the rumor?"

Fiona shook her head and took a sip of her margarita.

Denise glanced around dramatically, then lowered her voice. "You know. The one about her killing her husband."

Mia straightened in her seat, her interest clearly reignited.

"Oh, come on," Denise said, waving her hand as if it were common knowledge. "Charles Bates. The guy was supposedly having an affair. And then, poof, the mistress disappears, and Charles winds up dead not long after. Suspicious, right?"

Fiona set her glass down. "Where did this even come from?"

"Savannah gossip." Denise grinned, and her eyes gleamed with something sharper. "But there's usually some truth buried in it. They never proved anything, but people still whisper about it, especially when Dolores' name comes up."

Mia leaned forward, curiosity written all over her face. "Wait, who was the woman? The one he was having an affair with?"

Denise's tone dropped conspiratorially. "Sarah Mercer."

Mia folded her arms. "Sarah Mercer ... I feel like I know that name. What happened to her?"

"Like I said. She disappeared without a trace. Some people think Dolores found out about the affair and took care of both of them."

"Or she just had really bad luck."

"Savannah doesn't believe in luck," Denise said, leaning back. "It believes in secrets."

Fiona swirled her drink absently, her mind spinning. She'd heard whispers about Dolores' past, but this was the first time someone had laid it out so plainly. The scandal, the affair, the disappearance—it all felt like a puzzle begging to be solved.

"She didn't seem dangerous when I met her," Fiona said. "Just ... cold."

"Cold and controlling doesn't mean innocent," Denise said, raising her glass. "Here's to uncovering secrets."

Fiona forced a laugh, but the weight of the conversation lingered as she finished her drink. The name Sarah Mercer echoed in her mind, along with the cracks she'd noticed in the facade of Dolores' estate.

"Cheers to that," she said, clinking her glass with Denise's. But as the others moved on to lighter topics, Fiona's thoughts stayed firmly on Dolores, Sarah Mercer, and the story that was quickly becoming much more than she'd bargained for.

chapter
six

THE SAVANNAH PUBLIC Library was a quiet refuge on Saturday mornings, the kind of place where sunlight filtered gently through tall windows and dust motes floated lazily in the air. Rows of worn oak tables sat under high ceilings, their surfaces scarred with decades of use. In the back corner, the newspaper archives were tucked away like a forgotten treasure trove, the shelves stacked with brittle pages and microfilm reels waiting to be rediscovered.

Fiona settled in at one of the tables, her laptop, notebook, and a steaming cup of coffee arranged neatly in front of her. The events of the previous night still echoed in her mind, Denise's words replaying like a nagging melody. *Dolores killed her husband.* It was sensational, almost absurd—but the pieces Denise had mentioned, the affair, the disappearance of Sarah Mercer, Charles Bates' death, they all had weight.

It was enough to keep her awake, and enough to bring her here on a Saturday morning, chasing answers.

The musty scent of old newsprint filled Fiona's nose as she unrolled a microfilm reel and positioned it under the machine. The dim light of the screen glowed softly, illuminating the blocky headlines of decades past. She scrolled carefully, starting with any mention of Dolores Bates.

Her search turned up the usual articles about the Tour of Homes and Gardens, the occasional photo of Dolores at charity events, and clippings that alluded to the Bates family's scandals without delving too deeply. But it was a brief wedding announcement buried in the society pages that made Fiona pause.

Fiona flipped through the pages carefully. Most of the articles were mundane—announcements of charity galas, engagements, and high-society events that had long since faded from memory. But then, she saw it.

A photograph.

She nearly turned the page, expecting yet another stiff, posed portrait of Savannah's elite, but this one stopped her cold.

A younger Dolores Bates, laughing.

It was a candid shot taken on the beach, the sun casting golden streaks through her windblown hair. She looked young, vibrant, bare-foot in the sand with her white dress flowing around her as if caught mid-spin.

She looked carefree.

Fiona swallowed, her stomach twisting with something she couldn't quite place.

This woman—this girl—was not the Dolores Bates the world had whispered about for decades. She wasn't the poised, composed socialite with a reputation carved from scandal and suspicion. She wasn't the cold widow, the calculating matriarch, the woman who carried the weight of rumors like armor.

She was just a girl in love.

A girl who, at least at that moment, looked truly happy.

Fiona forced herself to tear her eyes away and glanced at the article beneath the photo.

Miss Dolores Wesley Wed to Charles Bates.

Fiona leaned closer, reading the details. It was a simple piece, noting that the couple had eloped despite her parents' disapproval. But what caught her attention was Dolores' maiden name.

Wesley.

Fiona sat back, tapping her pen against her notebook. The name tugged at her memory, familiar in a way she couldn't quite place. It wasn't until she jotted it down that the connection clicked. The Wesleys had been one of Savannah's most prominent families, known for their wealth and influence in the early 20th century. Her curiosity flared as she typed the name into her laptop, searching for more information.

The Wesley name appeared almost immediately, dominating the social pages of Savannah's golden era. They had been one of the city's wealthiest families, their fortune rooted in shipping and textiles. Articles painted a picture of opulence: grand parties at their estate, lucrative business ventures, and connections to Savannah's elite.

Dolores herself featured prominently in the coverage. As a young woman, she was described as poised, beautiful, and fiercely intelligent. Her debutante ball was the talk of the town. Her gown had been imported from Paris. There were photos of her attending charity galas with her parents, Thomas and Margaret Wesley, and one particularly striking image of her aboard a sailboat, her face lit with determination.

But Fiona's research took a darker turn when she uncovered a small, somber article about Andrew Wesley, Dolores' younger brother. He had died tragically at the age of thirteen, drowning in the family's private pool. The piece reported the incident as an accident, but Fiona lingered on the details. Andrew had been the heir to the Wesley legacy, the one who would have carried the family name forward. With his death, everything passed to Dolores.

Fiona scribbled notes as she pieced it together: *Wesley fortune— Dolores inherits after brother Andrew drowns at 13.*

From there, the narrative shifted to Charles Bates. Compared to the Wesleys, his background was unremarkable. He had grown up in Savannah, but without the privilege of wealth or connections. His charm and ambition, however, had earned him a place in the city's social circles, where he'd met Dolores.

An article detailing their elopement noted the strong disapproval of her parents. Her parents had been staunchly opposed to the match, a fact that became glaringly apparent as Fiona scanned a gossip-laden article from a 1970s edition of the Savannah Gazette. The headline read: *Wesley Heiress Elopes with Savannah Gambler: High Society Shocked by Secret Wedding.*

Fiona leaned closer, her eyes skimming the melodramatic text. The article practically dripped with scandal, painting Dolores Wesley as a rebellious debutante who had defied her family's wishes to marry Charles Bates, a man described as, "charming, but entirely unsuitable."

"Sources close to the Wesley family," the piece read, *"report that the union was strongly opposed by Mr. and Mrs. Thomas Wesley, who are said to have considered Mr. Bates' reputation as a gambler and social climber incompatible with the values of their distinguished lineage."*

The accompanying grainy photograph showed the newlyweds outside a modest courthouse, their hands clasped as they faced the camera. Charles was striking in a rakish way, his wide grin and slightly disheveled hair giving him the air of someone who knew how to charm his way out of trouble. Dolores, by contrast, looked radiant but defiant, her elegant coat and hat a clear reminder of her pedigree. Her expression seemed to dare the world to question her choice.

The article continued. *"Miss Wesley, the last surviving heir to the Wesley shipping and textiles empire, is said to have married without the knowledge of her family. The couple has declined to comment, though speculation abounds as to the rift this has caused within the Wesley household. Friends of the family suggest that her parents may have threatened to disinherit her, a claim the Wesleys have neither confirmed nor denied."*

Fiona scrawled notes in her notebook, her mind buzzing with the implications. The mention of disinheritance seemed pointed—whether it was a rumor or not, the article made it clear that Dolores had chosen love over loyalty to her family's expectations. But what had that choice cost her?

Another line caught Fiona's eye. *"Though Mr. Bates has yet to establish himself in Savannah's social or business circles, his charm and wit have earned him a reputation among acquaintances as a man of ambition. However, whispers of unpaid debts and frequent visits to card tables have raised questions about his ability to match the stability of his new bride's illustrious heritage."*

Fiona underlined the phrases "unpaid debts" and "card tables." It painted a picture of Charles Bates as a man with scandalous habits—quite at odds with the stoic, duty-bound Wesley family.

The final paragraph of the article was a masterclass in subtle venom. *"As the couple begins their life together, all eyes will be on the young Mrs. Bates to see whether her gamble on love will pay off—or if she will find herself left to clean up her husband's losses."*

Fiona leaned back in her chair, exhaling. The article wasn't just gossip; it was a window into how the world had viewed Dolores from the very start. It added a new dimension to the story she was uncovering —a woman who had inherited everything, only to marry someone who could potentially take it all away.

Could this really have given Dolores a reason to kill Charles? she thought to herself.

A sudden vibration jolted Fiona from her focus. Her phone buzzed on the table, its sound sharp in the library's stillness. She snatched it up quickly, glancing around at the few other patrons before answering in a hushed tone.

"Hello?" she whispered.

"Fiona, it's Henry Caldwell."

Fiona blinked, startled by the interruption. "Hi, Henry. What's up?"

"I wanted to check in about the Tour preparations and your involvement. Have you received the formal invitation yet?"

"No, not yet," Fiona replied, keeping her voice low. "I'm guessing it'll arrive soon?"

"I'll follow up on that," Henry said smoothly. "How's the article coming along? Anything you need from me?"

Fiona hesitated, glancing at the notes scattered across her table. "It's coming together. I'm still in the research phase, but I might have questions as we get closer."

"Great. How about we discuss it over dinner tonight? Say, seven o'clock? We can meet at the Bellwether downtown."

Fiona blinked. Dinner? With Dolores Bates' lawyer? It felt oddly personal. Was this simply efficiency on his part, or was he trying to soften her up somehow? Either way, the flutter of nerves in her chest caught her off guard.

But maybe it was just how Henry operated—charming, disarming, and quietly managing Dolores' interests. Then again, it was an opportunity. A dinner setting might make him more relaxed, less guarded. If she played her cards right, she might coax out details he wouldn't otherwise share.

"That works," she said, keeping her voice even despite the sudden swirl of thoughts. "I'll see you there."

"Looking forward to it," Henry replied before the line disconnected.

Fiona exhaled, setting the phone down and realizing just how long she'd been buried in the archives. A glance at her watch confirmed it—she'd been here all morning.

chapter
seven

FIONA STEPPED INTO THE BELLWETHER, one of Savannah's more understated yet elegant restaurants. Its warm wooden paneling and soft lighting gave it an intimate atmosphere, the kind of place where people could discuss serious matters or lose themselves in meaningless small talk.

Fiona spotted Henry at a table near the window, his jacket draped neatly over the back of his chair. He stood when he saw her, flashing that easy, practiced smile.

"Fiona," he said warmly, gesturing to the chair across from him. "Thanks for coming."

"Of course," she replied, sliding into the seat as he pushed it in for her. "Though I have to admit, I was a little surprised you suggested dinner."

Henry returned to his seat, adjusting his cufflinks. "Fair enough. I guess it's not the usual approach for a lawyer, is it? Scheduling a meal in lieu of sending an endless string of emails?"

"Not exactly," Fiona said with a smirk. "I'm guessing you're not one for efficiency?"

"Oh, I'm efficient," Henry said, grinning as he poured her a glass of wine from the bottle already on the table. "But I've learned that a lot of what I do can feel isolating. Drafting documents, handling estate details —it's important, but not exactly stimulating. So, when I find someone interesting to talk to, I might"—he paused, his grin turning playful —"stretch things out a little."

Fiona laughed lightly, taking the glass he offered. "So you admit it. Some of these meetings could've been emails?"

"Maybe. But where's the fun in that?"

She raised her glass. "Well, here's to your unconventional methods."

He clinked his glass gently against hers. "Cheers."

The conversation began easily, with Henry outlining the practicalities of Dolores' expectations. "She's very particular," he said, leaning back slightly as the waiter brought their first course. "Strict timelines, no invasive questions, and a heavy focus on the estate rather than her personal life."

"You're very good at this whole gatekeeping thing," she said, setting her pen down. "Do you ever get tired of it?"

"Constantly. But clients like Dolores come with challenges—and rewards. She's particular, but she values loyalty."

"She'd have to, with all the things people say about her."

Henry tilted his head but didn't respond immediately, instead choosing to refill their glasses. Fiona watched him closely. He was always careful, deliberate, but there was something else—a hint of weariness, perhaps.

"Your sister was involved in Anthony Bates' appeal. That must've been ... difficult," Henry asked suddenly, shifting the focus.

"Yes, it was. For her, for me ... for everyone." Fiona hesitated, swirling her wine as the memories of those tense months resurfaced. "Claire took a lot of heat for representing him, especially after his acquittal. And I'll be honest, I didn't support her at first."

Henry raised an eyebrow, his expression encouraging her to continue.

"I let public opinion sway me. It was hard to reconcile what people were saying with what Claire believed. She was so sure he deserved a second chance, and I wasn't. It strained our relationship for a while."

"But you worked through it," Henry said, his tone curious rather than judgmental.

"Yeah," Fiona said with a faint smile. "We had to. And honestly, it made us closer in the end. Now we're, I don't know, better equipped to support each other. She's my sounding board for a lot of things."

"That kind of relationship is rare. I envy it, honestly."

Fiona glanced at him, intrigued. "What about you? Any siblings?"

"None," Henry said, his smile faint. "Just me and my parents, though my father wasn't around much. He was consumed by work. Law was everything to him, and I think he assumed it would be for me, too."

"And was it?"

"Not at first. I went to law school because it was expected of me. I hated it, honestly. But somewhere along the way, I realized I was good at it. It's ... practical. Useful. And it's kept me connected to my family, even if it's in a roundabout way."

"What about your mom?" Fiona asked gently. "What'd she do?"

Henry's expression softened, a flicker of something unspoken crossing his face. "She had a hard life. Dad's work always came first, and she had to carry everything else. But she did her best for all of us. She passed a few years ago."

"I'm sorry," Fiona said quietly.

"Thank you," Henry replied, his smile returning, not quite reaching his eyes. "Anyway, enough about me. What about your parents?"

Fiona leaned back, considering the question. "My dad was a lawyer, too. Although he handled asbestos cases. He's retired now. My mom ..." She hesitated, then laughed softly. "Mom is kind of like Dolores in some ways. She was always focused on keeping everything perfect—our home, our image. I think it's exhausting, but she thrives on it."

"That does sound familiar," Henry said, his voice tinged with amusement. "Maybe you and Dolores are destined to cross paths then."

"Destined, huh?" Fiona teased, shaking her head. "Not sure that's the word I'd use."

Henry laughed, lifting his glass to take another sip. Their conversation meandered through lighter topics, from Savannah's quirks to shared gripes about their professions. But as the meal stretched on, Fiona couldn't help noticing the way Henry seemed to relax, especially as the level in his wine glass dropped.

Fiona motioned to the wine bottle, indicating they needed refills, but Henry started to shake his head. "It's Saturday. Relax," she suggested.

Henry hesitated, then relented with a grin. "All right. Twist my arm."

Their conversation flowed easily for a while, but Fiona remained attentive, noticing how Henry's guard began to loosen just a little more. When the topic shifted back to Dolores, she approached it cautiously.

"Can I ask you something about Dolores?"

Henry took a sip of wine, then nodded. "Depends on what it is."

"Her marriage to Charles," Fiona said. "It was ... complicated, wasn't it?"

Henry's smile faltered for a split second before he recovered. "You could say that."

Fiona leaned forward slightly. "There were rumors about their relationship, about finances and... other things. Is there any truth in them?"

Henry hesitated, the wine clearly loosening his tongue, but not enough to make him careless. "All marriages have their challenges. But Dolores and Charles ... their dynamic was unique."

"How so?"

Henry sighed, swirling the last of his wine. "Let's just say the elopement was the beginning of many complications. And there were ... documents later. Divorce agreements, things that would've left Dolores in a difficult position. But I shouldn't—" He stopped abruptly, his eyes widening as if realizing he'd said too much. "Forget I said that."

"I won't repeat it," she said quickly, her voice steady despite her heartbeat skipping. "I promise."

Henry exhaled, his shoulders relaxing. "Thanks. It's just a delicate subject. And she's my biggest client. I can't afford to lose her trust."

"I understand," Fiona said, but her mind was already racing.

Divorce agreements? It was a thread she hadn't even considered pulling before. One she didn't even know existed. The Savannah rumor mill had been notably quiet on that subject.

Henry set his glass down and glanced at her plate. "Done eating?"

Fiona nodded, folding her napkin and placing it on the table. "Yeah, I think I'm good."

He signaled to the waiter, who brought the check promptly. Henry reached for it, but Fiona raised a hand. "At least let me split it."

"No chance. Consider it part of my unconventional lawyering."

"You're making this a habit, aren't you?"

"Only with interesting company," he replied, signing the receipt with a flourish. He slid his jacket on as they rose from the table. "Ready?"

"Sure." Fiona grabbed her bag and followed him to the door. The cool night air was a welcome relief after the cozy warmth of the restaurant.

They flagged a cab to share, and the ride was quiet, both of them seemingly lost in their thoughts. When they reached Fiona's stop, Henry turned to her with a smile. "Thanks for humoring me tonight. It was nice to talk about something other than contracts for a change."

"Likewise," Fiona replied, stepping out of the cab. "Have a good night, Henry."

chapter
eight

FIONA DROPPED her bag onto the couch and sank down beside it, her head buzzing from the wine and her conversation with Henry. Glancing at her phone on the coffee table, her thoughts tumbled over each other, and she needed someone to help her sort through them.

She grabbed the phone, scrolling to Claire's name, and hit call. The line rang twice before her sister picked up.

"Fiona?" Claire's voice was soft but edged with fatigue.

"Hi," Fiona said, sitting up straighter. "Are you busy?"

"It's almost ten," Claire replied dryly. "What do you think?"

"Okay, yeah, but I had to call. I just got back from dinner with Dolores Bates' lawyer, and I think I learned something huge."

There was a beat of silence before Claire spoke again. "You went to dinner with her lawyer?"

"It's not like that. But I have to admit, he's a lot different than I expected—"

"Fiona."

"Right, sorry. Focus. So, we were talking about Dolores and the whole thing with Charles, and he slipped—like, actually slipped—something about a divorce agreement. Apparently, it would've left Dolores in a really bad position." Fiona paused. "Or, at least that's what it sounded like." She paused again. "The way he said it, it definitely didn't sound good."

Claire's voice sharpened. "He told you that?"

"Well, he didn't mean to," Fiona admitted, tucking her legs underneath her on the couch. "He clammed up immediately and begged me not to repeat it."

"I should hope so. That's a pretty big violation of attorney-client confidentiality."

Fiona waved her hand, as if her sister could see her. "I get it. Ethics. Boo on him. But Claire, this is huge. If Charles was trying to leave Dolores, that changes everything we know about their marriage. Maybe the rumors about a mistress are true."

"Fiona," Claire said, her tone careful, "you told me this was supposed to be a feature about the house and the Tour. Maybe something about her resilience after losing her son. Not a deep dive into her personal life."

"But don't you see? I really want it to be more than that. This is my chance to move away from puff pieces and write something that actually matters."

Claire sighed, her voice steady but tinged with frustration. "I get that. I do. But don't you think it's a little disrespectful? The woman just lost her son. She's grieving, even if she doesn't show it the way people expect. Digging into her personal life, especially now—it just feels like bad timing."

Fiona paused, the words hitting her harder than she wanted to admit. "I hadn't thought about it like that," she said softly. "But Claire, it's not about making her look bad. It's about the truth. People have been whispering about her for years—about Charles, about Sarah Mercer. This is my chance to get her story right."

Claire's voice sharpened slightly, though it remained calm. "You might be digging into things you shouldn't. Dolores Bates isn't just another society figure. She's connected, and people have been speculating about her for decades. But nothing ever comes of it."

Fiona bristled, her back stiffening. "This is what I've been trying to do, Claire. Move past the fluff and into real journalism. I thought you'd understand that."

"I do," Claire said evenly. "I'm just saying ... tread lightly. I've been in situations like this, where the story pulls you in deeper than you expected. Sometimes it's not worth the cost. People like Dolores have a way of protecting their secrets."

Fiona opened her mouth to respond but hesitated, letting Claire's words hang in the air. She felt a flicker of hurt at the lack of support, her voice softening as she spoke. "You know, I thought you'd be more excited for me. This is a big opportunity, Claire."

"I didn't mean to sound unsupportive, and I'm sorry if it came across that way. I just ..." She trailed off, and Fiona caught something in her voice—an exhaustion.

Fiona tilted her head, frowning. "You sound tired. Is everything okay?"

There was a long pause on the other end of the line before Claire finally spoke. "I've taken on some pro bono work at the Savannah Art Museum."

Fiona raised an eyebrow. "The museum? That's unexpected. What brought this on?"

"I needed a change. Something that doesn't involve criminal trials or appeals or anything too heavy. They were looking for help with contracts, donor agreements, and legal odds and ends. It felt like a good fit—low pressure, engaging, and a way to stay busy without getting overwhelmed."

"That actually sounds nice," Fiona said, leaning back into the couch. "Fun, even. How's it going so far?"

"It's different," Claire admitted. "There's a lot to catch up on. They've got a backlog of things—neglected donor files, disputes over exhibit pieces, you name it. I've been pulling long hours getting up to speed."

Fiona frowned. "You're supposed to be taking it easy, Claire. You told me you didn't want to overload yourself."

"It's not overload," Claire said, though there was a tired edge to her voice. "It's refreshing. No judges, no courtrooms. Just paperwork, some meetings, and getting to dive into Savannah's history in a way I haven't before."

Fiona softened. "Okay, fair. But don't forget why you took this on— to breathe a little."

"Don't worry. It's not like the museum is throwing scandals at me."

"Yet," Fiona quipped. "Give it time."

"Let's hope it stays quiet," Claire said, a note of warmth in her voice. "I'll admit, though, it's fascinating to see the way art and history intertwine here. There's so much I didn't know about the families who've shaped Savannah."

"I bet," Fiona replied, her curiosity already piqued. "You'll have to give me the full rundown sometime."

"Maybe when I have the energy. For now, I just need to survive the backlog."

"You will. And hey, if anyone can untangle centuries-old Savannah drama, it's you."

"Let's hope I don't have to. But thanks for the vote of confidence."

"Hey, speaking of old Savannah drama, will you come on the Tour through Dolores' house with me?"

"What a segue," Claire said, shaking her head.

Fiona smiled and shrugged her shoulders. "I was waiting for the right opportunity to ask."

"Clearly."

"Well?"

"Sorry, but no," Claire declined.

"Claire, come on. I need someone there who has a good eye for details. Plus, I could really use the moral support."

"You know how I feel about getting involved in things like this. Especially involving Dolores."

"You're already involved," Fiona pointed out. "You're the one who made the call that got me in the door. Now I need you to walk through the door with me."

"That's not the same thing," she countered.

"Please, Claire," Fiona said, her tone imploring. "Just this once. I promise I'll owe you."

Claire groaned. "Fine. But on one condition."

"Name it," Fiona said, already feeling triumphant.

"Come with me to Tybee Island for a week. You need a break too, and I'm not letting you wriggle out of it."

Fiona laughed. "Deal. I'll schedule it for after I publish this story. I'll buy the drinks because when it hits the newsstands, it's gonna be huge!"

"Alright, Donald," Claire laughed.

"Thanks, Claire. You're the best."

"Don't push it," Claire replied, but there was warmth in her voice. "Goodnight, Fiona."

"Goodnight," Fiona said, ending the call and placing the phone back on the coffee table. She sank deeper into the couch, her mind whirling with everything she'd learned. For the first time, she felt like the pieces were starting to connect. And as much as Claire's warning lingered in her mind, the pull to uncover the truth was even stronger.

chapter
nine

THE NEWSROOM BUZZED with its usual morning energy—keyboards clacking, phones ringing, and the occasional burst of laughter cutting through the din. Fiona was at her desk, scrolling through her notes on Dolores Bates when she heard Jacobs' familiar bark behind her.

"Stevens. How's the Bates story coming along?"

She turned, forcing a confident smile as she gestured to her laptop. "Good. Mrs. Bates has agreed to let me do the feature, and I'm already uncovering some interesting stuff."

"Interesting is good," Jacobs said, crossing his arms and leaning against the edge of her desk. "But remember, if it starts to stall or she shuts you out, you pull the plug. No wasting resources on something dead in the water."

"I know, I know," Fiona replied, waving a hand as if brushing off the thought. "But that's not going to happen. Plus, I've got an in with her lawyer. He's been surprisingly open with me so far."

Jacobs raised an eyebrow. "The family lawyer, huh? That's a lucky break. Lawyers usually clam up tighter than a bank vault. You should see how much you can get out of him. People close to the family tend to slip up if you keep them talking long enough."

"I'm working on it," Fiona assured him with a grin.

"Good." Jacobs pushed himself off her desk. "Keep at it. Sounds like you're off to a solid start."

As he walked away, Denise appeared almost immediately, sliding into the chair beside Fiona's desk. "So, what's the plan for today? Snooping around the Bates mansion again?"

"Not exactly," Fiona shook her head. "I've got a luncheon at noon. It's one of those socialite events at her house—charity stuff."

Denise's eyes lit up. "The gossip there is going to be juicy. Those women love to tear each other apart when they think no one's listening. You might want to prepare yourself."

"That's the plan." Fiona glanced at the clock. Her stomach dropped. "Wait, it's already—"

"Almost eleven," Denise said, biting back a laugh. "You might want to get going."

"Damn it," Fiona muttered, grabbing her bag. "I need to change and fix my hair first."

"Lucky for you, all those years with your mom must've made you a pro at pulling yourself together in record time."

Fiona chuckled internally. Gretchen was well known in Savannah for being a hardass. And while Fiona had an easier time navigating their mother growing up than Claire did, it still didn't mean she escaped a lot of her etiquette requirements.

"You're not wrong."

She made it home with just enough time to throw on a sleek dress and sweep her hair into a low chignon, her mother's voice echoing in her head as she pinned the last stray strand. *Always look polished, Fiona. People judge what they see before they ever hear what you say.* It was a mantra she resented growing up but found herself leaning on more often than she cared to admit.

Sliding on a pair of nude heels, she grabbed her bag and headed out the door. The streets of Savannah blurred past her as she drove, her thoughts spinning between the story, the luncheon, and the many questions still swirling around Dolores Bates.

When she arrived, the Bates estate was already buzzing with activity. Servers in crisp white shirts carried trays of champagne flutes, and clusters of women in pastel dresses and oversized hats gathered under the shade of the sprawling oak trees in the garden. Fiona scanned the crowd, hoping to spot Henry, but he was nowhere to be seen.

Her phone buzzed in her bag. She fished it out and saw a text from him. *Sorry, something came up. I can't make it today. Enjoy yourself, though. We'll catch up soon.*

Fiona sighed, slipping the phone back into her bag. She had been hoping Henry could help her navigate the tightly knit world of Savannah's socialites.

So much for that. Grabbing a flute of champagne from a passing server. She straightened her shoulders and forced her expression to stay open and approachable, even as nerves fluttered in her chest. If Henry wasn't going to be here to help, she'd have to figure out her own way to fit in—and more importantly, find out what these women knew.

She meandered from group to group, exchanging polite smiles and engaging in small talk. Her first stop was with an older man in a cream-colored suit who was discussing the historical preservation of Savannah's architecture.

He swirled a glass of bourbon as he said, "It's always a balancing act, you see. Restoring these old homes while keeping them functional for modern living. You can't just replace 19th-century windows with vinyl, no matter how much more efficient they are."

Fiona nodded, making a mental note of his name—James Lockwood, head of a local preservation society. "That's fascinating," she said. "I imagine the Tour must bring a lot of attention to those efforts."

"Indeed, it does," he replied, glancing over the rim of his glass. "Mrs. Bates' home is one of the crown jewels of this year's event. I can only hope people appreciate the history rather than just snapping pictures for social media."

After a polite laugh and a few more pleasantries, Fiona moved on, her champagne flute still nearly full. Her next conversation was with a couple of women in their early fifties, both impeccably dressed and clearly well-acquainted with the Savannah social scene.

"Did you hear about the gala next month?" one asked the other. "The Museum of Coastal History is hosting it."

"Oh, of course," her friend replied, adjusting her pearl necklace. "I think everyone in this crowd has been invited. It's the event of the season."

Fiona stepped in smoothly. "That sounds incredible. Do you know if Mrs. Bates will be attending?"

Both women turned to her with polite smiles, their expressions subtly evaluating her. "I imagine so," one of them said after a pause. "She rarely misses an event tied to the city's history. It's important to her family's legacy."

Fiona filed that away, thanking them for the information before excusing herself. As she moved on, she passed a few other groups—some chatting animatedly about their gardens, others discussing the latest arrivals at a local boutique.

She felt a flicker of frustration as the light chatter swirled around her. She took a swig of champagne to tamp it down. This wasn't what she had expected at all. Weren't these people supposed to be the worst gossips?

It wasn't until she drifted toward a trio of older women near the hydrangeas that her instincts kicked in. Their heads were tilted together, their voices low, and while their laughter was light, Fiona recognized the edge to it immediately.

"Good afternoon," she said brightly, stepping closer. The women straightened slightly, their smiles widening in that polite but wary way Southern women mastered. Fiona held up her glass. "Mind if I join you?"

"Of course not," one of them said, her eyes flicking briefly to the others. "You're the reporter, aren't you?"

"That's me," Fiona said, her tone disarming. "But don't worry, I'm off duty. Just here to enjoy the luncheon."

The women exchanged glances before one of them—a petite woman with sharp features and pearls that gleamed against her tan skin—spoke up. "We were just talking about how lovely the estate looks, weren't we?"

"Absolutely," said another, a taller woman with a honeyed drawl. "Dolores always keeps things so perfect."

Fiona smiled knowingly. "It must be hard keeping up with the estate after everything."

The women hesitated, their polite masks slipping just a little. Fiona tilted her head, her smile encouraging. "You don't have to sugarcoat it for me. I've heard the whispers."

That was all it took. The petite woman leaned in slightly, her voice dropping. "If you've heard the whispers, then you know the marriage wasn't quite as perfect as she liked to pretend."

"She's always been good at pretending," the taller one said with a smirk. "But everyone knows about Charles and Sarah."

"Sarah?" Fiona asked, feigning surprise.

The third woman, who had been silent until now, let out a soft laugh. "Sarah Mercer was the darling of Savannah for a time. Charles took quite a liking to her, and she didn't exactly mind the attention."

"She was younger," the petite woman added, her voice tinged with disdain. "Pretty, of course, not in the same league as Dolores. Still, Charles couldn't help himself."

"And then she disappeared," Fiona said, keeping her tone casual despite the spike of interest in her chest.

The taller woman shrugged delicately. "People say she left town to avoid the scandal. Others think ..." She trailed off, glancing around as if to make sure no one was listening. "Well, others think Dolores had something to do with it. You know how she is when she's crossed."

The petite woman nodded, her pearls catching the light as she shifted. "She's always had a temper. You wouldn't know it from the way she carries herself, but behind closed doors? Let's just say it's no surprise Charles didn't have the last word in their marriage."

The group dissolved into quiet laughter, but Fiona could tell they were only half-joking. Before she could press further, a shadow fell over them. She turned to see Dolores herself approaching, her expression unreadable.

"Ladies," Dolores said, her voice smooth but firm. "Enjoying yourselves?"

The women straightened instantly, their laughter cutting off as if on command. "Of course, Dolores," the petite woman said with a bright smile. "Everything is just lovely."

Dolores' gaze flicked briefly to Fiona. "And you? How are you finding everything?"

"It's wonderful," Fiona said, her words coming out stiffer than she intended. "Thank you for having me."

Dolores nodded, her lips curving into a faint smile that didn't reach her eyes. Without another word to the other women, she turned and walked away, her posture as rigid as ever.

As soon as she was out of earshot, the petite woman exhaled audibly. "See what I mean? That temper could strip paint off a wall."

The taller woman nodded, her voice low. "She never forgets a slight, either. Just be careful, Miss Stevens. Dolores Bates has a way of making problems disappear."

Fiona's stomach twisted at the remark, but she forced a polite smile and thanked the women for their company before slipping away. The weight of their words hung heavy in her mind as she wandered through the garden, the champagne in her hand barely touched.

How much of this is true? she wondered, her thoughts circling back to Sarah Mercer, the temper, the whispers about Charles. Dolores Bates had secrets—of that, Fiona was certain. The question was whether she could uncover them without becoming one of the whispers herself.

chapter
ten

THE AFTERNOON SUN filtered through the towering oaks that lined the driveway of Dolores Bates' estate, casting shifting patterns of light and shadow over the gathering crowd. Fiona adjusted her notebook in her bag and glanced at Claire, who looked less than thrilled to be there.

"This is ridiculous," Claire muttered, pulling her sunglasses down as they stepped out of the car. "Why did I let you talk me into this?"

"Because you love me," Fiona replied with a grin, ignoring Claire's glare. "And because I promised to go to Tybee with you."

"You're not getting out of it. A week of no work, no digging into anyone's secrets, just sand, sun, and margaritas."

"Sounds like a dream," Fiona said lightly. "But first, let's enjoy this little field trip."

Claire glanced toward the mansion. "You know this isn't easy for me."

Fiona sobered, slowing her pace to fall into step beside Claire. "I know. And I really appreciate you coming here with me, especially after everything with Anthony."

"It's hard to separate this place from the case, you know?" Claire's lips tightened, but she didn't look away from the estate. "But you're my sister, and if this is what you need for your story, I'll deal with it."

Fiona bumped her shoulder lightly. "That's why you're the best. I promise, I'll make it up to you. Maybe even with the fanciest dinner on Tybee."

Claire's mouth twitched into the faintest hint of a smile. "I'm holding you to that."

Fiona laughed, the tension easing between them as they joined a group milling about near the front steps. The ornate door opened, and the tour began, the crowd filing into the grand foyer under the watchful eyes of staff and security.

Inside, the house was just as grand as Fiona remembered, with its polished wood floors, high ceilings, and intricately carved molding. The faint scent of lavender lingered in the air, likely from the discreetly placed floral arrangements that graced each room so far. The tour guide, a composed woman in a crisp navy blazer, stood at the center of the grand foyer, her voice carrying effortlessly over the murmurs of the group.

"The estate was built in 1904 by Thomas and Margaret Wesley. Thomas Wesley was a key figure in Savannah's shipping empire, and Margaret was known for her philanthropy and social influence."

The guide gestured toward a large portrait above the marble fireplace. The painting depicted a tall, broad-shouldered man with stern features and piercing blue eyes, his hand resting on the back of a chair. Beside him stood a woman with auburn hair swept into an elaborate updo, her gown rich with intricate lacework.

The guide moved toward a side table, where a leather-bound book was displayed beneath a glass case. "The Wesleys were among the most prominent families of their time, and their contributions to Savannah's economy and society are still remembered today. Margaret Wesley, for instance, was instrumental in funding several of the city's earliest public schools."

Fiona trailed behind the group, her eyes darting to every detail. The house was immaculate. Her gaze snagged on a doorframe just off the main hallway. The paint looked fresh compared to the rest of the house. The wood underneath seemed to dip slightly, as if it had been hastily repaired. She slowed her steps, peering closer.

"Do you see that?" Fiona murmured, nudging Claire and gesturing toward the frame. "Right there by the hinge."

Claire glanced over, her brow furrowing. "Looks like it was kicked in," she whispered back. "And then patched up and painted over."

Fiona tilted her head, studying the faint grooves where the wood didn't quite line up. "Not exactly what you'd expect in a house like this. Think it's from the Wesleys' time?"

Claire sighed, her lips pressing into a thin line. "Don't make this a thing. The last thing we need is you going off-script."

Fiona smirked but didn't reply, her curiosity already spinning. Whatever had happened to that doorframe, someone had been in a hurry to cover it up.

The group followed the guide into the formal dining room, a stunning space with a crystal chandelier that cast a soft glow over the long mahogany table. The table was set with pristine china, and the chairs were upholstered in a floral fabric that looked as though it hadn't been touched since the 1930s.

"This room was often used for hosting Savannah's elite. The Wesleys were known for their grand dinner parties, where guests would discuss everything from local politics to international trade."

Claire lingered near a sideboard lined with silver serving pieces, her gaze caught by a photograph in a gilded frame. Fiona stepped closer and realized it was a picture of Dolores and her son, Anthony. Anthony was a teenager in the image, his sandy hair slightly tousled as he stood beside his mother. Dolores looked regal as ever, her hand resting lightly on his shoulder.

Claire's fingers brushed the edge of the frame as she stared at the photo for a beat too long. Fiona tilted her head, lowering her voice. "You okay?"

Claire blinked, pulling her hand back as though she'd touched something hot. "Yeah."

Fiona studied her sister, but Claire quickly turned away, refocusing on the guide, who was now leading the group into the next room.

"This way, please," the guide called, motioning toward a sitting room off the main hallway. The crowd followed, their footsteps muffled by an ornate Persian rug that stretched the length of the corridor.

"Stay with the group," Claire muttered under her breath, giving Fiona a pointed nudge.

"I am staying," Fiona whispered back. Her eyes traced the intricate woodwork along the doorframes, her mind spinning with thoughts of the people who had walked these halls.

The guide paused near another portrait, this one of a young man with an earnest expression and a navy blazer. "This is Andrew Wesley, Thomas and Margaret's only son. He was meant to inherit the family legacy. Tragically, he passed away at the age of thirteen in a drowning accident. The estate and all its holdings were passed to their daughter, Dolores, who has carried the Wesley name forward."

"Carried it forward," Fiona murmured, glancing at Claire. "More like married it into near ruin."

Claire shot her a warning look. "Keep your voice down."

Fiona kept quiet as the group moved on. Her gaze drifted to the edges of the rooms, where she noticed faint nicks in the furniture and small cracks in the plaster. She leaned closer to Claire. "Look at that—on the corner of the credenza. Do you think that's from years of use, or …?"

Claire squinted at the mark, her brow furrowing. "Maybe someone moving furniture. Or kids roughhousing?"

"Do you think Dolores would tolerate either?" Fiona whispered.

The guide led the group down another long hallway. The walls were lined with portraits and gilded mirrors, their reflections bouncing the afternoon light in uneven patterns.

"This hallway leads to several of the family's more private rooms," the guide said, gesturing to the closed doors they passed. She paused before a heavy wooden door with a brass handle, its dark surface gleaming under the overhead chandelier.

"This was Mr. Charles Bates' personal office," she continued, her tone dropping slightly, as if the space carried an unspoken weight. "He used this room for much of his business dealings and private correspondence. While it remains largely intact, it is not part of today's tour, and we ask that guests refrain from entering. You're welcome to take a moment and admire the door."

Fiona's curiosity flared. The door was different from the others around the house—sturdier, almost imposing. It radiated the kind of secrecy that begged to be unraveled. She glanced at Claire, who was studying the door with a frown.

"Charles' office," Fiona murmured under her breath, her mind already spinning with possibilities. "There's no way that room doesn't have something interesting."

Claire caught Fiona's expression with a glare. "Don't even think about it. We're guests here. Don't start something."

Fiona gave her a quick smile but said nothing, her attention snapping back to the guide, who was now directing the group toward the next room.

The group filed into a nearby parlor, but Fiona hung back near the hallway, her gaze fixed on the office door. The brass handle gleamed in the dim lighting, almost taunting her. Claire hovered nearby, her arms crossed.

"Fiona," she warned, her voice a low whisper. "Don't."

"I'll just take a peek," Fiona said lightly, but her pulse quickened as she edged closer to the door.

Claire stepped in front of her, blocking her path. "You're going to get us both kicked out. And for what? A locked desk drawer and a bunch of dusty books?"

"Maybe. Or maybe something more."

"You can't just snoop around someone's house like this. What if Dolores finds out? Then your story is ruined. She could destroy your entire career if she wanted to."

"She won't," Fiona said, brushing past her sister with more determination than caution.

She wrapped her hand around the brass handle and twisted. The door creaked open, and the scent of old leather and cedar wafted out, mingling with the faint mustiness of a room that hadn't seen much use.

"Fiona," Claire whispered urgently, glancing over her shoulder toward the group.

"It'll take two minutes."

The room was dimly lit, the only light filtering in through heavy drapes that muted the afternoon sun. A massive mahogany desk sat at the center, flanked by shelves filled with dusty books and scattered with framed photographs.

Claire followed reluctantly, her arms folded tightly across her chest. "This is crazy. What are you even looking for?"

"Anything," Fiona said, moving toward the desk. Her fingers brushed over its surface, trailing across the faint scratches in the wood. "Anything that might explain what really went on in this house."

"This is so inappropriate," Claire muttered again, her tone tense. She hovered near the door, peeking into the hallway. "If someone catches us—"

"They won't." Fiona crouched down to inspect the desk drawers. The first two opened easily, revealing nothing more than yellowed stationery and a few pens. The third drawer stuck slightly. Fiona tugged at it, her heart racing.

"Fiona, stop," Claire pleaded, her voice tight with exasperation. "You're pushing it."

"Almost got it."

She gave the drawer one final tug. It slid open with a faint scrape. Her heart pounded when she looked inside and saw—nothing. Some old receipts, an empty envelope, and a stack of blank file folders.

She sighed, her excitement fading as quickly as it had come. "Damn it."

"Feel better now?" Claire asked sharply, her frustration evident. "All that for nothing. Can we go before someone notices?"

Fiona straightened, giving the room one last glance. The weight of disappointment settled in her chest, but she couldn't shake the feeling that this office still held answers—it just wasn't giving them up yet.

"Fine," she said, stepping back toward the door. "I had to try."

Claire shook her head, holding the door open for her. "You're going to get yourself into trouble one of these days, you know that?"

"Wouldn't be the first time," Fiona said with a faint smirk, though her heart wasn't in it. She cast one last look at the desk before following Claire out, pulling the door softly closed behind her.

The tour concluded shortly after, with the group gathering on the back lawn for refreshments. Fiona scanned the crowd, her gaze searching for Henry, but once again, he was nowhere to be found.

"You're looking for someone," Claire said dryly, sipping her lemonade.

"No, I'm not."

Claire raised an eyebrow but didn't press further, shaking her head as she turned her attention to the crowd.

Fiona took a deep breath, fishing her phone from her bag as she stepped away from the chatter. She hesitated for a moment, her fingers hovering over the screen, before pulling up Henry's contact.

Hey, didn't see you at the tour today. Any chance we can meet tomorrow? I have some follow-up questions.

She hit send and tucked the phone back into her bag, trying not to overthink the casual tone of the message. As she stood there, watching the sunlight filter through the oak trees and listening to the soft murmur of the other guests, her phone buzzed in her bag.

She pulled it out to see Henry's reply.

Sorry about today. Busy morning. Tomorrow works—my office at 10?

chapter
eleven

FIONA PARKED in front of the small, unassuming building, her eyebrows lifting slightly. She double-checked the address Henry had given her, glancing at the converted one-story house. A discreet wooden sign by the sidewalk read Caldwell Law Office, the letters neat but understated.

She climbed out of the car, smoothing the front of her blouse.

The place was tidy, but it lacked the grandeur she'd imagined for someone representing one of Savannah's most prominent women. A small porch wrapped around the front and right side, and a potted fern sat in one corner, looking a little worse for wear. She pushed open the door, the faint chime of a bell announcing her arrival.

Inside, the office was quaint and practical, with a small waiting area that held two mismatched chairs and a coffee table stacked with magazines. The air smelled faintly of coffee and paper. Before she could take it all in, Henry appeared from a side room, a wide smile on his face.

"Fiona," he greeted warmly. "Come on in. Sorry, the receptionist is on leave for the week, so it's just me holding down the fort."

Fiona smiled, stepping further inside.

"She usually keeps me organized and running on schedule," Henry admitted, gesturing for Fiona to follow him. "Sorry again for missing the tour and the luncheon. I appreciate you coming by today."

Fiona shrugged as they walked. "It's fine. I managed. The luncheon and tour were ... illuminating."

They entered the main office space, a cluttered desk in the center of the room. Files were spread out in uneven stacks, sticky notes clung to the edges, and a laptop sat precariously on one corner. The desk itself was a worn wooden beast, likely having weathered decades of paperwork.

Henry followed her gaze and chuckled. "I'd apologize for the mess, but it's kind of unavoidable. I've been working on some things for Dolores—Bates and Wesley files everywhere."

Fiona's interest piqued at the mention of her maiden name but kept her expression neutral. "Seems like she keeps you busy."

"You could say that." Henry smiled and moved to the Keurig machine on a small cart in the corner of the room. "Coffee? It's not fancy, but it's fresh."

"That sounds great," Fiona replied, glancing at the walls while Henry prepped the coffee.

A framed diploma from law school hung beside a black-and-white photo of a younger Henry with an older man she assumed was his father. Other frames displayed generic landscapes—oceans, fields, and a foggy marsh.

Henry handed her a mug, steam curling lazily from the top. "Here you go. Let's sit down."

They settled into the chairs in front of the desk, and Henry leaned back slightly, cradling his coffee. "So, did the tour live up to the hype?"

"It was fascinating. The house is incredible—meticulously preserved." Fiona sipped her coffee, its sharp bitterness grounding her. "But I think the most interesting part of these tours is the people who attend them."

Henry chuckled. "That sounds about right."

Fiona hesitated, setting her mug on the edge of the desk. "I wanted to talk to you about Charles, actually. I know there's been a lot of speculation about him over the years, and I don't want to perpetuate anything unfounded in the article. I thought maybe you could help me navigate that."

Henry's expression softened, and he nodded. "You could've gone ahead without checking in, but you didn't. I appreciate that. What do you want to know?"

Fiona took a deep breath. "I've gotten wind of his ... habits. Gambling, the affair. I don't want to sensationalize, but I also don't want to ignore the things people clearly remember."

"It's tricky. Charles was a complicated guy—charming but flawed." Henry sighed, rubbing the back of his neck. "There are parts of his story I can't get into, for obvious reasons, but I'll help where I can."

Before Fiona could press further, Henry stood abruptly, setting his coffee down. "Hang on a second. Too much caffeine today—I'll be right back."

He disappeared down a narrow hallway, leaving Fiona alone in the office. The moment she was alone, her gaze dropped to the desk. Her eyes darted over the scattered files until landing on one near the edge, its label catching her attention: C. Bates - D. Wesley: Agreement.

Her breath hitched. She hesitated for only a second before reaching for the file, her fingers trembling as she slid it closer, glancing toward the hallway where Henry had disappeared. The muffled sound of a faucet running reached her ears, but the office was otherwise silent.

Just a quick look, she told herself, flipping open the cover.

The first few pages were dry—standard legal language about financial disclosures, property agreements, and assets. She scanned the headings quickly, her heart thudding in her chest. It looked like the kind of paperwork every lawyer would handle, but nothing stood out. Yet.

She flipped to the next document, her fingers brushing the edge of the paper. This one was older, the typewritten text slightly faded. It appeared to be a list of shared assets: accounts, properties, and even a note about a trust under the Wesley family name. Fiona's pulse quickened as she read, her mind racing with questions.

Why would this be included?

The next page was a letter. She skimmed the letterhead, noticing the name of a well-known Savannah law firm, and her eyes caught on a line near the bottom: *Regarding dissolution of marriage between Charles Bates and Dolores Wesley Bates.*

Fiona froze. Her hands tightened on the edges of the paper, her gaze darting back to the letterhead to confirm what she was seeing. She flipped to the next document, her movements more urgent now.

And then she found it.

Divorce Agreement.

The words seemed to leap off the page, stark and undeniable. Fiona stared, her breath catching in her throat. This wasn't speculation. It wasn't the usual Savannah whispers passed between society women at charity galas.

This was real.

She leaned in, scanning the document more closely, her pulse quickening. The signature lines at the bottom confirmed it—Charles Bates on one side, Dolores Wesley Bates on the other.

But the signatures weren't there.

The agreement had never been finalized.

Fiona exhaled slowly, her mind racing.

Rumors of marital discord had swirled for years, but no one had ever uncovered anything concrete. Charles was known for his wandering eye, his extramarital affairs quietly tolerated by Savannah's high society. But divorce?

That was something else entirely.

Dolores and Charles had remained married until the day he died. There had been no separation, no official parting of ways. And yet—this document existed.

Fiona's fingers skimmed over the fine print, the legal language a blur as her gaze caught on key phrases.

"Dissolution of assets in accordance with preexisting agreements..."

"Equitable division of marital property..."

Then—Dolores' handwritten note in the margins, ink pressed deeply into the paper, the words nearly carving themselves into the fibers.

"Protect Anthony's inheritance. Retain Wesley properties. Ensure estate remains intact."

Fiona's throat tightened.

This wasn't just some draft of an agreement that had been tossed aside. This was a battle plan.

Dolores had been fighting for control. Fighting to keep what was hers—to make sure that, no matter what happened between her and Charles, Anthony wouldn't lose his birthright.

But why hadn't the divorce happened?

Had Charles backed down? Had Dolores refused to sign?

Had something worse happened before it could be finalized?

Fiona pressed her fingertips into her temples. The woman Savannah had gossiped about for years wasn't this woman—the one whose desperate handwriting now stood out against cold legal terms.

This wasn't the calculated, power-hungry socialite people had painted Dolores to be.

This was a woman who had been backed into a corner.

She pulled out her phone with trembling hands and snapped a picture of the page. The camera's shutter sounded too loud in the quiet office. She winced, glancing toward the hallway. The faint creak of floorboards sent a jolt of panic through her, but the footsteps didn't come closer.

Fiona exhaled shakily and flipped through the remaining pages. Most were dry legal notes—clauses about property, custody, and confidentiality. She photographed several more documents, even as her nerves frayed with every passing second.

The faucet turned off, and Fiona's heart nearly stopped. She hastily shoved the papers back into the folder, smoothing them as best she could before closing it and sliding it back into its original spot. Her hands trembled as she picked up her coffee mug and tried to appear calm.

When Henry reentered the room, he was none the wiser, sitting down with a small sigh. "Sorry about that. Caffeine gets me every time."

"No problem." Fiona forced a smile. Her pulse still thundered in her ears, but she kept her voice steady. "We've all been there."

Henry leaned back in his chair, picking up his coffee again. "So, what other questions do you have? I figured you'd be here grilling me for at least an hour."

Fiona's fingers tightened slightly around her mug. Her mind was still racing, and the last thing she wanted was to linger and risk giving herself away. Her voice was a touch higher than usual when she said, "Actually, I think I've got what I need for now."

Henry's eyebrows lifted in mild surprise. "Really? That's it?" He grinned, setting his coffee down. "Wow. Guess this really could've been an email."

Fiona let out a nervous laugh, her fingers twitching as she tucked her hair behind her ear. She wanted to get out of there fast and take a closer look at the photos that were burning a hole in her phone. "Yeah, well, you've been super helpful. I'll be sure to let you know if I need anything else."

Henry studied her for a moment, his grin softening into something friendlier. "Anytime. I appreciate you coming to me for guidance before diving into the article. Not everyone would do that."

"Of course. I want to make sure I'm being fair."

Henry rose as Fiona stood and grabbed her bag, walking her to the door. "I meant what I said—if you need anything else, just call. And good luck with the story."

"Thanks, Henry."

As she stepped outside, he paused, his hand resting lightly on the doorframe. "Are you planning to attend the regatta this summer? Dolores is a big donor, and it's ... let's just say it's an event worth covering if you're writing about her."

Fiona hesitated, caught off guard. "The regatta?"

"A lot of the city's power players will be there. It's not just about the boats—it's a networking goldmine."

She nodded slowly, her mind already working through the logistics. "I hadn't planned on it, but it sounds like it could be worth checking out."

Henry gave her a knowing look. "Let me know if you decide to go— I can make sure your name's on the list."

"Thanks," Fiona said, appreciative despite the whirlwind of thoughts buzzing in her head.

As she walked to her car, her mind flickered to Claire. She'd promised her sister a week in Tybee Island as a break after finishing this story, but maybe she could work the trips together—spend a few days at Tybee, then head to the regatta. Claire wouldn't be thrilled about sharing the time with her work, but Fiona could make it up to her.

chapter
twelve

FIONA SAT cross-legged on her couch, the dim glow of her desk lamp casting long shadows across the room. Her coffee table was a chaotic mess—scattered printouts of the photos she'd taken at Henry's office covered nearly every inch of space, some overlapping, others crumpled at the edges from where she'd gripped them too tightly.

At the center of it all, staring back at her in crisp black-and-white detail, was the divorce agreement.

Finalized Divorce Agreement.

The bold header loomed over columns of clauses and subsections, a wall of legal jargon that might as well have been written in another language. Fiona understood the general premise—that Dolores and Charles had been negotiating a divorce—but the finer details were murky at best.

She leaned in, tracing a finger over the dense, unyielding paragraphs. Words like *irrevocable*, *distribution of assets*, and *contingencies for transfer of property* blurred together as her eyes skimmed line after line, trying to make sense of the tangled mess of conditions and agreements.

And then there was the note.

Dolores' handwriting—elegant, precise, yet unmistakably rushed— was scrawled in the margins of one of the pages, its ink slightly smudged, as if written in haste.

Protect Anthony's inheritance. Retain Wesley properties. Ensure estate remains intact.

Fiona swallowed hard, her fingers tightening around the edge of the paper.

This wasn't a standard note left by a woman casually discussing the end of a marriage. This was a directive. A plea. A mother making sure her son wouldn't be left with nothing.

She exhaled, pressing her knuckles into her forehead. *How did this never come out before?*

The divorce agreement—if it had been finalized—would have shattered everything. The preserved wealth of the Wesley family, passed down through generations, would not have gone to Dolores or Anthony at all.

It would have gone to Charles.

Or worse—to Sarah Mercer and her unborn child.

Fiona's breath caught as she read the words again. *Protect Anthony.*

She let out a frustrated sigh, dragging a hand through her hair. This wasn't the cold, calculating woman Savannah had whispered about for decades. This wasn't the "power-hungry widow" who had destroyed a man to keep her fortune.

This was a woman desperately trying to hold on to what little she had left.

Dolores had known Charles was trying to take everything from her. She had known he was planning to leave her for Sarah, to start over, to erase the life he had spent years building with Dolores and Anthony and replace it with another.

She must have felt the walls closing in, the ground shifting beneath her feet, the realization that she had spent years in a marriage that was now dissolving like smoke—and there'd been nothing she could do to stop it.

Fiona's gaze drifted back to the note. The inked words stood out against the cold, sterile document. A raw, deeply personal plea buried in legal formalities.

Dolores had not been a wife clinging to power, nor a woman seeking revenge.

She'd been a mother fighting to protect what was hers.

Fiona swallowed against the lump forming in her throat.

The implications were staggering. If Charles had succeeded, the Wesley legacy would have been fractured, perhaps irreparably. Generations of careful stewardship would have been undone in a single legal maneuver. No wonder Dolores had been desperate to prevent it.

But how far would she have gone? The question lingered in Fiona's mind, persistent and troubling. Would a woman who'd scrawled that desperate note in the margins of a divorce agreement take even more desperate measures to protect her family's legacy?

Fiona shook her head, trying to clear her thoughts. She needed more information, more context. Without the full picture, she was just speculating.

Her phone buzzed on the table, and she glanced at the screen.

"Hey," Fiona said, picking up. "I was just about to call you."

"That's always a good sign," Claire said dryly. "What did you get yourself into this time?"

"Nothing," Fiona replied, biting her lip. "Not yet anyway. I need your help. I've got some documents I need you to look at. Legal stuff."

"Legal stuff? You're not being sued, are you?"

"Why would I be sued? It's related to the story. I just can't make sense of it, and you're the only person I trust with this."

Claire sighed on the other end of the line. "I've got a few things to finish here first—working on donor lists for an upcoming event at the museum—but I'll come over after. Give me an hour."

"Thanks, Claire. I owe you."

"You really do," Claire said, her tone half-joking. "See you soon."

Fiona spent the next hour cleaning her apartment—a habit she defaulted to whenever her nerves got the better of her. She scrubbed the kitchen counters until they gleamed, organized her bookshelf by color (a system she'd abandon within days), and even dusted the ceiling fan that had been collecting grime for months.

The physical activity helped channel her restless energy, but her mind kept circling back to Dolores, to Charles, to the web of secrets that seemed to grow more tangled with each revelation.

By the time Claire knocked on the door, the apartment was spotless, and the coffee table was cleared except for the photos and a fresh pot of coffee.

"Wow," Claire said as she stepped inside, glancing around. "Nervous or procrastinating?"

"Both," Fiona admitted, gesturing to the table. "Come on in. I need you to take a look at this."

Claire set her bag down and took off her jacket, glancing at the photos as she poured herself a cup of coffee. "What am I looking at?"

"Before I explain, I'd appreciate it if you didn't ask where I got these."

Claire gave her a sharp look, then waved her hand. "Fine. I don't need to know. Let's just get this over with."

She sat down, pulling the photos closer, and began to read. Fiona perched on the edge of the couch, watching Claire's expression shift from mild curiosity to something more serious.

"Fi," Claire said after a moment, her voice low. "Wherever you got these ... this is bad. Like, really bad."

"What do you mean?" Fiona asked, leaning forward.

Claire tapped the handwritten note. "This is Dolores trying to hold on to what she could, but if this divorce agreement had gone through as it's written here, she would've been left with almost nothing. Charles was planning to strip her of the Wesley properties and most of the inheritance, leaving her with just a fraction of what her family was worth."

A chill crept up Fiona's spine. "You're saying he was trying to ruin her?"

"It looks that way. If this agreement had been finalized, Dolores would have been in a terrible position."

"But how?" Fiona asked, leaning forward. "How could Charles have pulled something like this off? The Wesley fortune belonged to Dolores' family—it wasn't his."

"It's more complicated than that." Claire exhaled, rubbing her temple. "When Dolores married Charles, he was given certain positions within the Wesley family's businesses—board seats, executive roles, that kind of thing. On paper, it probably seemed harmless, but those positions gave him significant control over the family's assets."

"So, you're saying he used that control against her?"

"Essentially, from what I can tell, Charles was slowly transferring certain Wesley assets to himself under the guise of managing them. It looks like he leveraged his positions in the Wesley businesses to move things around without raising suspicion."

Fiona tensed, her shoulders tightening with each new revelation. "I knew they didn't have a prenup because they eloped, but this—this is so much worse. He wasn't just taking advantage of Dolores; he was setting her up to lose everything."

Claire nodded, her brow furrowed as she scanned another page. "It gets messier. This divorce agreement suggests that part of the negotiations involved a potential deal—Charles relinquishing his claim over certain Wesley assets in exchange for the family agreeing not to pursue fraud charges against him."

Fiona's eyes narrowed. "Fraud charges?"

"It looks like the Wesley family uncovered what he was doing, or at least part of it. There are references here to 'mismanagement' and 'breach of fiduciary duties.' If the divorce had gone through, Charles would've walked away with a substantial payout, but the Wesleys would've avoided the scandal of a public legal battle."

"And Dolores?"

"She would've been left with scraps." Claire's expression darkened. "The divorce agreement doesn't explicitly state what she'd retain, but it heavily favors Charles, especially when it comes to liquid assets. It's no wonder Dolores fought so hard to protect the estate."

Fiona picked up the photo of Dolores' handwritten note again. *Protect Anthony's inheritance. Retain Wesley properties. Ensure estate remains intact.*

"This wasn't just a divorce," Fiona said softly. "This was a power struggle. She wasn't just fighting for herself—she was trying to salvage everything her family had built."

"It's even more than that." Claire set the papers down and looked at Fiona. "If this agreement had gone through, the damage wouldn't have been limited to Dolores. It would've tarnished the Wesley legacy entirely."

Fiona exhaled slowly, the weight of the revelations settling over her. "No wonder she's so guarded. If this is what she'd been up against."

Claire nodded, her expression grave as she examined another document. "The legal maneuvering here is sophisticated. Charles must have had excellent counsel—someone who knew exactly how to exploit the vulnerabilities in the Wesley family's financial structure."

"And Dolores would have been blindsided," Fiona murmured, the pieces falling into place. "She trusted him with her family's legacy, and he was planning to dismantle it."

Claire's lips thinned into a tight line. "It's not just about the money, though that's significant. It's about the betrayal of trust. Charles didn't just cheat on his wife—he systematically positioned himself to take everything from her."

Fiona felt a wave of unease wash over her. "Doesn't this make it more likely that Dolores had something to do with Sarah's disappearance? I mean, she had the motive, right?"

"Don't go there. You don't know what happened." Claire frowned, putting the photos down. "Don't get in over your head with this."

Before Claire could say more, Fiona's phone rang. She glanced at the screen, her heart skipping when she saw Henry's name.

chapter
thirteen

"IT'S HENRY," Fiona whispered, picking up the phone.

Claire gave her a pointed look. "Tell him you'll call back."

Fiona shook her head, putting a finger to her lips before answering. "Henry? Everything okay?"

"Fiona," Henry slurred, his warm voice thick and unmistakably drunk. "I just ... I needed someone to talk to. You're good at listening."

Fiona exchanged a glance with Claire, who mouthed, *Hang up*.

"Of course," Fiona said, ignoring Claire's silent protests. She hit the speakerphone button and set the phone on the table.

"Henry, are you okay?"

"Just been working too much. It's all this estate stuff for Dolores ... it's too much sometimes, you know?"

Claire gave Fiona a sharp look, but Fiona waved her off, mouthing, *Let him talk*.

"You sound exhausted," Fiona said gently. "What's been so overwhelming?"

Henry let out a bitter laugh. "Everything. Dolores is ... she's difficult. You've met her, right? Always needs things done yesterday, always needs things perfect. It's like walking a tightrope every day. I mean, I get it— her whole life is about appearances—but sometimes I feel like I can't breathe."

Fiona exchanged a glance with Claire, who still looked wary. "That sounds rough. What's been the hardest part lately?"

"The estate," Henry said, his voice pitching upward with frustration. "Always the estate. Wesley this, Wesley that. Do you know how many documents I've had to go through just to make sense of everything? And it's all a mess—fraud here, disputes there. I didn't sign up for this."

Fiona leaned forward slightly. "Taking this all over from your father must be really hard."

Henry laughed bitterly. "My dad was everything I didn't want to be. Cold. Distant. Everything was about work. He used to drag me to his office as a kid, making me sit there while he worked. I swore I'd never do what he did. I wanted to be ... I don't know, anything else."

"But you went to law school."

"Yeah," Henry muttered, his voice softening. "Because he made me. Said it was the only way to 'secure a future.'" He laughed again, the sound hollow. "I hated it. Still do, honestly. But what do you do when it's the family business, right? You just ... suck it up and do it."

Claire arched an eyebrow at Fiona, silently asking if they were really letting this continue, but Fiona gave her a subtle shake of the head. She didn't want to stop him.

"And now," Henry continued, his voice growing louder, "I'm stuck sorting out this mess with Dolores and the Wesley estate. Everything's about the damn Wesley fortune. Do you know how many times I've read over these agreements? And then there's Sarah."

Fiona's heart jumped. She forced her voice to stay calm. "Sarah Mercer?"

"Of course, Sarah Mercer. Charles was obsessed with her. Everyone knew it. Young. Artist. He was going to leave Dolores for her. Can you imagine? Blow up everything, throw away the Wesley fortune for someone like her. And then—poof—it's like it never happened. Sarah just disappears. Like magic."

Fiona's pulse quickened. "Disappeared how?"

No one knows. One day, she's there, and the next, she's gone. And everything just ... resolves itself. Charles dies. Dolores keeps the estate. It's like someone pressed a reset button."

Fiona exchanged a wide-eyed glance with Claire, who looked like she wanted to intervene. "That sounds convenient. Did anyone ever look into it?"

Henry sighed heavily. "What was there to look into? No body, no clues. Just rumors. Savannah loves its rumors. And Dolores—she plays the grieving widow like a pro. Keeps everything under lock and key. Always in control."

He paused, his breathing audible through the phone. "Sometimes I think about just walking away. Forgetting the whole thing. But she's my biggest client. If I lose her, I lose everything."...

Henry's voice grew slower, his words blending together. "You know, I didn't think I didn't think I'd end up like this. Sorting through everyone's mess. My dad was always telling me what to do... and now Dolores..." His words trailed off, followed by a heavy sigh.

"Henry?" Fiona prompted gently, exchanging a wary glance with Claire.

"Sorry, I'm just ..." Henry mumbled, his voice softening as if he were slipping into a half-daze. "I've had too much to drink, I think ... too much ... and too much of all this work. It's just so much. She doesn't make it easy, you know?"

"It sounds like you've been carrying a lot. Why don't you take a break for tonight?"

Henry didn't seem to hear her, his speech becoming heavier. "It's not just her, though. It's all of it. Charles ... he made such a mess. And then there was Sarah. And then poof, gone. Like magic. And Dolores ... always Dolores."

Claire's eyebrows shot up as she whispered, "He's half asleep. End the call."

Fiona shook her head slightly, mouthing, *Not yet.*

Henry's voice drifted further. "It's all just gone. All that drama. All the trouble. Sarah disappears, Charles dies ...... Dolores wins, you know? Keeps it all. But at what cost?"

His words slurred more as he continued. "I should just ... just stop. Dolores would kill me if she knew I ... but it's just too much, Fiona. Too much."

"Henry," Fiona said softly, her chest tightening at his vulnerability. "Maybe you should get some rest."

There was a long pause on the other end before he finally muttered, "Yeah ... yeah, maybe. Thanks, Fiona. You're a good friend. You always ... you always listen."

"Anytime." She waited until the line went dead before setting her phone down and exhaling sharply.

Claire turned to her, her expression a mix of disbelief and exasperation. "You are unbelievable."

Fiona's gaze stayed fixed on the phone, her thoughts spinning. "Unbelievable or not, we might have just cracked this wide open."

Claire leaned back in her chair, crossing her arms tightly over her chest. "You better know that you can't repeat or use any of that."

Fiona looked at her, frowning. "What are you talking about?"

"That." Claire gestured sharply toward the phone on the table. "The drunk ramblings of an overworked attorney. You cannot treat that like it's some big revelation. He's obviously burned out, and you just let him talk himself into a hole."

"Didn't you hear him?" Fiona sat up straighter, her eyes flashing. "He practically admitted Dolores killed Sarah."

Claire's jaw tightened. "What he said was muddled nonsense. He's been working too hard, drinking too much, and you let him vent. That doesn't mean it's fact."

"Come on, Claire. He as much as admitted he feels like Dolores could kill him. He is scared of her!"

"And you don't think that could just be his paranoia talking? Do you realize what you're saying? You're taking the word of a man too drunk to string together a coherent sentence and trying to turn it into some kind of smoking gun."

Fiona stood, pacing in front of the couch. "What about what he said about Sarah being an artist? That's new, Claire. I didn't know that before."

Claire blinked, caught off guard. "And?"

"And you're working with the museum. You have connections there. You could look into it—see if they have anything about her."

Claire's face hardened. "Absolutely not."

"Why not? You have the access, and this could be a huge lead."

"Because it's not right. This story you're chasing. It's crossing the line. You're digging into a family, a woman that's already been through enough hell. Dolores Bates has lost her husband, her son, and you want to drag her through the mud over something that happened decades ago? Have you even thought about what that might do to her?"

"Of course, I've thought about it. But don't you see? This is important. People deserve to know the truth."

"Important to who? You? Because it's your big break? This is not justice, Fiona—it's gossip wrapped in a fancy package."

Fiona's cheeks flushed with anger bubbling inside of her. "You don't get to say that to me. Not after what you did for Anthony. You thought that was the right thing to do, didn't you? You fought for him, even when everyone told you not to."

"That was different," Claire said through gritted teeth. "He was alive. He deserved a second chance."

"And what about the truth?" Fiona asked, her voice trembling. "Doesn't that matter?"

Claire exhaled sharply, grabbing her bag from the chair. "You need to think long and hard about what you're doing. You're going to destroy someone's life if you're wrong."

"I'm not wrong," Fiona said quietly, but Claire was already heading for the door.

Claire paused with her hand on the doorknob, her voice softer but no less serious. "Just think about it, okay? Before you stir up old rumors and gossip that could ruin a woman who's already been through enough."

The door clicked shut, leaving Fiona in silence.

She sank back onto the couch, her legs suddenly too heavy to stand. The call history from Henry was still on her phone screen, his name sitting there like a challenge. She stared at it, her mind spinning.

What if he remembers? The thought made her tense. What if he woke up tomorrow and realized how much he'd let slip? She had to be ready—ready to explain, to deflect, to handle whatever fallout might come.

A soft chime broke her thoughts, and she glanced at her screen. A calendar reminder: *Interview with Dolores Bates—2 Days.*

Fiona sighed, rubbing her temples. She had to prepare for that, too

—decide which questions to ask, how far to push. It would be her only chance to confront Dolores directly, and she needed to make it count.

Her gaze fell to the stack of papers still spread out on the coffee table. The photos of the divorce agreement, the notes she'd scribbled, the fragments of information that felt like pieces of a puzzle she couldn't quite fit together.

She gathered the papers into a neat pile, her movements slow and deliberate. Her body ached with exhaustion, but her mind refused to settle.

"Tomorrow," she whispered to herself. "I'll figure it out tomorrow."

For now, she shuffled into her bedroom, her feet dragging beneath her, and collapsed onto the bed. The unanswered questions swirled in her mind, pulling her deeper into the mystery even as sleep began to claim her.

chapter
fourteen

FIONA WOKE with the morning sun streaming through the blinds, its warmth doing little to soothe the tension knotting inside her. She stared at the ceiling, replaying Henry's drunken phone call in her mind. His slurred words looped endlessly. *Charles dies. Dolores keeps the estate. Sarah disappears, just like that.*

Claire's warning rang in her ears. *This isn't justice—it's gossip.* But Fiona couldn't shake the feeling that this was bigger than idle speculation. She needed perspective.

Her fingers hovered over her phone before finally dialing her father's number.

"Morning, Fi," Roy answered, his deep voice tinged with surprise. "To what do I owe the pleasure?"

"Hey, Dad. I ... I need your advice on something. Are you free this morning?"

There was a pause before he replied. "How about breakfast? It's been too long since we've had a proper catch-up."

Fiona hesitated, picturing her mother listening in from the next room, ready to weigh in with her usual commentary. Roy seemed to sense her hesitation.

"Not at home," he added quickly. "Let's go to Morningside Café. It'll be easier to talk there."

Relieved, Fiona agreed. "Sounds perfect. I'll see you in half an hour."

. . .

The café buzzed with soft morning energy, the clink of mugs and murmur of conversation creating a comforting backdrop. Fiona spotted Roy immediately, sitting at a corner table by the window. He was impossible to miss, with his full head of silver-white hair and a neatly trimmed beard that gave him the air of a distinguished Southern gentleman. His broad frame filled the chair easily, but Fiona noticed he'd grown a bit leaner over the past year.

Roy's presence seemed to command the room. Even as he sat casually, his jacket draped over the back of his chair, he carried an undeniable gravitas. His booming laugh rolled through the café as he exchanged a word with the waitress, who smiled at him like he was an old friend. That was Roy—a man who could charm anyone, whether it was a judge in the courtroom or a barista on her first shift.

When Fiona approached, he stood, spreading his arms wide. "There's my girl! Come here and give your old man a hug."

She couldn't help but smile as she leaned into his embrace, the faint scent of cigars lingering on his clothing. "Hi, Dad."

"Sit, sit," Roy said, gesturing to the chair across from him. "Order whatever you want—it's on me. A man doesn't get to have breakfast with his daughter often enough."

The waitress arrived moments later, smiling warmly. "What can I get for you today?"Fiona scanned the menu quickly. "Just coffee and the veggie omelet, please. Oh, and wheat toast."

"Make that two omelets," Roy said, handing the menu back. "And bring some of those biscuits. They'll tide us over."

The waitress nodded and walked away, and Roy leaned back, studying Fiona with a thoughtful expression. His sharp eyes, still vibrant despite his years, seemed to miss nothing. "You look good, Fi. A little tired, though. What's on your mind?"

Fiona shrugged, trying to play it casual, but Roy wasn't the type to let things slide. He leaned forward, folding his hands on the table. "Spill it. You don't call me for a breakfast meeting unless there's something other than coffee brewing."

She hesitated before diving in. "Last night, I got a call from the Bates family lawyer."

Roy arched an eyebrow, a familiar mischievous grin creeping onto his face. "Uh-oh. Let me guess—he billed you for the call? Lawyers are like that, you know. Every minute costs a fortune."

Fiona chuckled, shaking her head. "No, Dad, it wasn't like that."

"Or maybe he called to offer you a retainer? I mean, who wouldn't want you on their team?" He leaned back with a satisfied chuckle, clearly amused by his own wordplay.

Fiona couldn't help but smile, despite the weight of the conversation she was about to have. Her father loved dad jokes and puns with a passion that bordered on theatrical. If there was an opportunity to insert one into a conversation, Roy Stevens would find it.

"Are you done?" Fiona asked, her tone teasing.

"For now," Roy replied, still grinning. "But I reserve the right to throw in a few more before my coffee gets cold."

Fiona's smile faded as her tone shifted. "Well, brace yourself, because this is serious."

Roy's grin faded instantly, replaced by a look of sharp concern. He leaned forward, resting his hands on the edge of the table. "What's going on?"

Fiona exhaled, running a hand through her hair. "Okay, so I've been working on this feature piece for the Chronicle. It started as something straightforward—a piece about the Bates estate for the Tour of Homes and Gardens. But ... it's turned into something else. Something bigger."

The waitress returned with their coffee, and Fiona paused, waiting as Roy thanked her and doctored his own coffee with sugar. Fiona took hers black, savoring the warmth as she continued. "I was given the contact information for Dolores Bates' attorney to help with the story. To make sure I had everything right. The logistics, permissions, that kind of thing."

Roy frowned. "Henry Caldwell, right?"

"Yes," Fiona said slowly, watching her father's reaction. "Why? Do you know him?"

"Of course I know him."

"He was drunk, Dad. Really drunk. And he said some things that ... well, I don't know what to make of them."

"Henry Caldwell is one of the most respected attorneys in Savannah. I'm surprised he'd act so carelessly."

"That's the thing. I couldn't believe it either. He was slurring his words, rambling about how stressful everything's been. And then he started talking about Dolores. And Sarah Mercer."

The waitress returned with their food, setting down the plates. Roy murmured a polite thank you before turning back to Fiona, his large brow furrowed. "What did he say?"

Fiona hesitated as she spread butter on her toast. "It's not just what he said—it's how he said it. He sounded scared of Dolores. Like he thought she was capable of ..." She stopped herself, choosing her words carefully. "He implied that Dolores might've had something to do with Sarah Mercer's disappearance."

Roy sat back in his chair, picking up his fork but not eating. "That's a serious accusation, Fiona. And it's not something you can base on a drunken phone call."

"I know," Fiona admitted, taking a bite of her omelet. "But don't you think it's strange? If someone like Henry—someone with his reputation—is saying things like that, doesn't it mean something?"

Roy shook his head, finally cutting into his food. "It means he's tired and overwhelmed. The Wesley family has always been a high-pressure client. If Henry's slipping like this, it's because the work is getting to him. Maybe he should think about stepping back, even retiring."

Fiona frowned at the comment, a flicker of confusion crossing her face. "Retirement? That's a surprising statement."

Roy shrugged as he chewed his omelet. "Some people just don't know when to call it a day. Work like that, it takes a toll after a while."

Fiona tilted her head. *Henry doesn't seem like the type who'd want to retire*, she thought, but she let it go. Roy had always been one to preach balance, even if he didn't always practice it himself.

Roy didn't seem to notice her confusion. "If you're planning to pursue this story, you need to tread carefully. The Wesley family has faced enough scandal over the years. You don't want to fuel baseless rumors that could hurt people—or your career."

"I know. But if there's truth to this—if Dolores really did—"

"You don't know that. And you can't act like you do."

As they finished their meals, Roy leaned forward. "You've got a formal interview with Dolores tomorrow, right?"

"Yeah," Fiona said, setting down her fork.

"Then that's your chance. Ask the right questions. See what she says. And above all, get the facts before you act."

Fiona nodded reluctantly. "You're right. I need to go in prepared."

"That's my girl," Roy said, his voice softening. "You've got good instincts, Fi. Trust them, but don't let them cloud your judgment."

Fiona managed a small smile. "Thanks, Dad. And Claire's doing well, by the way. She's been busy with her pro bono work at the museum."

"That's good to hear," Roy said, sitting back with a faint smile. "You both deserve a little peace and quiet. Not that I expect either of you to actually take it."

Fiona laughed lightly, feeling a flicker of relief. "Probably not. But I should get home and start prepping for tomorrow."

"Take care, Fi." Roy stood as she gathered her things, giving her a warm hug before she left. "And remember—don't chase the smoke. Chase the fire."

chapter
fifteen

THE BATES ESTATE LOOMED AHEAD, its sprawling facade as imposing as ever. Fiona parked at the end of the circular driveway, her nerves tightening with each step toward the entrance. She'd spent the entire night rehearsing questions, but now, standing at the threshold of Dolores Bates' home, they all felt inadequate.

A housekeeper—Margaret, according to her nametag—let her in and led her through the grand entryway. Fiona noticed how the woman's eyes darted around the space, as if checking that everything was in its proper place.

Dolores appeared in the sitting room, dressed in a tailored navy dress and pearls that gleamed against her skin. Her smile was polite but thin, the kind of smile that didn't quite reach her eyes. "Ms. Stevens. Punctual as ever. Please, have a seat."

Fiona perched on the edge of an antique armchair, trying not to fidget. Dolores gestured to a tray of tea and cookies set on the coffee table between them. "Help yourself," she said, sitting down with an elegance that only heightened Fiona's unease.

"Thank you for having me," Fiona said, trying to keep her tone steady. "I appreciate you making time during the Tour. I know how busy you must be with all the visitors."

"We did agree to full coverage," Dolores replied, a note of resignation in her voice. She furrowed her brow slightly, studying Fiona. "But why did you decide to write this article, Ms. Stevens? What drew you to my home?"

Fiona opened her mouth, then closed it, scrambling for an answer that wouldn't sound callous or opportunistic. Saying, *I really wanted to use the gossip surrounding your estate to build my career* wasn't exactly the right angle. She cleared her throat, forcing a smile.

"I wanted to highlight your resilience," she said carefully.

Dolores stiffened but maintained her smile. "Resilience is a necessity, Ms. Stevens. Not a choice."

Fiona nodded. "And your home is always being talked about in Savannah, isn't it? It's absolutely stunning."

"Yes, it is. Five generations of careful preservation will do that."

"I'd love to hear about some of the restoration work you've done," Fiona began, pulling out her notebook. "I understand you personally oversaw the renovation of the east wing after the fire in '98?"

Something flickered across Dolores' face—a flash of something unreadable, gone just as quickly as it appeared. Surprise, perhaps, that Fiona had done her homework. Annoyance, maybe, that she was bringing up a subject better left untouched.

"Yes," Dolores said, her tone measured. "Though that was a trying time. We lost several original pieces in that fire." She paused, stirring her tea with slow, deliberate movements. "The insurance investigation was extensive."

Fiona tapped her pen lightly against the page. "They had questions about how it started, didn't they?"

Dolores' stirring stopped. The spoon rested against the delicate china for a long moment before she set it down with just a little too much precision.

"I believe the official report determined it an accidental electrical fire. Of course, when one has a home as old as this, such things are not entirely unexpected. Wiring fails. Unfortunate things happen."

"There were rumors, though," she continued. "That it started in the master bedroom. That—"

"Ancient history. And not relevant to your article, I presume?"

Fiona hesitated, debating whether to push further. But the sharpness in Dolores' gaze was a clear warning: she was done discussing it.

She could feel the shift, the way the air in the room seemed to tighten around them.

Time to change direction.

Fiona cleared her throat and pivoted. "Actually, I'd love to hear about your husband's contribution to the decor. Charles had quite the eye for paintings, I understand?"

Dolores' expression softened after a flicker of something unreadable crossed her face. "He did," she said slowly. "The Sheraton in the library was his pride and joy. He always said it brought warmth to the room."

"And the Wesley collection? I've read it's one of the more remarkable private collections in Savannah."

"It is. The Wesley family has always valued the arts."

"And Charles' role in expanding that? I've heard he had an interest in more modern works. Even commissioned a few pieces."

Dolores stiffened slightly, her fingers curling around the armrest of her chair. "He did, from time to time. Though his focus was always on maintaining the family's legacy, not chasing trends."

"Still, he must have had a keen eye," Fiona said lightly. "I noticed a few names associated with the Savannah Art Museum tied to donations in his name. I think Sarah Mercer was mentioned?"

Dolores' face froze, her lips pressing into a tight line. "Sarah Mercer was an artist. She was involved in several exhibitions during that time."

"And her work? Was it part of your collection?"

"I wouldn't know." Dolores' eyes darkened, her voice dropping a degree in warmth. "Charles handled those matters."

"Of course," Fiona said, leaning forward slightly. "But you must have some thoughts. I mean, with his reputation for supporting local artists, Sarah Mercer must have been a significant connection—"

"Ms. Stevens," Dolores interrupted, her voice sharp. "I think we're straying from the purpose of this interview. You wanted to discuss the estate, not ancient gossip."

In the hallway beyond the sitting room, Fiona caught a glimpse of Margaret whispering urgently to another staff member, their heads bent close together. The second woman's eyes widened at whatever Margaret was saying.

"Of course," Fiona said smoothly, her pulse quickening. "I just thought it was interesting how Charles' contributions to the arts have tied into the Wesley family's legacy. The Savannah Art Museum even credited him for commissioning Sarah Mercer's last major piece."

Dolores' knuckles whitened against the armrest. "I wasn't aware of that."

Fiona pressed, her voice tinged with curiosity. "That's surprising, given how involved you've always been with maintaining the family's reputation."

"I don't care to discuss Sarah Mercer, Ms. Stevens. She is irrelevant to the history of this estate, and to my family."

Fiona hesitated, then pressed forward. "It's been said that Charles had an affair with Sarah. That she knew things about the family's finances that made her ... dangerous."

Dolores' jaw tightened, her hands still gripping the armrests of her chair. "I see. And what does this have to do with the Tour of Homes?"

"It is part of the story," Fiona said carefully. "The history of the estate, your family, everything that shaped it. Including Sarah's disappearance."

Out of the corner of her eye, Fiona saw Margaret hovering in the doorway again, wringing her hands.

Dolores' voice hardened. "My family is not a tabloid headline, Ms. Stevens. Charles is gone. My son is gone. And yet people like you insist on dragging their names through the mud."

"I'm not trying to drag anyone's name," Fiona said quickly, leaning forward. "I'm trying to understand what happened. The timing of everything—Charles' death, Sarah's disappearance, the truth has to be—"

"The truth?" Dolores snapped, her composure cracking. "The truth is that people will believe whatever lies suit them. And Sarah Mercer was a liar, through and through."

"Then what did she lie about?" Fiona asked, her voice quieter but no less pointed. "What was she threatening to reveal?"

Dolores stood abruptly, the movement so sudden that Fiona flinched. "Enough!" She grabbed a small porcelain vase from a nearby table and hurled it across the room. Fiona ducked, and the vase shattered against the wall behind her, pieces scattering across the floor like jagged confetti.

Margaret rushed in immediately, as if this were a well-rehearsed scene. Another maid appeared with a dustpan and brush, already moving toward the broken pieces.

"Check the wall," Dolores snapped at them. "Last time it took three coats to cover the mark."

She turned back to Fiona, her face livid. "Someone is feeding you lies, Ms. Stevens. Manipulating you. And I won't have it. You are not authorized to publish anything about me or my family. My lawyer will ensure that."

Fiona swallowed hard, her voice barely above a whisper. "I didn't mean to upset you."

Dolores pointed a trembling finger at her. "You listen to me, young lady. My life has been picked apart by people like you for years. I won't tolerate it anymore. Watch your back."

The words sent a chill down Fiona's spine. She nodded stiffly, gathering her notebook and pen with trembling hands. "Thank you for your time," she murmured, her voice barely audible.

Margaret hurried to escort her out, leaving the other maid to deal with Dolores, who had turned away, gripping the back of a chair to steady herself, her shoulders heaving with uncontrolled breaths.

As they reached the door, Margaret glanced over her shoulder before whispering, "Be careful, Ms. Stevens. Please."

chapter
sixteen

FIONA'S HANDS trembled as she gripped the steering wheel, her knuckles white against the leather. She'd practically fled the estate, her heart pounding in her chest and her thoughts spinning uncontrollably. The immaculate driveway with its manicured hedges had disappeared in her rearview mirror as she sped away, desperate to put distance between herself and Dolores Bates. Now, as she navigated through Savannah's streets, Dolores' outburst replayed in her mind—her sharp words cutting through the air, the violent crash of the vase against the wall, and the unspoken menace behind her warning to watch her back.

The memory of those eyes—cold and calculating one moment, wild with fury the next—sent another wave of panic through her. Dolores hadn't just been angry; she'd been threatening. And that threat felt all too real.

Pulling her phone from the cupholder, she dialed Claire, her fingers fumbling slightly against the screen. The phone rang twice before her sister answered, the familiar voice a momentary comfort in the chaos.

"Hey, Fi," Claire said casually. "What's up?"

Fiona's words tumbled out in a rush, her voice high-pitched and frantic. "She threatened me! Dolores Bates threatened me! She threw something across the room and I ducked out of the way and it shattered. I think she's going to come after me."

There was a pause on the other end of the line. Claire's tone sharpened, her casual greeting replaced by immediate concern. "Fiona, slow down. Where are you?"

"Driving. I just left her house," Fiona said, her grip tightening on the wheel as she swerved around a slower car. "It was horrible. As I was asking her questions, she completely lost it. She said I wasn't allowed to publish the story, and then she—" Fiona's breath hitched, the memory fresh and terrifying. "She told me to watch my back."

"Okay, hang on," Claire said, her voice calm but firm. "Take a deep breath. You sound like you're panicking."

"I am panicking!" Fiona snapped, her voice catching as she tried to steady herself. The truth was, she couldn't remember the last time she'd felt this shaken. Her journalistic instincts had always pushed her to chase stories, to dig deeper, but she'd never faced something like this—someone like Dolores Bates.

"Okay, okay," Claire said gently, her tone softening. "Find a safe spot and pull over. You can't drive like this."

Fiona exhaled shakily, glancing in her rearview mirror. The car behind her honked loudly as she realized she was drifting into the next lane, the driver's angry face visible in her mirror. "Crap!" she muttered, jerking the wheel to correct herself, the tires of her car catching the edge of the road.

"Fiona!" Claire's voice was urgent now. "Pull over before you hurt yourself—or someone else."

Spotting a gas station up ahead, its faded red and white sign a beacon of momentary safety, Fiona flicked on her turn signal and steered into the lot, her tires crunching on the loose gravel. She parked near the edge of the property, away from the pumps and the few customers milling about, and slumped against the seat, her heart pounding relentlessly in her chest.

"I'm stopped," she said, her voice barely above a whisper, the adrenaline that had carried her this far beginning to ebb, leaving exhaustion in its wake.

"Good. Now, tell me what happened. Slowly."

Fiona inhaled deeply, forcing herself to speak more evenly, though her hands still trembled as she gripped the phone. "I went to interview Dolores, and at first, it was fine. We were talking about the house, the

Tour, everything I was supposed to cover. But then I asked her about Charles—about his connection to Sarah Mercer and the art donations."

Claire groaned softly, the sound carrying a clear note of disapproval. "You didn't."

"I had to!" Fiona protested, frustration bubbling up alongside her fear. "That's the real story, Claire. But she completely shut down—no, worse than that. She snapped. She said someone was feeding me lies, manipulating me, and then ... then she threw a vase. It smashed against the wall right behind where I was sitting. The maids cleaned it up like this was a regular occurrence. And she told them last time it took three coats of paint to cover up. So I think this has happened before, Claire. This wasn't her first outburst. She looked ... unhinged."

Claire was quiet for a moment, her tone measured when she finally spoke. "And you think she might actually, what? Come after you?"

Fiona hesitated, glancing at the rearview mirror again, half-expecting to see Dolores Bates' car pulling into the gas station behind her. The thought sent a shiver down her spine. "I don't know. But I can't shake the feeling that she's hiding something significant. The way she reacted—it wasn't normal, Claire. It was intense, calculated even. Like she'd been waiting for someone to ask these questions so she could put them in their place."

"You were accusing her of having knowledge about someone's disappearance. In her own home. Don't you think it's reasonable for someone to get upset about that? Especially given everything she's been through?"

Fiona blinked, taken aback by her sister's response. Her free hand curled into a tight fist against her thigh. "You think it was reasonable for her to throw a vase across the room and scream at me to watch my back? Are you serious right now?"

"I'm not saying that. I'm saying people have limits. If someone came into your home and started poking at the worst parts of your life, the tragedies and scandals you've tried to move past, wouldn't you lash out, too?"

Fiona shook her head vigorously, even though Claire couldn't see her. "It wasn't just lashing out, Claire. It was more than that. There was something calculated about it, something deliberate. Like she knows something terrible and doesn't want anyone else to find out. And the way her staff reacted—they've seen this before. They know what she's capable of."

Claire sighed, her tone patient but firm. "Or," she said gently, "it's just a woman who's been through hell and doesn't want her life picked apart anymore. People have breaking points, Fiona. Maybe you hit hers. She lost her husband in tragic circumstances, her son was falsely accused of murder then killed after his release—these aren't small hardships. These are life-altering traumas."

"This wasn't just some temper tantrum! This was different. Please believe me!" Fiona's voice rose in pitch, desperation coloring her words. She needed her sister to understand, to validate what she'd experienced. Claire was always the rational one, the voice of reason, but this time her logic felt like a betrayal.

Claire exhaled, the sound crackling through the phone. "You're emotional right now, and I get it. But try to think about this logically. Dolores has been through more than most people could handle—losing her husband, her son, the rumors that have followed her for decades. Is it really so surprising that she'd snap when someone brings all of that up in her own home?"

Fiona opened her mouth to argue but stopped. Claire's words rung in her ear, rational and cutting. Was she being fair to Dolores? Had she crossed a line in her pursuit of the truth? Fiona's mind raced with everything she'd seen and heard, her thoughts tangling together in a confusing knot of suspicion and doubt.

Before she could respond, her phone buzzed in her hand and beeped in her ear. She pulled the device away from her face to glance at the screen, and the name she saw made her pulse quicken with a mix of anticipation and dread.

"Claire, it's Henry," Fiona said quickly, her voice taut with tension.

Claire's tone sharpened immediately. "Don't pick up. You don't need to talk to anyone connected to Dolores right now. Not when you're this rattled."

Her finger hovered over the screen as her heart raced. *Claire doesn't get it*, she thought, biting her lip. *Henry's the only one who might actually tell me the truth. Everyone else is too careful, too controlled. He's already opened up to me once—if I ignore him now, I might lose my chance to get more answers.*

She watched the phone continue to buzz, torn between her sister's cautious advice and her own burning curiosity. The call would go to voicemail in seconds if she didn't decide.

She knew Claire was right in some ways. The situation with Dolores was volatile, and every instinct told her to tread carefully. But there was something about Henry—his honesty, even in his drunken ramblings—that made her feel like he was holding pieces of the puzzle she desperately needed. *If I want the real story, I can't afford to shut him out. This could be my only chance.*

"I'll call you back," Fiona said quickly, ending the call before Claire could argue further. She swiped to answer Henry's call, her heart pounding in her ears.

"Henry?"

"Fiona," Henry said, his voice warm but tinged with concern. "I heard about what happened."

"How did you—?"

"Dolores called me. She told me you were asking all sorts of questions about Charles and Sarah. She's furious," he continued, his words measured but somehow urgent. "She was practically incoherent when she called. I've never heard her like that before."

"I wasn't trying to upset her," Fiona said quickly, feeling a flicker of guilt despite herself. "I just wanted the truth. People have been whispering about this for years, and I thought—"

"And you did the right thing," Henry said firmly, cutting through her explanation. "Don't let her scare you, Fiona. She's been keeping this buried for too long. The secrets, the lies—they've been eating away at everyone involved. Maybe it's time someone finally shined a light on all of it."

"What do you mean?" Fiona asked, her voice dropping to barely a whisper, as if Dolores might somehow hear her through the phone.

There was a pause on the line, as though Henry was weighing his words carefully, deciding how much to reveal. "I mean, Dolores isn't who she pretends to be. I have proof, Fiona—proof that she killed Sarah. And Charles ... well, let's just say their last argument wasn't as innocent as she'd like people to believe. That fight led to his heart attack."

Fiona's breath hitched, her free hand gripping the steering wheel so tightly her knuckles whitened. "You have evidence? Why haven't you come forward?"

"I'm her lawyer," Henry said, a note of resignation in his voice. "I'm supposed to keep these secrets. Attorney-client privilege is sacred, you know that. And it isn't my story to tell. But it is yours. The world deserves to know the truth, Fiona. You can't let her get away with this anymore."

"I don't know, Henry." Fiona pressed a hand to her forehead, her thoughts spinning in dizzying circles. The enormity of what he was suggesting overwhelmed her. "I don't know if I can do this. What if she really does come after me? You didn't see her today. The way she looked at me ..."

"She won't. You're stronger than you think. But if you're nervous, we can talk about this in person. I'll explain everything. How about I come to you?"

"Come to me?" Fiona asked hesitantly, glancing around the deserted corner of the gas station where she'd parked.

"Sure," Henry said, his tone soothing, almost hypnotic in its reassurance. "You don't have to go anywhere. I remember your address from when we shared the cab. I'll text you when I'm close."

Fiona hesitated, weighing her options. Meeting with Henry meant committing to this path, to uncovering whatever dark secrets lay at the heart of the Bates estate. But staying silent meant letting those secrets remain buried—perhaps forever.

"Okay," she said finally, her decision crystalizing. "But I need to understand everything, Henry. No more half-truths or vague implications. I need the whole story."

"You'll get the full story. I'll see you soon."

The call ended, and Fiona sat there for a moment, her mind racing with possibilities and fears. A notification flashed across her screen—Claire calling her back, probably worried after their abrupt disconnection.

She swiped the call away and quickly typed out a text. *I'm fine. I overreacted. Talk later.* The lie tasted bitter, but she couldn't deal with Claire's caution now—not when she was so close to the truth.

Her thumb hovered over the send button for a moment before she pressed it, guilt gnawing at her conscience. Claire would be hurt when she found out, but Fiona couldn't let that stop her. Not when she finally had a chance to uncover what really happened to Sarah Mercer, to Charles Bates—and to discover who Dolores Bates truly was beneath her carefully constructed facade.

Starting the car, she pulled back onto the road with renewed determination. Whatever Henry was about to tell her would change everything—she could feel it. And she had to be ready.

chapter
seventeen

FIONA'S HANDS gripped the steering wheel tightly as she pulled into her apartment complex. Her heart leaped and her pulse quickened when she spotted Henry leaning casually against the wall near her door, his hands in his pockets and a bottle of wine in one hand.

"Hey," Henry said, straightening when he saw her. His smile was easy, but there was tension in his eyes. "Are you okay?"

Fiona got out of the car and slung her bag over her shoulder, walking toward him. "I don't know."

Stepping forward, he wrapped his arms around her in a quick, firm hug. She stiffened slightly at first, then let herself lean into it. His embrace was steady, comforting.

Henry pulled back and gestured toward her door. "Let's get inside. You've had a day."

As Fiona unlocked the door, she glanced at the bottle of wine in his hand. "You brought alcohol? That's your big plan to fix everything?"

Henry chuckled, his grin softening the tension in her shoulders. "Alcohol's the universal cure for lawyers. Stress? Alcohol. Bad day? Alcohol. Existential dread? You guessed it—alcohol."

Fiona managed a small laugh as she fumbled with her keys, her fingers trembling slightly as she unlocked the door. "You might be onto something. But I think existential dread requires whiskey, not wine."

"Noted. I'll bring whiskey next time."

They stepped inside and she headed to the kitchen. Henry followed her in. Her hands refused to steady as she pulled glasses from the cabinet, despite her best efforts.

Before she could stop fumbling, the glass slipped from her fingers and crashed to the floor, shattering. "Oh my God," she muttered, her voice breaking as she crouched to pick up the shards. "I'm so sorry—"

"Hey, hey, don't worry about it," Henry said gently, crouching down beside her. He placed a steady hand on her arm to stop her. "I'll take care of it. Just sit down, okay?"

Fiona hesitated, then nodded, her cheeks flushing as she stepped back and sat on the couch. She watched as Henry calmly swept up the broken glass, wiped the counter, and pulled a fresh glass from the cabinet. He poured the wine with measured ease before joining her.

"Here," he said, handing her a glass.

"Thanks," Fiona replied, taking a sip. The bold red wine warmed her throat, but it didn't do much to settle her nerves.

Henry sat beside her, his gaze steady. "Tell me what happened."

Fiona stared at the liquid in her glass before taking a deep breath. "I started asking questions about Charles. Donations to the Savannah Art Museum, his connection to Sarah Mercer. Dolores completely lost it. She threw a vase across the room, Henry. I felt like she was going to—" She stopped, shaking her head. "I don't know. It was terrifying."

Henry nodded, rubbing the back of his neck. "Yeah, that would do it. Dolores doesn't like being cornered. Especially not about Sarah."

"I saw things around the house—damaged doorframes that were patched up, scratches on the furniture, covered repairs in the walls. And then she throws a vase like it's nothing. It's like she's done this before."

Henry nodded slowly, his expression grim. "She has a temper. Always has. But it's not just about the outbursts—it's what's underneath them."

"Henry, I need you to tell me the truth." Fiona set her glass on the coffee table, leaning toward him. "You keep hinting at things, but right now, it's all just hearsay. I'm not a lawyer, but even I know that doesn't hold up."

"You're right." Henry's shoulders sagged, and he let out a long breath. "And you deserve the truth. All of it."

He took a sip of his wine before continuing. "Sarah Mercer didn't disappear. Dolores killed her."

Fiona's breath hitched, but she forced herself to stay calm. "How?"

Henry set his glass down, his gaze distant as he spoke. "Sarah had been pushing Charles to leave Dolores. She was ambitious—convinced she could take over the Wesley fortune if she played her cards right. But Dolores found out."

Fiona leaned forward. "And?"

"They had a confrontation," Henry said, his voice steady but low. "Sarah went to the estate to demand that Charles finalize the divorce agreement. Dolores caught her there, and things got heated. According to what my father pieced together, Sarah threatened to expose something about Dolores—something damaging. Dolores snapped."

He hesitated, then added, "She killed Sarah. Strangled her in the study."

Fiona's hands trembled as she picked up her glass again, needing something to anchor her. "And the body?"

"Dolores dumped it in the marshes near the estate. She used weights to make sure it sank. My father discovered some of this later, through documents and ... conversations Dolores probably thought were private."

"And you have proof of this?"

Henry nodded. "Letters, notes. Copies of things my father kept, probably to protect himself if anything ever came to light. He passed them down to me when he retired."

Fiona stared at him, her thoughts racing. "Why haven't you come forward? Why didn't your father?"

"Because when you work for a family like this, you're not just an employee—you're a hostage." Henry's jaw tightened, his hand gripping the armrest of the couch. "Dolores is powerful, Fiona. My father knew that crossing her could ruin him. But she's the reason his firm thrived. Losing her would've meant losing everything."

He leaned forward, his elbows resting on his knees. "If I—or my father—were ever accused of revealing something considered attorney-client privileged, that would be the end of our careers. Forget reputation —we'd lose our licenses. We'd never be able to practice again."

Fiona blinked, absorbing his words. "But if you have proof, isn't there a way to, I don't know, work around that?"

Henry shook his head, a bitter smile tugging at the corner of his lips. "That's the problem with privilege. Even if the proof was left lying around, if it's connected to anything Dolores shared with my father in confidence, I can't touch it without risking everything."

He rubbed a hand over his face, the weight of the admission dragging him down. "My dad always said the Bates family was both the best and worst thing that ever happened to him. They made his career, but they also put him in an impossible position. And now, I'm in the same one."

"Then why tell me this?" Fiona tilted her head, studying him. "If it's so dangerous for you, why trust me?"

Henry met her gaze, his voice quieter but resolute. "Because I can't live with this anymore. And you're not bound by the same restrictions I am. You're a journalist, Fiona. You can tell the truth without Dolores completely ruining you."

Fiona's breath came in shallow bursts as she processed his words, her thoughts spinning. "You'd really trust me not to reveal where all this came from?"

"I wouldn't have told you otherwise."

Fiona held his gaze, searching for any trace of doubt, but all she saw was sincerity. And something unspoken that made her pulse quicken. The room was quiet, save for the faint hum of the fridge in the kitchen and the soft ticking of the clock on the wall.

"I don't know how you do it," she murmured, her voice barely above a whisper.

He leaned in, his expression both curious and cautious. "Do what?"

"Keep all of this inside. Carry it around, knowing what you know."

Henry gave a small, humorless laugh, his hand moving to rest on the back of the couch near her shoulder. "You get used to it. Or at least, you tell yourself you do." His voice dropped slightly, softer now. "But maybe that's why I needed to tell you. I couldn't carry it alone anymore."

Fiona's chest tightened at the vulnerability in his tone. The tension between them was palpable, undeniable and electric. Her gaze flicked to Henry's mouth, lingering before darting back up to meet his eyes. She didn't know who moved first, whether it was his hand brushing her shoulder or her leaning toward him, but his lips were on hers, warm and insistent.

Her breath hitched as the kiss deepened, her wine glass tilting dangerously in her hand. Henry's hand shot out, steadying the glass and setting it safely on the table without breaking the connection between them. His other hand found her waist, his touch firm yet gentle as he pulled her closer.

Fiona's fingers tangled in his shirt, clutching the fabric as her heart raced. The world outside disappeared, leaving only the heat between them and the soft sounds of their breathing.

The kiss slowed, turning softer, more deliberate, but the tension between them didn't fade. It simmered, a promise of more to come.

Henry pulled back just enough to rest his forehead against hers, his breath warm against her cheek. "Are you okay?" he asked quietly, his voice laced with concern and something deeper.

Fiona nodded, her voice catching as she whispered, "Yeah."

The rest of the night blurred together in a haze of wine, whispered confessions, and soft touches. Fiona felt herself letting go of the tension that had gripped her all day, surrendering to the moment and the man who had trusted her with more than she'd ever expected.

chapter
eighteen

FIONA SAT AT HER DESK, staring blankly at her computer screen. Her hands hovered over the keyboard, frozen in place as her mind replayed the events of the past twenty-four hours.

That morning, Henry had kissed her goodbye before leaving her apartment. He'd woken early, murmuring something about meetings and paperwork, but not before pausing by the door. With a lingering smile, he had cupped her face, his thumb brushing her cheek. "I know you'll do the right thing, Fiona," he'd said softly. "About the story. About everything."

The words echoed in her mind. Did he really trust her judgment that much? Or was it his way of nudging her toward publishing the article, ensuring that his truth finally came out?

Dragging herself to the office had been a monumental task. Now, as she sat in the muted din of the newsroom, the blinking cursor on her blank screen taunted her. What was she supposed to do? How could she write a story that could destroy another woman's life—and possibly her own, if she wasn't careful?

She placed her hands on the keyboard, her fingers hesitating over the keys. Taking a deep breath, she began typing.

Dolores Wesley Bates has spent decades as one of Savannah's most respected social figures, but beneath the veneer of Southern grace lies a story of deception, loss, and ...

Fiona stopped, her pulse racing as she read the words. She hit the backspace key, watching the sentence disappear. Her hands hovered over the keys again, trembling slightly.

She tried another angle.

The disappearance of Sarah Mercer is one of Savannah's enduring mysteries, but new evidence suggests ...

Fiona's fingers hovered over the keyboard, her thoughts twisting in knots.

She hesitated, then pressed the backspace key, watching the words disappear from the screen as doubt crept in again.

What if she was wrong?

What if this wasn't the story she thought it was?

She exhaled sharply, rubbing a hand over her face. Her mind was a mess—a tangled web of contradictions.

On one hand, she saw the Dolores Bates that Savannah whispered about. The woman who had exploded in fury, who had thrown a vase against the wall like it was nothing. The woman who had glared at her with barely contained rage, who had told her in no uncertain terms to stay out of her affairs. The woman who, if the rumors were to be believed, had murdered Sarah Mercer in a blind rage.

But then there was the other Dolores.

The one who had scrawled that desperate note in the margins of the divorce agreement, the woman fighting to hold on to her family's legacy, the mother trying to protect her son from being erased by a husband who had already moved on.

Fiona leaned back in her chair, staring at the blank document in front of her, her frustration bubbling just beneath the surface.

It didn't add up.

The woman who had clawed to keep the Wesley estate intact—who had fought to make sure Anthony got what was his—wasn't the same woman Savannah gossiped about. That woman—the cold, unfeeling widow, the one people claimed had killed for power—was a fabrication. A story that had taken on a life of its own.

And yet, she had seen the anger firsthand. She had seen the cracks in Dolores' armor, the way her temper could ignite in an instant.

Which was the real Dolores Bates? Fiona clenched her jaw, shaking

her head. She didn't know anymore. Her mind flashed back to Henry—
to his quiet encouragement, his insistence that she was doing the right
thing.

But was she?

Or was she playing into a narrative she wasn't sure was true
anymore? She sighed and pressed the backspace key again. More words
disappeared.

"Stevens." Jacobs' voice broke through her fog.

Fiona startled, looking up to see him standing by her desk, his usual
no-nonsense expression softened with curiosity. "Got a minute?" he
asked.

"Uh, yeah," Fiona said, quickly minimizing the blank document on
her screen.

"Let's talk in my office."

Jacobs' office was cluttered but familiar, the smell of coffee and ink
permeating the air. Fiona sat in the chair opposite his desk, her hands
clasped tightly in her lap as he settled into his chair.

"Okay," he began, leaning back slightly. "So, what's the deal with the
Bates story? If it's dead, just say so. No shame in cutting your losses and
moving on."

"It's not dead," Fiona said quickly. Her heart raced as she blurted
out, "It's the opposite. I have a source who says he can prove that
Dolores Bates killed Sarah Mercer."

Jacobs froze, his eyebrows shooting up. "Shit."

Fiona opened her mouth to utter a reply, but it wouldn't come out.
She hadn't meant to share this so soon. Her hands trembled in her lap.

Jacobs leaned forward, his elbows on the desk. "Do you trust this
source?"

"Yes," she said firmly, meeting his gaze.

Jacobs nodded, but his expression remained cautious. "Okay, so
what exactly does he have?"

Fiona hesitated. "Documents, letters, evidence passed down from
his father, who worked with Dolores for years. He says it's enough to
show she killed Sarah and covered it up. That, plus he knows where she
buried the body."

"Jesus," Jacobs muttered, rubbing his temples.

Fiona continued, her voice quieter now. "I went to Dolores' house yesterday for the interview. She ... she threw a vase across the room. It shattered. She told me I wasn't authorized to publish anything and that her lawyer would be in touch. She said I should 'watch my back.'"

Jacobs sat back, his eyes widening slightly. "That's ... a lot."

Fiona nodded, her hands twisting in her lap. "I don't know what to do. This story—it's huge. It's important. But it's dangerous."

"What do you want to do, Fiona?" Jacobs studied her for a moment, then leaned forward again, his tone serious. "Because if you're going to write this, you need to be all in. No second-guessing halfway through. If you're out, we drop it now and move on."

She straightened in her chair, her hands still trembling slightly. "This story needs to be told, no matter the consequences."

Jacobs didn't speak immediately, letting her words settle. Fiona's own voice echoed in her mind, and she took a deep breath, trying to steady herself. Her thoughts churned, weighing the gravity of what she was about to undertake.

"This isn't just a story about an old scandal or some long-forgotten affair," Fiona continued, her tone growing firmer. "This is about a woman who was murdered, a life that was stolen, and justice that was never served. If I don't write this, who will? Who else even knows what I know?"

She glanced at Jacobs, her throat tightening. "I can't walk away from this, Jacobs. If I do, then Sarah Mercer just becomes another victim of Savannah's gossip machine—another name lost to time, another person who didn't matter enough to get the truth."

Jacobs leaned forward, watching her. "And you're sure, Fiona? Because this isn't just about the article—it's about what comes after. The fallout, the scrutiny, the pushback. Are you ready for that?"

Fiona nodded, her fingers gripping the edge of her chair. "No one's ever ready for something like this. But if there's a chance to set the record straight, I have to try."

Fiona swallowed hard, her chest tightening as she considered his words. She thought of Claire, of the risks her sister had taken when she decided to represent Anthony in his appeal. This must have been what Claire felt like when she'd taken Anthony's case. Everyone told her it was a mistake, that it wasn't worth it. But she believed in what she was doing, and she fought for it.

Jacobs sat back, exhaling. "You've thought this through."

"I have. And I know it's not going to be easy. But this is bigger than me. It's bigger than any of us."

Jacobs gave her a small, approving nod. "All right, then. Write it. Make it airtight. No loopholes, no gaps. We'll deal with the fallout when it comes. But in the meantime—" He gave her a pointed look. "Don't be alone when you're walking to your car, or anywhere, for that matter. Got it?"

Fiona exhaled, her shoulders easing just slightly. "Got it."

As she stood to leave, Jacobs stopped her. "I'm proud of you. Not everyone has the guts to chase a story like this."

Fiona smiled faintly. "Thanks, Jacobs."

Back at her desk, Fiona opened a blank document again, staring at the blinking cursor as she gathered her thoughts. Her phone buzzed, and she glanced at the screen.

Claire.

With a sigh, she answered. "Hey."

"Hey?" Claire's voice was sharp, frantic, instantly setting Fiona on edge. "I've been trying to reach you all morning. Where have you been?"

Fiona hesitated, shifting in her chair. She hadn't checked her phone at all. "I've been busy," she said, keeping her tone neutral.

Claire let out an exasperated huff. "Busy? Busy with what, exactly? Tell me you haven't done something reckless."

Fiona winced. Too late for that.

"I'm handling it," she muttered.

"That's not reassuring. Tell me you didn't answer the phone for that so-called lawyer."

Fiona stayed silent.

Claire groaned. "Jesus Christ, Fiona! Are you serious?"

"Claire—"

"No. You do not pick up the phone for him. You do not engage. And you sure as hell don't—"

"Why don't we just meet up?" Fiona pinched the bridge of her nose.

"Clearly, you're in a mood, and I don't feel like getting chewed out over the phone."

Claire huffed, but her frustration was laced with worry. "Fiona, I swear to God, if you—"

"Let's just meet at the coffee shop. That way you can yell at me in person instead of my eardrums ringing for the next hour."

There was a pause, then a reluctant, "Fine. Ten minutes."

"Try not to break any speed limits on the way."

Fiona hung up, exhaling as she shoved her phone into her bag. Her nerves tightened, but she pushed the feeling aside.

She had bigger things to worry about now.

chapter
nineteen

THE COFFEE SHOP was packed with the usual mid-morning rush—business professionals grabbing caffeine before heading to the office, students hunched over laptops, tourists lingering near the pastry case debating between croissants and muffins. The air smelled like roasted espresso beans and warm cinnamon, a scent Fiona usually found comforting.

Today, it barely registered.

She sat across from Claire in the farthest booth, tucked away from the bustle, but even with the relative privacy, her nerves were frayed. The hum of conversations, the clinking of mugs against saucers, the hiss of the espresso machine—it all blurred into meaningless noise as she stirred her coffee, the spoon clinking softly against the ceramic.

Claire, on the other hand, sat perfectly still, her hands wrapped around her own mug, her eyes sharp and unwavering as she studied Fiona like she was trying to pick her apart molecule by molecule.

Finally, Claire sighed and set her cup down, tilting her head. "Let's start with the obvious: You answered the phone for Dolores' lawyer. Even though I warned you not to."

Fiona winced. There was no point in lying. Claire would see right through her. She glanced down at her coffee before giving a small, reluctant nod. "I did."

Claire exhaled, leaning back against the booth and crossing her arms.

Fiona lifted her cup, taking a small sip, but it did nothing to loosen the tightness in her throat.

Claire arched a brow. "And then what?"

Fiona set her spoon down on the napkin beside her plate, the small metal clink sounding deafening. "He came over."

Claire's eyebrows shot up.

Fiona held up a hand to preempt whatever lecture was brewing. "And before you say anything, it wasn't weird. He wanted to explain everything, and I let him."

Claire let out a slow, measured breath. "Fiona ..."

"I know how it sounds," Fiona rushed to say, pressing her palms against the table. "But I needed answers. And he gave them to me."

Claire narrowed her eyes. "And you trust the answers he gave you?"

Fiona hesitated. Because the truth was—she didn't know.

"But I just needed to hear him out, okay?"

Claire shook her head, her lips pressing together in clear disapproval.

Fiona bristled. "I didn't say it was a good idea, Claire. But what was I supposed to do? Ignore him? Pretend I wasn't already in the middle of this?"

"Yes!" Claire said, exasperated. "That's exactly what you should have done."

"You don't get it."

"Then explain it to me."

Fiona shook her head, looking down at her coffee, watching the steam curl into the air. She glanced around the bustling coffee shop, her gaze darting to the couple at the counter and the barista chatting with a customer. Lowering her voice, she leaned forward and gestured for Claire to do the same.

Claire frowned but obliged, leaning in until they were nearly nose-to-nose across the small table.

"He told me Dolores killed Sarah Mercer." Fiona glanced around one more time, even though her voice was a low whisper. "He said she hid the body in the marshes near the estate. He has proof, all passed down from his father."

Claire's eyes widened, her mouth opening before she quickly snapped it shut. She glanced over her shoulder, stiffening as she checked their surroundings. "You're serious?"

"Dead serious. He said Sarah and Dolores had a confrontation, it got physical, and Dolores killed her. Then she dumped the body in the marshes."

Claire sat back, her hand brushing her temple as she processed the information. "And you believe him?"

"Why wouldn't I? He's her lawyer, Claire. Coming forward with this could destroy him. He has everything to lose."

Claire was quiet for a moment, her gaze searching Fiona's face. "That's true," she admitted. "But it also makes me wonder why now? Why tell you instead of the police?"

"Because he feels trapped. He said his father was too scared of Dolores to come forward, and now he's in the same position. But I'm not bound by attorney-client privilege."

"I guess that makes sense. But this is big. Bigger than I think you realize."

"I do realize it," Fiona said softly, her voice trembling slightly. "I talked to Jacobs about it, and he's on board. He thinks I should write the story."

Claire's gaze softened. "And how do you feel about it?"

Fiona hesitated, her fingers curling around her coffee mug. The warmth seeped into her palms, but it did little to steady the tremble in her hands. "If I don't write this, who will? This isn't just some tabloid piece. It's justice—for Sarah, for the truth."

Claire pressed her lips into a thin line, her fingers idly tracing the edge of her napkin. She was silent for a moment, her gaze distant, as though weighing every word. Finally, she leaned forward, her arms resting on the table, her voice quiet but firm. "If you believe this is right, I'll support you."

Fiona's breath caught. She opened her mouth to speak, but Claire held up a hand, stopping her.

"No one stood by me when I took Anthony's appeal," Claire continued, her tone softening but carrying an unmistakable weight. "It was lonely, and it was hard. Everyone told me I was wasting my time, that I was wrong for even trying. But I knew what I was doing was right, and I couldn't walk away from that. It didn't matter what anyone else thought."

Claire met Fiona's gaze, her expression a mix of vulnerability and resolve. "You're fighting for something bigger than yourself. And if that's what you believe in, then I'm going to stand by you."

Fiona blinked, emotion tightening her throat. Her voice wavered as she said softly, "Thank you. That means a lot."

Claire gave her a faint smile, but she fiddled with the edge of her napkin again. "You're braver than I was at the start of Anthony's case."

Fiona shook her head, her voice heavy with regret. "I wasn't brave then. I didn't stand by you at the beginning. I wasn't there for you when you needed me most."

Claire's brow furrowed, and she reached across the table, placing a hand over Fiona's. "We don't need to revisit all of that. We've moved past it."

"But I still feel bad," Fiona said, her voice breaking slightly. "You were doing the right thing, and I didn't support you."

Claire squeezed her hand gently. "I forgive you. I forgave you a long time ago. And honestly? You made it up to me by being there when it mattered most. You stood by me when the verdict came through, and you've been my biggest cheerleader ever since."

Fiona managed a faint smile, but something about her sister's words cut deeper than she expected.

Because the truth was—she had always admired Claire.

Her whole life, Claire had been the fearless one. The one who had taken risks, who had put herself on the line for the things that mattered. She had taken on Anthony Bates' appeal when the world told her not to, when everyone told her she was making a mistake. Had stood her ground when people whispered about her, when the rumor mill tried to grind her down.

And Fiona?

Fiona had always played it safe.

She had built her career on observing, reporting, staying neutral. She had done what was expected, taken the assignments that wouldn't ruffle feathers, written the stories that stayed within the boundaries of what was acceptable.

But now, she wasn't sure that was enough anymore.

For the first time, she was stepping over a line she wasn't sure she could come back from.

And she wanted to believe it was worth it.

Blinking, her throat tightened as she forced herself to hold Claire's gaze. "I just want to make you proud."

Claire's expression softened, her smile faltering just slightly. "Fi, You already do. You always have."

Fiona swallowed, nodding, but deep down, she wasn't sure that was true. Because Claire had fought for what was right, even when it cost her everything. And Fiona was just starting to understand what that felt like.

Claire sighed, squeezing Fiona's hand once more before letting go. "But that doesn't mean I'm not worried. This is dangerous. Dolores Bates is not some small-town socialite. She is powerful, and she will not play nice if you back her into a corner. Look at my history with her. She essentially manipulated everyone so that I would take Anthony's appeal."

"It all worked out, though," Fiona said.

Claire nodded. "Sure. But, what I'm saying is that she's used to getting her way with things."

Fiona exhaled slowly, feeling the weight of Claire's words settle deep in her chest. She wasn't playing it safe anymore. But for the first time, she didn't want to. "Yes, I know. And to be honest, I'm struggling. I've been sitting at my desk all morning, trying to start the story, but I can't. I feel like I'm paralyzed."

"Maybe it's the setting," Claire said after a moment. "You're stuck in your head, stuck at your desk. You need a change of scenery."

Fiona frowned slightly. "Like what?"

"Tybee Island," Claire said, her tone decisive. "Let's take that trip early. You can bring your laptop, and I won't even complain. But getting out of the city, being near the ocean—it might help."

Fiona's lips curved into a small smile. "You'd really let me work on vacation?"

Claire rolled her eyes. "Within reason. Besides, it'll be good for me to get away before the museum's big art festival."

"You know what?" Fiona leaned back in her seat, the idea settling over her like a soft blanket. "You're right. Let's do it."

chapter
twenty

FIONA TOSSED clothes into her suitcase haphazardly, her mind swirling. She barely noticed what she was packing—T-shirts, jeans, maybe a dress. All she could focus on was the story. The truth. And the nagging fear that she might not get it right.

The sharp chime of her doorbell pulled her from her thoughts. She glanced at the clock. Claire was early.

"Coming!" Fiona called, zipping her suitcase halfway before hurrying to the door.

She opened it with a smile, expecting her sister's face, but was met instead by a tall, imposing man in a navy blazer. His expression was blank, professional, but his presence made her tense.

"Fiona Stevens?" he asked.

"Yes," she replied cautiously.

He handed her a thick stack of papers. "You've been served."

Fiona blinked, stunned. "What? Wait—what is this?"

The man didn't answer. He nodded, turned on his heel, and walked briskly down the hallway, leaving her standing in the open door with the papers clutched to her chest.

Her breath caught in her throat. Moving to the kitchen, she set the stack on the counter as if it might bite her. Taking a deep breath, she began flipping through the pages. The legal jargon swam in front of her eyes—motion for preliminary injunction, plaintiff, defamation—and none of it made sense.

Her fingers trailed over the embossed seal on the first page, her mind racing. *This has to be a mistake. Doesn't it?*

She barely registered the sound of footsteps approaching.

"Why is your door wide open?" Claire's voice cut through her haze. "After everything you just told me, you really need to be more careful about your surroundings."

Fiona looked up, startled, the papers trembling in her grip. "I don't know—I was just. Someone just handed me these." She gestured helplessly to the stack of papers. "They said I've been served."

Claire stepped inside, closing the door firmly behind her and clicking the lock. She set her bag down and crossed to the counter, her sharp gaze flicking to the papers. "Let me see."

Fiona handed them over, her nerves tightening as Claire flipped through the documents. Her sister's face grew more serious with every page she scanned.

"This," Claire said finally, her tone measured, "is a lawsuit."

Fiona's chest tightened. "What kind of lawsuit?"

"A motion for a preliminary injunction." Claire held up the front page. "Dolores Bates is suing you to stop you from publishing any articles about her."

"What?" Fiona's voice cracked. "That doesn't make sense. Henry told me I should publish the article." She froze, her mind spinning. "Maybe she hired a different lawyer."

Claire's expression darkened as she flipped to the last page, her eyes narrowing as she examined the signature. "It's signed by Henry Caldwell."

"Why would he do this?" Fiona whispered, her breath catching. "He told me to publish the article. He said I was doing the right thing!"

Claire raised an eyebrow, her tone sharp. "I told you not to pick up the phone for him. But you didn't just pick up—you let him come over. And now this happens?"

Fiona winced, her hands tightening around the edge of the counter. "I thought he was helping me, Claire. He told me things—things about Dolores, about Sarah Mercer."

"And you believed him?" Claire let out a frustrated sigh, setting the papers down. "Lawyers say a lot of things. That doesn't mean they can always be trusted."

"Why wouldn't I trust him?" Fiona shot back, her voice rising. "He gave me evidence! He put himself on the line—"

"Did he, though? Or did he just tell you what you wanted to hear? Think about it, Fiona. He's Dolores' lawyer. He and his father have worked for her for years. Do you really think he'd betray her like that without an ulterior motive?"

Fiona opened her mouth to argue, but no words came out. Her mind raced, replaying every conversation she'd had with Henry. He'd seemed genuine, honest, even vulnerable—but now, doubt seeped into the cracks of her trust.

"I ... I don't know," Fiona said finally, her voice quieter. "It felt real. He felt real."

Claire's expression softened, but her tone remained firm. "Look, I get it. You wanted to believe him because he told you what you needed to move forward. But you need to be smart about this. Right now, he's filing lawsuits with Dolores' name on them. That doesn't scream ally."

Fiona frowned, her gaze dropping to the papers on the counter. "There's got to be another explanation."

"Okay," Claire murmured, sitting down at the counter and flipping through the pages of dense legal text. "Let's figure out why Henry Caldwell is filing this lawsuit."

Fiona watched her sister's focus intensify, her heart racing as Claire muttered phrases like "preliminary injunction" and "irreparable harm" under her breath. The tension in the room felt like a weight pressing on Fiona's chest.

"You're right," Claire said, frowning as she turned another page. "None of this makes any sense. If he's been working with Dolores all this time, why would he be encouraging you to publish and then file this? It's contradictory."

Fiona crossed her arms, her voice tight. "Maybe Dolores forced him. He could be under pressure, right? You said it yourself—lawyers have to protect their clients."

Claire didn't answer immediately. Instead, she flipped to the last page, her fingers stilling as her eyes narrowed on the signature line. She tilted the paper toward the light, her gaze zeroing in on something small.

"What's wrong?" Fiona asked, leaning forward.

"Look at the bar number next to his name."

"What about it?"

"It's low," Claire said, her tone sharpening. She tapped the page. "Usually, the higher the bar number, the younger the attorney. A number this low means the attorney has been practicing for decades."

Fiona's stomach dropped. "But ... Henry's not old. He's ... I mean, he's in his thirties."

"If he's in his thirties, then he went to law school in utero."

"I'm just going to call him," Fiona said, grabbing at her phone. "He can explain what all of this is about."

Claire closed the folder with a decisive snap. "Listen to me. You cannot call Henry about this. Not now. Not until we figure out what's going on."

Fiona's finger hovered over the call button. "He can explain what is going on."

"You're being sued, Fiona. This isn't just a friendly conversation. It's a legal matter. If you say something to him, he can use it against you in court."

Fiona clenched her fists at her sides. "I can handle it—"

"No, you can't," Claire interrupted, her tone softening but no less firm. "You're not a lawyer, Fi. You don't know the implications of this, but I do. You need to trust me on this."

Fiona exhaled shakily, her shoulders slumping. "Okay. So what do we do now?"

Claire relaxed slightly, flipping the folder open again and scanning the pages with a focused intensity. "First, we'll go through this document thoroughly. Then I'll contact the lawyer who filed it. You'll have no further contact with anyone about this unless I'm present. Understood?"

Fiona nodded reluctantly, her hands gripping the edge of the counter. "Understood."

Claire tapped the signature line on the last page, her brow furrowing. "Also, we need to verify this Henry Caldwell. There's a public database where you can look up any lawyer's bar number. It'll show their licensing information, current contact details, and the firm they work for. It's how lawyers make sure they're dealing with the right person."

Fiona tilted her head, her curiosity piqued. "Anyone can access that?"

Claire nodded. "It's designed to keep things transparent. If this guy isn't who he says he is, we'll know pretty quickly."

"And if he is?"

"Then we figure out why someone who's supposedly helping you is also filing lawsuits against you. Either way, we're going to get answers." Claire pulled her phone from her bag. "Looks like we'll have to put Tybee on hold for now."

Fiona's heart sank at the mention of the trip. "Guess the beach will have to wait until I'm not being sued."

Claire smirked faintly. "It's not going anywhere, Fi. We'll sort this out first, and then we'll go. Hopefully before I'm drowning in prep for the art festival."

Fiona managed a small smile, her chest tightening as the weight of everything settled again. "Okay. So ... takeout?"

"Chinese?"

"Chinese," Fiona agreed, a flicker of relief breaking through her anxiety.

Claire nodded, scrolling through her phone. "Good. Food first, answers second. It's going to be a long night."

chapter
twenty-one

THE MORNING SUNLIGHT filtered through the blinds, casting soft stripes across Fiona's face. She stirred as a gentle nudge roused her from a restless sleep. Blinking groggily, she looked up to see Claire standing over her, a steaming mug of coffee in hand.

"Morning," Claire said softly, handing her the mug. "Thought you could use this."

Fiona pushed herself up on the couch, her neck stiff from the awkward position she'd slept in. The coffee's aroma was comforting, cutting through the haze of exhaustion. "Thanks," she murmured, taking a cautious sip. "Did I fall asleep here?"

Claire nodded, her hair slightly disheveled but her sharp eyes showing no sign of fatigue. "You did. You were out cold."

"Guess I needed it." She glanced around the room, taking in the half-empty takeout containers and the stack of legal papers Claire had meticulously combed through. "Did you even sleep?"

Claire sat down on the edge of the couch, letting out a small sigh. "A little. I crashed in your bed—I didn't want to wake you. I finished going through everything first."

"You stayed up all night working on this while I just ... passed out?" Guilt washed over her as she set the coffee mug down on the table, her fingers fidgeting with the hem of her sweatshirt. "I'm sorry, Claire. I should've stayed up to help."

Claire waved her off, a faint smirk tugging at the corner of her mouth. "Don't beat yourself up about it. Staying up all night is something you learn to master in law school. It's practically a requirement for survival."

Fiona managed a weak laugh, though the knot of guilt in her chest didn't loosen. "Still, I feel bad. I dragged you into this mess, and now you're losing sleep over it."

Claire shrugged, leaning back slightly. "It's not the first mess I've been dragged into, and it probably won't be the last. Besides, you're my sister. If anyone gets to lose sleep over your problems, it's me."

"Thanks." Fiona gave her sister a small smile, the warmth of Claire's words momentarily cutting through her anxiety. "I mean it."

"You'd do the same for me, Fi. Now, drink your coffee."

Fiona picked up her mug again, bracing herself. "What'd you find?"

Claire leaned back, resting her head against the couch as she rubbed her temples. "Well, once you wade through all the extraneous stuff us lawyers love to throw into these things, it's exactly what you'd expect—a preliminary injunction to stop you from publishing, plus a lawsuit alleging libel and defamation. Nothing unusual for a journalist dealing with a story this big."

Fiona set her coffee down on the table, her hands trembling slightly. "So, what do we do now?"

Claire straightened, her tone matter of fact. "The next step is to contact the Henry Caldwell who filed this and set up a meeting. I pulled his information from the database so that we know we have the right Henry. We need to understand his position and see what's going on here."

Fiona glanced at the clock, realizing it was only past 9 a.m. "Isn't it too early to call?"

Claire shook her head, pulling out her phone. "Not at all. Lawyers are used to early mornings."

Fiona watched as Claire pulled up the phone number from the lawsuit. Before dialing, she shot Fiona a pointed look. "I'm putting it on speakerphone, but do not say a word."

Fiona nodded, clasping her hands tightly in her lap.

Claire dialed the number, and after a few rings, a pleasant voice answered. "Henry Caldwell's office. How may I direct your call?"

"Good morning," Claire said smoothly, her tone professional. "This is Claire Stevens. I'm calling regarding a lawsuit Mr. Caldwell filed against Fiona Stevens. I'd like to speak with him directly."

"One moment, please," the receptionist replied before placing them on hold.

As soft instrumental music filtered through the speaker, Fiona leaned toward Claire. "What do you think—"

Claire shot her a sharp look, raising a hand to silence her. Fiona sank back into the couch, biting her lip.

A moment later, the receptionist returned. "I'm transferring you to Mr. Caldwell now."

The line clicked, and a deep, booming voice came through. "This is Henry Caldwell."

Fiona froze, her breath catching. The voice was nothing like the Henry she knew—it was older, richer, more commanding.

"Mr. Caldwell, this is Claire Stevens. I'm calling on behalf of my client, Fiona Stevens, regarding the lawsuit you filed against her."

"Ah, yes," Henry said, his tone polite but measured. "It's unfortunate that it came to this. Dolores was very insistent, and truthfully, it's on me. I didn't have the chance to reach out to your sister directly when Dolores asked me to. Maybe if I had, this could've been avoided."

Fiona's heart raced, her mind spinning as she tried to process his words. She glanced at Claire, her confusion mirrored in her sister's sharp expression.

Claire leaned forward, her voice even. "I think it would be helpful if we could all sit down and discuss this in person. Perhaps we can come to a resolution that works for everyone."

"That sounds reasonable," Henry replied. "I can clear some time this afternoon. Would that work for you?"

"It would," Claire said. "We appreciate your flexibility."

"Of course," Henry said. "I'll transfer you back to my receptionist to provide the address and confirm a time."

"Thank you," Claire said smoothly.

After the call ended and Claire jotted down the details from the receptionist, she hung up the phone and turned to Fiona.

Fiona stared at her sister, her mind racing. "That ...That's not the Henry I know."

The words felt hollow even as they left her mouth. She was still trying to process the deep, unfamiliar voice she had just heard over the phone—the one that claimed to be Henry Caldwell.

Claire's expression remained unreadable as she leaned back against the couch, crossing her arms. "I noticed."

Fiona let out a breath, rubbing her temples. "Maybe it's his father?" she offered weakly. "I thought Henry said his father retired, but maybe he hasn't. Maybe they've been working on this together, and I just didn't know."

The theory sounded desperate even to her own ears.

Claire shook her head, unconvinced. "We can speculate all day, but it won't get us anywhere." She hesitated, her sharp eyes studying Fiona like she was trying to figure out just how much she was unraveling. "You look like you're about to spiral. Don't."

Fiona let out a humorless laugh. "I'll just go ahead and turn off the part of my brain that's freaking out, thanks."

Claire exhaled, pushing herself up so she was sitting straight again. "The meeting this afternoon will give us answers. Until then, I need you to take some deep breaths and focus. You can't afford to be distracted."

Fiona nodded slowly, though the tightness in her chest didn't loosen. "Okay. You're right. I'll try."

"Good," Claire said, standing and stretching. "Let's clean up a little around here and get ready. We'll need to be sharp for whatever's coming."

Fiona took another sip of her coffee, her hands still trembling slightly around the mug. The warmth didn't reach her fingers, and the knot in her chest only twisted tighter.

She had thought she was playing the game. Thought she was the one chasing the truth.

But now?

Now it felt like she had been playing right into his hands all along.

And the certainty she had clung to for weeks was slipping through her fingers like sand.

chapter
twenty-two

THE HUM of the car engine filled the silence as Claire drove. Fiona stared out the window, the blur of passing streets doing little to distract her from the knot tightening in her chest. She traced her finger along the edge of the folder resting in her lap, her thoughts churning.

"You okay?" Claire asked, breaking the quiet.

Fiona glanced over at her sister, her fingers stilling. "Just nervous."

Claire gave a small nod, her eyes fixed on the road. "We'll figure it out, Fi. For now, just let me do the talking, okay?"

Fiona looked back out the window. "Yeah, I know."

When they pulled into the parking lot, Fiona's breath caught. The law office was housed in a sleek brick building with manicured landscaping and a polished sign out front that read Caldwell & Associates, Attorneys at Law.

Claire parked and turned to her sister. "Recognize it?"

Fiona shook her head, the unfamiliarity of the building heightening her unease. "No. This isn't the same place I met him."

Claire raised an eyebrow but didn't say anything. Instead, she unbuckled her seatbelt and gestured toward the entrance. "Come on. Let's see what's going on."

Fiona followed Claire into the building, her shoes clicking softly against the pristine marble floor of the lobby. The space was bright and modern, with floor-to-ceiling windows letting in streams of sunlight.

Plush leather chairs were arranged neatly around a glass coffee table adorned with glossy legal magazines. A receptionist sat behind a sleek mahogany desk, her smile professional and welcoming.

"Good afternoon. How can I help you?"

"Claire Stevens. We have an appointment with Mr. Caldwell regarding the Bates matter."

The receptionist nodded, typing into her computer. "Of course. He's expecting you. Please have a seat, and I'll let him know you're here."

Claire thanked her, and the sisters sat in the leather chairs. Fiona fidgeted with the folder in her lap again, her gaze darting around the room. The upscale surroundings only made her feel more out of place.

"Relax," Claire whispered, giving her a sidelong glance.

Before Fiona could respond, the door to the inner office opened, and an older man stepped out. He was rounder, grayer, and much more imposing than the Henry she knew. His tailored suit strained slightly against his frame, and his booming voice filled the lobby as he greeted them.

"Ms. Stevens?" he asked, his tone warm but authoritative.

Claire stood, extending a hand. "Yes. Claire Stevens, and this is my sister, Fiona."

Fiona rose hesitantly, shaking his hand when he turned to her. Her mind raced as she studied his face. *There's no resemblance at all*, she thought, her chest tightening. *How could this man possibly be related to the Henry I know?*

"Thank you for coming," Henry said, gesturing toward the hallway. "Let's head to the conference room."

The sisters followed him through a corridor lined with framed diplomas and certificates. The conference room itself was spacious, with a long mahogany table, high-backed chairs, and a view of the city through a wide window.

Henry settled into one of the chairs at the head of the table and motioned for them to sit. "As I mentioned on the phone," he began, "I had intended to reach out to your client earlier, but I got bogged down with work. You know how it is for lawyers."

Claire smiled politely. "I do. But don't you think resorting to a lawsuit and a motion for a preliminary injunction is a little extreme, especially when Dolores had agreed to the interview?"

Henry sighed, spreading his hands. "I'm really just the messenger here. Dolores was very upset—obviously something happened during your interview that pushed her to this point. She demanded we act quickly, and here we are."

Fiona's fists clenched under the table as she fought the urge to speak. Claire gave her a quick glance, as if sensing her tension, and subtly shook her head.

"I understand," Claire said smoothly. "But don't you think it would have been more productive to have a conversation first? Filing a lawsuit escalates things unnecessarily."

Henry shrugged, his smile rueful. "It's not ideal, I agree. But when a client insists, you follow their instructions. I'm sure you know how it goes."

Before Claire could respond, Henry's phone buzzed. He glanced at the screen and stood. "Apologies, but I need to take this—it's the clerk's office. I'll be back in a moment."

As soon as the door closed behind him, Claire leaned toward Fiona, her voice low. "Tell me that isn't the man you spent the night with."

Fiona's cheeks flushed, and she shook her head vehemently. "Of course not. But maybe he's ... I don't know, his dad? I mean, Henry said his father retired, but what if he didn't? What if they're working together?"

Claire arched an eyebrow. "You're grasping at straws, Fi. It's starting to sound more and more like the 'Henry' you know might be an imposter."

Fiona's nerves coiled tighter. "Should we ask him? Maybe just to be sure?"

"I'll fish a little more," Claire said. "But let's not jump the gun."

The door opened, and Henry reentered, his expression apologetic. "Sorry about that. Just something I was waiting on from the clerk's office."

"Not a problem," Claire said. "I'll just come out and say it. I wanted to see if we can come to some sort of agreement to avoid litigation. Perhaps Dolores could review the article before publication?"

Fiona stiffened, her chest tightening as she stared at her sister. *She can't be serious.* But Claire gave her a quick look, silently warning her to stay quiet.

Henry nodded thoughtfully. "That could work. Let me take it back to Dolores, and we'll hold off on moving forward with the preliminary injunction in the meantime."

"Great," Claire said with a smile as they all stood. She gathered her bag and extended a hand to Henry. "Thank you for your time. I'll follow up once you've spoken with Dolores."

Henry shook her hand firmly. "Sounds good. Hopefully, we can resolve this without too much hassle."

As they walked toward the door, Claire slowed slightly, her tone casual. "By the way—I think I might've run into your son at the last bar meeting. A younger Henry Caldwell, right?"

Henry chuckled, his brow furrowing in confusion. "No, no son. I've got three daughters, but we never did get that boy."

Claire stopped, feigning surprise. "Ah, my mistake. Must've been someone else. Long hours blur everything together, you know how it is for lawyers."

Henry laughed warmly, nodding. "Don't I ever. Happens to the best of us."

Claire gave him a polite smile as they stepped into the lobby, exchanging goodbyes. Once they exited the building and headed for the car, Fiona finally spoke, her voice low and urgent.

"Claire ... if he doesn't have a son, then who the hell have I been talking to?"

Claire's face was tight as she unlocked the car. "That's exactly what we need to figure out, Fi. And we need to do it fast."

chapter
twenty-three

THE HUM of the car engine filled the tense silence as Claire drove, her gaze fixed firmly on the road ahead. Fiona stared out the window, the cityscape blurring into an indistinct smear of color. Her thoughts were a cacophony of confusion and anxiety, and her hands fidgeted in her lap.

Claire broke the silence. "Fiona, I need you to focus."

Fiona didn't respond, her eyes still trained on the passing streets.

"Fi," Claire said, her tone more forceful this time. "I'm serious. Get my notepad from the backseat and write down everything you can remember about the Henry you've been dealing with. Every detail. His appearance, his mannerisms, his office—anything."

Fiona hesitated, her hands still. "I don't know where to start," she said softly.

Claire glanced at her, her jaw tightening. "Start anywhere. We can't afford for you to shut down right now. Someone impersonating Dolores' lawyer isn't just strange—it's dangerous. You need to snap out of it."

Fiona turned to Claire, her voice trembling. "You think I'm in danger?"

"Yes. And we're not going to ignore that possibility. You might not see it but look at what I lived through. These things can escalate in situations like this."

"Or is that your past talking?" Fiona frowned, her anxiety giving way to defensiveness. "Are you letting what happened to you make you see things that aren't there?"

"You're right," Claire said after a moment, her voice quieter but no less firm. She inhaled deeply, gripping the steering wheel tighter. "What happened to me probably does affect how I see things. But these things do happen. What matters now is making a paper trail. If this guy isn't who he says he is, we need to document everything."

"And then what? File a police report? Make this public? Claire, if I do that, my career is over. I'll lose all credibility as a journalist. Everyone will see me as the idiot who trusted a fraud."

Claire bit back her response, her lips pressed into a thin line. "Better than losing your life over it."

Fiona shook her head, her voice rising. "No. You were in this position not so long ago, and you didn't torch your career. I'm not going to either. I won't end up some helpless Savannah debutante, beholden to a man because I destroyed my career and have nothing else to fall back on."

"Fine." Claire exhaled slowly, her shoulders stiff. "Maybe I can pull some strings at the department. Quietly. See what we can find without blowing this wide open."

Fiona relaxed slightly, but the tension in her chest wasn't too eager to leave.

The car's speakers rang as Claire's phone lit up with an incoming call. She pressed a button on the steering wheel. "Claire Stevens."

"Hi, Claire," a friendly voice said. "This is Abigail from the museum. I was wondering if you could stop by to pick up a few things we need you to review."

Claire glanced at Fiona, mouthing, *Do you mind?*

Fiona shook her head. "Go ahead," she whispered back.

"Sure thing," Claire said. "I'll be there in about ten minutes."

The museum was quiet, the air cool as a few patrons milled about, their footsteps echoing in the open hallways. Fiona followed Claire inside, her own footsteps tapping against the polished floors. The space was vast and filled with vibrant exhibits—paintings, sculptures, and artifacts that seemed to whisper stories of the past.

"Just give me a few minutes," Claire said, nodding toward the office wing. She adjusted the stack of papers in her arms. "Stay here. Don't get into trouble."

Fiona rolled her eyes but gave a small smile. "I'll try."

Claire disappeared down a hallway, leaving Fiona in the main exhibit. The quiet of the museum wrapped around her like a cocoon, muffling the chaotic thoughts that had plagued her all day. She took a deep breath and wandered through the space.

It struck her how long it had been since she'd last been here—years, at least. Maybe not since that school field trip in fifth grade, when her class had been herded through the galleries with a bored guide pointing out famous local artists. Back then, she'd been more focused on her friends than the artwork, their whispers and giggles echoing in the vast halls. Now, the museum felt different—larger, quieter, heavier. Time had given it a weight she hadn't noticed as a kid, and for a moment, she felt strangely out of place, as though the walls themselves were watching her.

The walls were lined with paintings, a mixture of serene landscapes and expressive portraits. Some depicted Savannah's iconic marshes, their muted greens and blues blending seamlessly into the horizon. Others captured moments of life—a woman hanging laundry, a child playing on a cobblestone street.

Fiona paused in front of a portrait of an elderly man seated on a porch swing, his gnarled hands resting on his knees. His eyes seemed to follow her, full of unspoken wisdom. She glanced down at the nameplate. *Henry Folsom, 1982.* A wave of sadness crept over her. So much life, frozen in a single frame.

Her gaze shifted to a sprawling depiction of the Savannah River at sunset, the water reflecting the fiery orange and deep purples of the sky. The artist's brushstrokes were deliberate, almost aggressive, as though the scene had been captured in a moment of intensity rather than tranquility.

She moved on, letting her fingers trail along the railing that separated the gallery floor from the walls. The nameplates below each piece caught her eye—many of the artists' names unfamiliar. Then, one painting made her stop mid-step.

It was different from the others. Striking in its simplicity, yet unsettling in its details. The canvas depicted a grand Southern home, its pristine white facade framed by oak trees draped in Spanish moss. The house was elegant, picture-perfect.

Fiona stepped closer, narrowing her eyes as she studied the details. The first-floor windows gleamed in the sunlight, their shutters perfectly aligned. The porch swing hung motionless, a glass of iced tea resting on a nearby table. But as her gaze traveled upward, she noticed a single open window on the second floor.

Smoke curled from the window, faint and wispy, almost easy to miss. Fiona leaned in, her breath catching. The edges of the curtains were charred, faint flames licking at the window frame. The fire was subtle but unmistakable, a quiet chaos hidden within the picturesque scene.

Her pulse quickened. The wide porch, the symmetrical windows, the towering oaks—it bore an uncanny resemblance to Dolores' estate. Fiona's rational mind tried to dismiss it. Many Savannah homes shared that classic architectural style. It was probably just a coincidence.

But as her eyes fell to the nameplate beneath the painting, her heart dropped.

Sarah Mercer.

The room seemed to tilt as Fiona's breath came faster. Her hand moved to her bag, pulling out her phone. She glanced around, her movements quick and nervous, before snapping a picture of the painting.

"Excuse me."

Fiona jumped, spinning around to see a museum employee approaching her. The tension in the room felt suffocating, her chest tightening as she clutched her phone.

"I'm sorry," the employee said, their tone polite but firm. "We ask that visitors refrain from taking photographs of the artwork."

Fiona nodded quickly, her face flushing. "Of course. I'm sorry—I didn't know."

The employee gave her a small smile. Fiona exhaled shakily, tucking her phone back into her bag.

"Ready?" Claire's voice startled her.

Fiona turned to see her sister approaching, another stack of papers tucked under her arm. Claire glanced between Fiona and the employee before raising an eyebrow. "Everything okay?"

"Yeah," Fiona said quickly, her voice tight. "Let's go."

As they left the gallery, Fiona cast one last glance at the painting. A flicker of movement in her peripheral vision made her pause, her breath catching. She turned her head sharply, but there was nothing there.

She shook her head, dismissing it as nerves, and hurried to catch up with Claire.

chapter
twenty-four

FIONA PUSHED OPEN the door to her apartment, her nerves still raw from the museum and the unsettling discovery of the painting. Claire followed close behind, setting her stack of museum papers on the counter before sighing and crossing her arms.

"There's nothing else we can do tonight," Claire said. "We should head out to Tybee. Clear our heads and figure this out when we're not so wound up."

Fiona hesitated, her hands lingering on the strap of her bag. The thought of leaving was both appealing and terrifying. "I don't know, Claire. What if something happens while we're gone? What if ... I don't know, this 'Henry' shows up here again?"

"And that's exactly why we need to go somewhere he's not. Somewhere with no connection to your apartment, to Dolores, or to any of this mess. Tybee is perfect. It's quiet, and no one's going to bother us there."

Fiona opened her mouth to argue but stopped herself. Instead, she pulled out her phone and stared at the screen. No messages. No missed calls. Nothing from Henry.

Claire tilted her head. "I know what you're thinking. And no, you should not call him. Or text him. Or email him. Or send a damn carrier pigeon."

"I wasn't going to," Fiona said defensively, locking the phone and shoving it back into her pocket. "I just ... I can't stop thinking about him. About what information he might have on me. About who he even is. What if he's been in my apartment before? What if he's listening to us right now?" Her voice wavered, and she looked around the room. "I mean, he was here while I was asleep, Claire. What if he planted something?"

"That's exactly why we need to get out of here, Fi. You're spiraling." Claire sighed and placed a steadying hand on Fiona's shoulder. "Tybee will give us space to breathe and figure this out with a clear head." She paused and looked at the door. "But also, you should consider getting a doorbell camera."

"Thanks for the reassurance."

"I'm just saying, then you'll know for sure whether imposter Henry is breaking and entering."

"Right." Fiona blew out a long stream of air. "In the meantime, let's get out of here."

The cool evening air greeted them as they stepped outside, Fiona pulling her suitcase behind her. Claire popped the trunk of her car, loading her own bag inside before turning to Fiona.

"I'll drive," Claire said, her tone leaving no room for argument.

Fiona frowned. "Are you sure? You've done most of the driving lately."

"I don't think you're in the best headspace to be behind the wheel right now, anyway."

Fiona sighed, but she couldn't argue with that. "Fine."

She climbed into the passenger seat, buckling herself in as Claire started the engine. As they pulled away, the familiar streets of Savannah gave way to quieter roads, the urban buzz fading into the soft hum of tires on asphalt.

Fiona stared out the window as the landscape blurred past her. The golden light of the setting sun bathed the trees and marshes in a warm glow, but she couldn't appreciate the beauty. Her thoughts were tangled, like a web tightening around her.

Who is he? She wondered, her mind circling back to Henry—or whoever he was. She replayed every interaction with him, tried to pick apart his words, expressions, anything that might have been a clue.

He'd been so convincing, so earnest. How could she have been so blind?

And then there was the painting. Sarah Mercer's name lingered in Fiona's mind, refusing to let go, the ghost of an unfinished story. The missing woman, the whispered rumors, the affair that had sent shockwaves through Savannah's most powerful circles. And now, Henry—or whatever his real name was—had fed her just enough information to make her question everything. He knew something about Sarah's fate. Whether it was firsthand knowledge or just another manipulation, she couldn't tell. But the connection was there.

And then there was Dolores. The way her temper had flared, raw and unchecked, how easily she had shattered that vase, her voice laced with warning. That was real. That wasn't just high society poise cracking—it was something deeply buried breaking through. But was it the weight of guilt, or the weight of a past she never escaped? Had Fiona been digging up the truth, or just ripping open old wounds?

Fiona pressed her forehead against the window, the cool glass grounding her. Her chest tightened with a wave of unease. *What if I've gotten it all wrong? What if Henry, or whoever he is, set me up to ruin Dolores—and I'm just a pawn in his game?*

She glanced sideways at Claire, who was focused on the road, her expression calm and determined. Fiona envied her sister's composure. Claire had always been the steady one, the one who could untangle the messes that seemed to follow Fiona wherever she went.

But even Claire doesn't know everything about this. Not yet.

The car bumped gently as the road changed to sandier terrain. Fiona looked up, startled to see the first glimpses of the coast. The salty air wafted in through the cracked windows, mingling with the faint scent of pine.

"We're here," Claire announced, pulling into the gravel driveway of a small cottage.

Weathered shingles and blue shutters lined the house with a cozy, lived-in feel. A wide inviting porch spanned the front, adorned with a swinging bench and a small potted palm.

Fiona stepped out of the car, taking a deep breath of the ocean air. For the first time that day, her shoulders eased.

"What do you think?" Claire asked, grabbing her bag from the trunk.

"It's perfect," Fiona said softly, but the tension in her chest hadn't entirely loosened. She grabbed her suitcase, following Claire up the steps and into the cottage.

Inside, the space was quaint but bright. Whitewashed walls and nautical decor gave it a relaxed feel, with seashells and starfish scattered across the shelves. The kitchen was small but functional, with a window that looked out toward the dunes.

Fiona dropped her bag near the couch and sat down, running her fingers through her hair. "Okay," she said, exhaling. "We're here. Now what?"

Claire set her own bag on the dining table. "Now, we take a breath. Let's settle in, and then we'll figure out our next steps."

Fiona nodded, but her mind remained restless. The ocean might be soothing, but the questions she carried with her weren't so easily quieted.

chapter
twenty-five

THE SALTY OCEAN breeze ruffled Fiona's hair as she stepped out of the cottage early the next morning. The quiet hum of Tybee Island was a welcome reprieve from the chaos swirling in her mind, but it did little to calm her nerves. She hadn't slept well, her thoughts circling endlessly around Henry, and the growing weight of the mystery surrounding Dolores and Sarah Mercer.

Claire was still asleep, her door closed when Fiona had crept out of the cottage. Sitting idle wasn't something she was good at, especially when her mind refused to settle. Wandering the island felt like a good way to clear her head—or at least distract her for a while.

Her footsteps crunched softly on the sandy path as she headed into town. Tybee had a charming, almost nostalgic feel, its streets lined with pastel-colored shops, weathered beach houses, and the occasional bicyclist pedaling lazily by. It was the kind of place that seemed untouched by time, its beauty lying in its simplicity.

Fiona spotted a small breakfast deli nestled between two gift shops. A hand-painted sign above the door read The Driftwood Café, and the smell of fresh coffee wafted through the air as she approached. The interior was warm and inviting, with mismatched furniture, shelves lined with books and knickknacks, and walls adorned with photographs of Tybee's history.

The shop was quiet, save for the soft murmur of a couple at a corner table and the low hum of a ceiling fan. Fiona approached the counter, her eyes flicking over the chalkboard menu written in colorful, looping script. The aroma of freshly brewed coffee filled the air and mingled with the faint scent of pastries displayed in a glass case.

"Good morning!" The cashier, a woman in her late forties with short, spiky hair and a friendly smile, greeted her. "What can I get started for you?"

"Just a latte, please," Fiona said, scanning the pastry menu. "Maybe a blueberry muffin, too."

"We're not fancy like that." The cashier smiled. "We've got good ol' drip coffee, though. Strong and hot. That work for you?"

Fiona blinked, then smiled. "That's perfect. Coffee's coffee, right?"

"Now you're speaking my language," the woman said, punching the order into the register. "And the muffins are fresh this morning—you'll love 'em. Visiting, huh?"

"What gave me away?"

"I know all the locals, and I don't recognize you." The woman grinned. "Plus, you've got that look about you—taking it all in like it's new."

Fiona laughed softly, feeling a bit exposed but not unkindly. "You got me. I'm visiting with my sister. We're staying at a cottage near the beach."

"Well, welcome to Tybee," the cashier said, sliding the muffin into a small paper bag. "How long are you here for?"

"Just a few days," Fiona replied. "We're taking a little break from the city."

"Good for you." The woman handed over the muffin and turned to pour her coffee. "Nothing beats the island for some R&R. You two should check out the lighthouse if you haven't already. Best view on the whole coast."

"I'll keep that in mind."

Fiona glanced around the café. Her eyes lingered on the walls, lined with black-and-white photos, faded newspaper clippings, and bits of local memorabilia.

The woman followed her gaze as she placed the coffee on the counter. "That wall's a bit of a time capsule," she said, nodding toward the photos. "A lot of history in this town. Some of those pictures go back decades."

"It's really interesting," Fiona said, picking up her coffee. "Thanks for the suggestion."

"Anytime," the cashier said with a friendly wave.

Fiona gave a small nod and retreated to a table near the back, setting her coffee and muffin down as she settled into a chair. Her eyes returned to the gallery wall, drawn to the stories they seemed to hold.

There were images of fishermen hauling in their catches, families posing on the beach, and faded shots of old regattas, the sails of small boats billowing in the wind. Fiona's gaze traveled across the collection, then paused.

The photo she'd landed on showed a group of boys standing on the deck of a sailboat, their smiles wide and carefree. The boat's name, *The Mariner*, was painted on the side in bold letters. Fiona leaned in, her breath catching as she studied the faces.

Her heart began to race. She stepped closer to the photo, her gaze locking onto the boy on the far left. There was something familiar about him—the shape of his jaw, the tilt of his head, the quiet confidence in his stance. His hair was lighter, his features softened by youth, but there was an unmistakable sense of recognition stirring in her chest.

Fiona frowned, trying to place him, to connect the blurred edges of memory to something concrete. She knew that face—or at least, she thought she did. But from where?

Fiona's hands trembled as she searched for a caption beneath the photo. *Local Sailing Club, Summer 1985*. No names, no details. Just a date and the faint echo of a past that suddenly felt far too close.

"Nice picture, isn't it?"

Fiona jumped, spinning around to see an older man standing a few feet away. His wiry frame and weathered skin suggested a lifetime spent under the Georgia sun. He held a steaming cup of coffee in one hand and a newspaper in the other.

"Uh, yeah," Fiona stammered, leaning back slightly. "It caught my eye."

The man chuckled, his voice warm and rough around the edges. "That one's a favorite around here. Brings back a lot of memories."

Fiona hesitated, then gestured toward the photo. "Do you know anything about it? The boys, I mean. Were they from around here?"

The man nodded, setting his coffee down on a nearby table. "Oh, sure. Most of 'em grew up right here on the island. That was the old sailing club. Just a bunch of kids back then. They used to race in the regatta every year."

Fiona's pulse quickened. "Do you remember any of their names?"

He squinted at the photo, leaning in slightly. "Let's see... that's Tommy on the right there. His folks owned the bait shop down by the pier. The one in the middle, that's Danny. He was always the best sailor of the bunch. And him..." He tapped the boy on the far left. "He was a Mercer, I think. His mama grew up here. Not sure what became of him, though."

"Mercer?" Fiona swallowed hard, her heart thudding in her chest. "Are you sure?"

"Pretty sure," the man said, his brow furrowing. "That name ring a bell for you?"

"Kind of. I think I might've met someone from that family. Do you know if they still live around here?"

The man shook his head. "Can't say for certain. Folks come and go, you know. But if you're curious, you might check out the library. They keep records on just about everyone who's lived on Tybee."

"Thanks," Fiona said, her voice barely above a whisper.

The man smiled. "No problem. You take care now."

As he walked away, Fiona turned back to the photo, her mind racing. Her skin prickled as though someone were watching her, despite the nearly empty café. She took a deep breath, snapping a quick picture of the photo with her phone before slipping out the door.

The warm ocean breeze greeted her as she stepped outside, but it did little to calm her nerves. She quickened her pace, heading back toward the cottage.

By the time Fiona reached the porch, her thoughts were a tangled mess of questions and half-formed theories. She pushed the door open, calling out softly, "Claire? You up?"

She heard movement from the kitchen, and Claire appeared, a mug of coffee in hand. "Hey. Where'd you go?"

"I went into town." Fiona glanced over her shoulder as if expecting someone to appear behind her. "Claire... I think I found something. Something about him."

Claire raised an eyebrow, setting her mug down. "What do you mean?"

Fiona sank onto the couch, her hands trembling as she unlocked her phone and pulled up the picture of the sailboat. "Look at this."

As Claire studied the photo, Fiona exhaled shakily, the weight of the discovery pressing down on her. "Who is he, Claire? And why do I feel like I'm being watched everywhere I go?"

chapter
twenty-six

CLAIRE SAT across from Fiona at the small dining table in their cottage, her coffee resting in front of her. The salty, sandy air drifted in through the open windows, mingling with the faint scent of sunscreen and the remnants of breakfast. Outside, the rhythmic sound of waves breaking against the shore provided a deceptively peaceful backdrop to their tense conversation.

"So," Claire began, setting her drink down, her voice laced with caution, "you're saying this guy told you the last name of one of the boys in the photo was Mercer?"

Fiona nodded, her fingers tightening around her cup. "Yeah, he seemed pretty sure about it. He mentioned the sailing club and said a Mercer was part of it."

Claire leaned back in her chair, her expression skeptical. "That doesn't mean it has anything to do with Sarah Mercer. Mercer isn't exactly a rare name, Fi. It could be anyone."

Fiona frowned, staring into her coffee as the steam curled upward. "I know. You're probably right."

"I am," Claire said firmly. "And you need to stop getting caught up in every little connection. It's easy to see patterns when you're already suspicious, but that doesn't mean they're real."

Fiona let out a slow breath, nodding reluctantly, but the doubt gnawed at her. She traced the rim of her mug with her finger, her mind refusing to let go of the possibility.

Maybe Claire was right. Maybe this was nothing more than a coincidence, a common last name thrown into a sea of overanalyzed details.

But then again, Claire had spent years trying not to see the connections in her own life, convincing herself that the worst possibilities weren't real—until they were.

And Fiona?

Fiona had spent her life playing it safe, looking at things from a distance, never trusting her gut to lead her in the right direction.

Maybe Claire was right.

But maybe, this time, she wasn't.

"Look," Claire said, softening her tone as she noticed Fiona's distant expression, "I know you're invested in this story. But sometimes coincidences are just that—coincidences. Mercer could be related to Sarah, but it's equally likely they have no connection at all."

"But what if they are related?" Fiona pressed, leaning forward. "What if Sarah has family here in Tybee? People who might know what happened to her?"

Claire sighed, rubbing her temple. "Even if that's true, what then? You'll knock on every door on the island asking if they're related to a woman who disappeared decades ago? How do you think that would go over?"

Fiona bit her lip, knowing Claire had a point. "I just can't shake the feeling that there's something here," she said quietly. "Call it journalistic instinct or whatever, but I feel like I'm close to understanding ... something."

"Your instincts have gotten you mixed up with a man pretending to be someone he's not," Claire reminded her gently. "Maybe it's time to take a step back and look at this with fresh eyes."

The words stung, but Fiona couldn't argue with them. She had been fooled—completely and utterly taken in by whoever was masquerading as Henry Caldwell. The shame of it still burned.

Claire stood, stretching her arms overhead. "I'm going to take a walk on the beach. Want to come? Might help clear your head."

Fiona hesitated, glancing toward the window where the waves rolled lazily onto the shore. The ocean did look inviting, its blue expanse promising temporary escape from the chaos in her mind. "I'm okay for now. Maybe I'll join you later."

"Suit yourself. Don't overthink this, Fi. We're supposed to be relaxing, remember?"

Fiona gave her a small smile. "I'll try."

Claire grabbed a hat from the hook by the door and slipped on her sandals. "We're going to figure this out, you know. All of it. But running yourself into the ground won't help."

"I know," Fiona said, grateful for her sister's unwavering support despite their disagreement.

"Come find me if you change your mind," Claire said before stepping onto the porch and disappearing down the sandy path toward the shore.

Fiona sat in the now-silent cottage, her fingers tapping absently on the table. The quiet was oppressive, leaving too much space for her thoughts to spiral. She reached for her phone, unlocking it with a swipe. The first thing she saw made her heart skip a beat—a new text message. From Henry.

Sorry I haven't messaged sooner. Things at the office got a little busy. Do you have time to get together again soon?

Her chest tightened as she read the words, alarm bells ringing in her head. Her first thought was that he didn't know. He couldn't have known about the lawsuit filed by the real Henry Caldwell. If he did, why would he be texting her so casually, pretending like nothing had changed?

A chill ran down her spine. It meant this man—this imposter, whoever he was—was still operating as though everything was normal between them. That he thought he still had her trust.

Her fingers hovered over her phone, her thoughts spiraling. *If he doesn't know, then he's still playing his game. But why? Why reach out now? Is he trying to keep me on his side? Does he know I've been asking questions? Does he suspect I'm starting to figure him out?*

She bit her lip, her pulse quickening as she stared at the message. It was so casual, so normal—as if they were just colleagues checking in with each other. As if he hadn't deceived her, manipulated her, potentially put her in danger.

What if he does know about the lawsuit but is pretending he doesn't? What if this is some kind of test?

Fiona glanced toward the window, her gaze darting to the beach where Claire had disappeared moments ago. The thought crept in unbidden. *What if he's watching me right now? What if he knows I've been asking about him?*

She gripped the edge of the table, forcing herself to breathe. *Stop. You're letting your paranoia get the best of you. He's not here. He doesn't know. He can't know.* But even as she told herself this, her hands trembled, and she shivered.

Her thumb hovered over the screen as doubt crept in. *I shouldn't respond. I shouldn't keep engaging with him. Claire would tell me to ignore it, to cut all contact.* But what if this was her chance to figure out who he really was? To turn the tables and gather information of her own?

Before she could talk herself out of it, she typed back: *I'm out of town right now, but I'll be back in a few days.*

The response came instantly, as if he'd been waiting for her reply, which only heightened her unease.

Got it. Any progress on the article?

Fiona's nerves tightened. Such an innocent question on the surface but loaded with implications given everything she now knew—or suspected. She hesitated, her pulse quickening as she typed a response to the loaded question: *Yeah, I'm working on it. I want to make sure it has an impact, so I'm taking my time with it.*

The three dots signaling his reply appeared almost immediately, but before his next message could come through, the door creaked open behind her. Fiona jumped, stuffing her phone into her pocket and turning to see Claire standing in the doorway, slightly damp from the ocean spray.

"I forgot sunscreen," Claire said, walking to the counter. She grabbed the bottle and turned back toward Fiona, her eyes narrowing as she took in her sister's tense posture. "What were you doing?"

Fiona forced a laugh, waving her hand dismissively. "Nothing. Just scrolling."

Claire didn't look convinced, her gaze lingering on Fiona's face. She could always tell when Fiona was hiding something—a skill honed through years of sisterhood. But she just shrugged and headed back toward the door. "Okay. Don't get too lost in it."

As the door closed again, Fiona exhaled, her hands trembling as she pulled her phone back out. The notification of Henry's next message was there, its presence taunting her from the screen. For a long moment, she stared at it, torn between curiosity and caution.

Just don't overwork yourself. These stories can consume you if you let them. Trust me, I've seen it happen.

The words sent a chill through her. Was it a veiled threat? A warning? Or just an innocent comment from someone who had no idea she was onto him?

She couldn't bring herself to reply. Instead, she shoved the phone into her bag and stood, pacing the small space of the cottage. The walls felt like they were closing in, the cozy interior suddenly claustrophobic.

Her thoughts churned, paranoia creeping in with each step. *He asked about the article. Is he trying to gauge how much I know? Could he be watching me somehow? He was in my apartment while I was asleep. What if he planted something? What if he's tracked my phone?*

She shook her head, trying to steady herself. *No. Get a grip, Fiona. You're spiraling.*

But the unease refused to let go, wrapping around her like a vise. She glanced out the window at the beach again, where Claire's figure was still visible against the shoreline. Her sister looked peaceful, carefree —everything Fiona wasn't feeling right now.

Fiona needed answers—answers she wasn't going to find sitting in the cottage letting her imagination run wild.

Her gaze drifted to her bag, where her notepad waited alongside her phone with its unanswered message. She grabbed her keys from the hook by the door, her decision made. That old man had said there was information on the residents at the library. Maybe she'd try her luck there.

With one last glance at the beach, she stepped out onto the porch, pulling the cottage door closed behind her. The warm island air greeted her, carrying the scent of salt and sunscreen. She took a deep breath, willing it to calm her nerves.

I'm done being manipulated, she thought, a new determination steadying her hands as she headed toward her car. *Time to find out who's really pulling the strings.*

chapter
twenty-seven

THE TYBEE ISLAND LIBRARY was modest but welcoming, its white brick facade partially shaded by the twisting branches of an old live oak. Fiona climbed the short set of steps to the entrance, the salty breeze clinging to her as she pushed open the glass door. Inside, the air was cool and smelled of aged paper and pine cleaner.

Rows of organized shelves stretched out before her, the muted hum of the fluorescent lights adding to the hushed atmosphere. A small reading area by the front window featured a few well-worn armchairs and a circular table stacked with local newspapers. A colorful bulletin board near the entrance displayed flyers for community events: yoga on the beach, a craft fair, and a notice about Savannah's upcoming art festival.

The librarian behind the front desk glanced up as Fiona entered, offering a polite smile. She was a petite woman with salt-and-pepper hair pulled into a low bun. "Good morning," she greeted. "Can I help you find anything?"

Fiona hesitated for a moment, adjusting her bag on her shoulder. "Actually, yes," she said. "A gentleman told me that the library keeps records of residents?"

The librarian tilted her head, her brow furrowing slightly. "I'm not sure what you're referring to?"

Realizing how odd that sounded, Fiona quickly added, "I'm just doing some research on the area. You know, the families that influenced the island. It's for a ... project." She smiled, hoping it made her seem less suspicious.

The librarian's expression relaxed, and she nodded. "Ah, I see. We do have a local history section. There's some material there on the island's families and businesses, as well as old newspapers on microfilm. Would that help?"

"That would be perfect."

"Right this way," the librarian said, stepping out from behind the desk. She led Fiona to a section near the back, where tall windows let in soft, diffused light. The shelves were lined with binders, books, and labeled boxes. Nearby, an older microfilm reader sat atop a sturdy wooden desk, its screen slightly yellowed with age.

"This is the history section. If you need anything specific, let me know. I'll be up front."

"Thank you," Fiona said, giving her a polite nod.

As the librarian walked away, Fiona sank into the chair by the microfilm reader. The room was quiet, amplifying the nervous energy thrumming through her. She pulled a few books from the shelf labeled *Tybee Island Families & History* and began flipping through them.

The pages were filled with old photographs, maps, and genealogies, but nothing immediately caught her eye. Her fingers lingered on a few entries, but the names meant nothing to her. She let out a small sigh. *This isn't going to be easy, and I don't even know what I'm looking for.*

She spent nearly an hour poring over the historical volumes, searching for any mention of the Mercer family. The books offered glimpses into Tybee's past—accounts of storms that had reshaped the coastline, descriptions of fishing communities that had thrived for generations, and stories of summer vacationers who had eventually become permanent residents. But nothing that connected directly to her investigation.

Pushing the books aside, she turned her attention to the microfilm index. She searched for the last name Mercer and found only two entries. Her pulse quickened as she loaded the first reel into the machine and scrolled through the faded scans.

The first article was from the Savannah Gazette, dated summer 1985. It was a report on the sailing club's participation in the annual regatta hosted by the Savannah Yacht Club.

Local Sailing Club Shines at Annual Regatta, Savannah Gazette, July 15, 1985

The Savannah Yacht Club hosted its highly anticipated annual regatta this past weekend, drawing competitors and spectators from across the region. Among the standout participants was the Tybee Island Sailing Club, whose young sailors earned praise for their skill, teamwork, and sportsmanship during the event.

The regatta, a longstanding tradition in Savannah, featured a series of races across multiple age divisions. Competing under sunny skies and steady coastal winds, the Tybee team performed admirably, securing top finishes in several heats.

One of the highlights of the day was the spirited performance by the club's junior division, sailing aboard The Mariner, a sleek craft that cut through the water with ease. The team of four boys showed exceptional coordination and determination, finishing third overall in their category.

Coach Gerald Fisher, who has been with the Tybee club for over a decade, praised the boys for their efforts. "They worked hard all summer preparing for this regatta, and it showed out there today," Fisher said. "This is what sailing is all about—teamwork, perseverance, and a love for the water. I'm proud of each and every one of them."

Parents and spectators gathered on the docks to welcome the boys back as they returned from the race. "It's such a joy to see these kids out there doing something they love," said Sarah Mercer, mother of Samuel. "They've put so much into this, and it's wonderful to see them thrive."

The regatta also served as a social occasion, with guests enjoying refreshments and live music on the club's expansive grounds. For many, the event is as much about celebrating Savannah's vibrant sailing culture as it is about the competition.

"This regatta is a cornerstone of the community," said Yacht Club Commodore Edward Blackwell. "It's a chance to bring people together and highlight the incredible talent we have here, both on and off the water."

As the day wound to a close, the boys from The Mariner were seen laughing and exchanging high-fives, already talking about next year's race. Their camaraderie and spirit were a reminder of what makes Savannah's sailing tradition so enduring.

The Tybee Island Sailing Club's junior team will return to their training schedule next week, already setting their sights on upcoming competitions.

Fiona scanned the names listed in the caption beneath a photo of the boys on the sailboat:

Participants: Tommy Graham, Danny Bishop, Samuel Mercer, and Mark Haney.

Fiona's eyes locked onto the name Samuel Mercer, her chest tightening. She carefully examined the grainy photograph accompanying the article, trying to make out the features of the young sailors. Though the image quality was poor, she could see that one of the boys bore a striking resemblance to the one she'd noticed in the café photo.

She jotted the names into her notebook before moving to the second article. Her breath caught as she read the headline. *Local Woman Reported Missing, The Search for Sarah Mercer Continues.*

The article, dated three years after the first, was a plea for residents to help in the search for Sarah Mercer. Fiona's fingers traced the words on the screen as she read.

Sarah Mercer, a resident of Tybee Island, was last seen in Savannah but frequently returned to Tybee, where her son Samuel attended school. Friends and family have described her as vibrant and outgoing. She was last spotted near Forsyth Park late on Friday evening. Authorities urge anyone with information to come forward.

The article ended with a call for volunteers to join search parties combing the island and surrounding marshlands. Fiona leaned back in her chair, her heart heavy. *Sarah Mercer was never found. Whatever happened to her, it's as if she vanished into thin air.*

Her mind raced as she pieced together the fragments. Could Henry —her Henry—be connected to this? Could he be telling the truth about Dolores killing Sarah? And what about Samuel? What happened to him?

Fiona straightened, leaning back into the microfilm machine. She searched for more on Samuel Mercer, but the name didn't appear in any subsequent articles. It was as if he, too, had disappeared.

She continued scrolling through the archived newspapers, searching for any other mention of the Mercers. There were birth announcements, wedding notices, and obituaries for other island families, but after Sarah's disappearance, the Mercer name seemed to vanish from the records. It was as if the family had been erased from Tybee's history.

The silence of the library pressed in around her as she worked, broken only by the occasional turning of pages or the soft footsteps of other patrons. Time seemed to stretch as she immersed herself in the search, determined to find some thread that would lead her back to Sarah and Samuel Mercer.

Her gaze shifted to her phone on the desk, the unread message from the imposter Henry still sitting there like a weight. *Who is he? And why does he care so much about this article? Why now after all this time?*

Fiona sighed, rubbing her temples. She needed answers, but nothing here was giving her clarity—just more questions. She closed her notebook, pushing her chair back from the desk.

As she stood, she felt the faintest chill, as though the air in the room had shifted. She glanced toward the tall windows, their light no longer warm but muted, almost cold. Shaking off the sensation, she waved at the librarian as she left.

"Find what you were looking for?" the librarian asked, her voice kind.

"Not quite," Fiona admitted. "But thanks for your help."

"Come back anytime," the woman said, her smile warm.

Fiona stepped out into the sunlit street, but the warmth did nothing to chase away the uneasy chill creeping up her spine. The questions churned in her head, looping over and over—Henry, Sarah, Samuel.

chapter
twenty-eight

FIONA PUSHED OPEN the door to the cottage, the soft creaking of hinges cutting through the sound of distant waves. She stepped inside, still clutching her notebook, her thoughts tangled with the fragments she'd pieced together about Sarah and Samuel Mercer.

"Claire?" she called, glancing around. She dropped her bag onto the dining table, the gentle clink of her keys breaking the quiet.

Claire was in the living room, her back to Fiona, speaking into her phone. Her tone was clipped, professional, but there was an undercurrent of something else—concern? Irritation?

"Yes, I understand," Claire said. "Please keep me updated if anything else comes to light." She paused, listening, before adding, "I'll check in tomorrow. Thanks."

She ended the call and turned, her shoulders tensed up to her ears. Fiona frowned, stepping closer. "What's going on? You look like you've seen a ghost."

Claire sighed, running a hand through her hair. "Someone broke into the museum last night."

"What?" Fiona's eyes widened. "Did they steal anything?"

"That's the odd part. They didn't. At least, nothing obvious. But ..." Claire folded her arms. "One piece of artwork was vandalized."

Fiona tilted her head. "Was it random?"

"No, it wasn't. Whoever did it was looking for something specific." Claire hesitated, her jaw tightening. "It was a Sarah Mercer painting."

Fiona's chest tightened, her pulse quickening. The same painting she had seen on her visit to the museum, the one that had caught her attention with its subtle depiction of fire in the window of what looked like the Bates estate.

Claire gave her a pointed look, as if sensing her sister's adrenaline spike. "And before you run away with this, let me explain. The painting wasn't just slashed or destroyed—it was taken down, and the back of the frame was ripped open. Like they were searching for something hidden in the frame."

"Did they find anything?"

"Apparently, yes. There's video footage showing someone running out of the museum with what looked like an envelope. That's all we know so far."

Fiona sank into one of the dining chairs, her heart pounding. What could've been inside? Her mind leapt to the imposter Henry, the unease from earlier bubbling back to the surface. What if it had been him? What if he'd been searching for something connected to Sarah Mercer all along?

"Do you have any idea what they were looking for?" Fiona asked, her voice low.

Claire shook her head. "No clue. And honestly, I'm not sure I want to know. Right now, it's a police matter. I'm just helping with some legal admin. It's not my case, and I don't plan on taking it on if it escalates."

Fiona frowned, her paranoia creeping in. "But what if this is connected to everything? What if—" She stopped herself, clenching her fists. She didn't want to say it out loud, but her mind was racing. What if imposter Henry had something to do with this? What if he'd been the one at the museum?

Claire pulled out a chair and sat down across from Fiona. "Look," she said gently. "I get that this is unsettling, but let's not jump to conclusions. We don't know who did this or why. The best thing we can do is stay out of it."

"But what if it is related?"

"And what if it's not?" Claire sighed, leaning back in her chair, her fingers idly tracing the edge of her coffee mug. "This isn't something we need to solve right now. The police are handling it, and if anything significant comes up, I'll hear about it."

Fiona opened her mouth to argue but stopped, her shoulders slumping. She stared at the table, her fingers curling around the edge. "So, what do we do now?"

Claire studied her for a moment, then tilted her head slightly. "First, you can tell me where you've been."

Fiona blinked, looking up quickly. "What do you mean?"

"You've been gone for hours. Where were you?"

Fiona hesitated, biting her lip. "The library."

"The library?" Claire repeated, her voice rising slightly. "This trip was supposed to be about relaxing. You know, taking a break? Not running off to dig up dirt."

"I know, I know," Fiona said quickly, holding up her hands. "I just ... I needed to know more about Sarah Mercer. About her disappearance. And I found some things, Claire. Things that might be important."

Claire pinched the bridge of her nose. "We're not here to solve some decades-old mystery. You're making this your whole world, and it's going to eat you alive if you let it."

"I get it," Fiona said softly, lowering her gaze. "I really do. I just ... I feel like I'm so close to understanding something, and I can't turn it off. It's like this itch I can't stop scratching."

"Well, you need to find a way to turn it off," Claire said firmly. She softened slightly, leaning forward. "Look, I know this is important to you. But this vacation wasn't supposed to be about Dolores or the Mercers or your mystery Henry. It was supposed to be about relaxing, remember?"

Fiona nodded reluctantly. "I remember."

"Good." Claire stood, placing her hands on her hips, and gave Fiona a pointed look. "Then here's what we're going to do. We're going to get dressed, go out for a nice dinner, and leave all of this—Dolores, Mercers, Henrys, all of it—off the table for the night. Deal?"

Fiona gave her a small smile. "Deal."

Claire reached over, nudging Fiona's shoulder playfully. "And I mean it, Fi. If you so much as say the word Mercer, I'm throwing your phone in the ocean."

Fiona laughed lightly, rolling her eyes. "Fine. But I'm holding you to the same rule."

"Fair enough," Claire said, grabbing her bag and heading toward her room. "Now, go get ready."

Fiona hesitated, her anxiety gnawing at her. But Claire was right. There was nothing they could do about the break-in or the painting. At least, not tonight.

She headed to her own room, closing the door softly behind her. The space was small but comfortable, with a twin bed covered in a blue quilt and a nightstand adorned with seashells. Through the window, she could see the sun beginning its descent toward the horizon, casting long shadows across the sandy path to the beach.

As she changed into a sundress, her mind drifted back to the library, to the articles she'd discovered about Sarah Mercer and her son. The connection was there, she knew it—Sarah, the missing woman from Savannah gossip, had a life on Tybee Island. She had a son. And now, decades later, her painting had been targeted at the museum.

It couldn't be a coincidence. Not all of it.

Fiona slipped on her sandals and ran a brush through her hair, trying to focus on the present moment. Claire was right—she needed a break from the investigation, even if just for one evening. She needed to step back, clear her head, and approach it all fresh tomorrow.

But as she set the brush down on the dresser, her gaze fell on her phone. The last message she'd sent to the imposter Henry remained unanswered, a silent reminder that this mystery wasn't going away, no matter how much she tried to ignore it for the night.

With a deep breath, she tucked her phone into her purse and joined Claire in the living room. Her sister had changed into a flowing maxi dress, her hair pulled back in a loose braid.

"Ready?" Claire asked, keys in hand.

"As I'll ever be," Fiona replied with a small smile.

As they walked out to Claire's car, the evening air wrapped around Fiona like a cool blanket. The sound of waves crashing on the shore soothed her, but not enough to quiet the storm in her mind.

She glanced at the cottage before climbing into the passenger seat, half-expecting to see a figure watching them from the shadows. Of course, there was no one there. Still, the thought lingered.

As Claire started the engine, Fiona stared out the window, her grip tightening around her phone. The last message she'd sent to Henry still sat unanswered, the silence stretching longer than she'd expected.

It gnawed at her.

Had he seen it and chosen not to respond? Had something changed? Or was he just waiting, biding his time, knowing that she'd come to him when she was ready?

What if he was the one at the museum? The question gnawed at her, refusing to be dismissed. If he was so intent on her writing the article, maybe he'd needed something from Sarah Mercer's painting to strengthen his story. Or maybe it was something else entirely—something he didn't want her to know.

The car jolted slightly as they backed out of the driveway, and Fiona forced herself to take a deep breath. Claire was right. She needed to let it go for now.

The sun dipped lower on the horizon as they drove into town, casting the island in a golden glow. For tonight, at least, she would try to focus on the beauty around her rather than the mysteries that had followed her from Savannah. But even as she made that promise to herself, she knew that tomorrow would bring her right back to the questions that refused to let her go.

chapter
twenty-nine

THE REST of the week on Tybee Island had been exactly what Fiona needed—a chance to step back, clear her head, and, for the most part, avoid the swirling mess of questions surrounding Dolores, Sarah Mercer, and the imposter Henry. Even Claire had seemed to enjoy the break, her usual sharp edges softening, her posture more at ease as they spent their days by the water and their nights sharing quiet meals without the weight of Savannah pressing down on them.

But now that they were back, the unease returned like a tidal wave, crashing over Fiona the moment the city skyline came into view. The questions she had pushed aside refused to stay buried, creeping back in with every mile they drove closer to home.

At her desk, Fiona twirled a pen between her fingers, staring at the blank document on her computer screen. Her phone buzzed with a text from Jacobs, asking for an update on the article. She hadn't responded yet. What could she say? That she'd uncovered enough tangled threads to weave a novel, but no clear answers?

To make matters worse, her inbox was still full of unresolved issues: the lawsuit from Dolores hung over her head; imposter Henry had texted her twice since she got back; and now, an elegant cream-colored envelope sat on her desk—a formal invitation to the regatta, allegedly from Dolores Bates herself. The timing couldn't have been more bizarre.

She picked up the envelope, her thumb running over the embossed edges. *Why would she invite me to this?* Fiona thought. Was it a trap? A show of power? Or was the invitation even real? It didn't make sense, not with the lawsuit still in play.

Her thoughts were interrupted by Denise's voice, snapping her out of her spiral.

"Earth to Fiona," Denise said, leaning over the edge of her cubicle. "What's going on in that head of yours? You look like someone stole your dog."

Fiona blinked, startled, and set the invitation down. "Nothing," she said quickly. "Just busy."

"Uh-huh," Denise said, clearly unconvinced. Their other friend Mia appeared behind her, balancing two cups of coffee.

"What are we gossiping about?" Mia asked, handing one of the cups to Denise.

"Fiona's mysterious mood," Denise replied, folding her arms. "We're trying to figure out if it's work-related or boy-related."

"It's neither."

"Uh-huh," Denise repeated, giving her a pointed look. "Well, whatever it is, we're going out for drinks tonight, and you're coming with."

Fiona shook her head. "I can't. I've got too much to do."

Denise tilted her head, studying her. "Okay, what's actually going on? You've been weird since you got back from Tybee. Are you in trouble or something?"

Fiona hesitated, glancing around the office to make sure no one was within earshot. The newsroom buzzed with its usual activity—phones ringing, keyboards clacking, the occasional burst of laughter from across the room. It was both comforting and concerning; familiar enough to put her at ease, yet public enough to make her cautious about what she said.

"It's complicated," she finally said, lowering her voice.

"Complicated how?" Denise pressed, sitting on the edge of Fiona's desk, her expression a mix of concern and curiosity.

Fiona sighed, running a hand through her hair. "You can't say anything, okay?"

"Scout's honor," Denise said, holding up two fingers.

Fiona glanced at Mia, who nodded encouragingly. "You've got my word ...too."

Fiona exhaled slowly. "A source I was relying on turned out to be ... someone he wasn't. And now I'm not sure what to do about it."

Denise frowned, her interest clearly piqued. "What do you mean, 'someone he wasn't'? Like, he lied to you?"

"More like he's not who he claimed to be," Fiona said carefully, choosing her words. "And now I don't know if I can trust anything he told me."

Denise leaned forward, her eyes narrowing. "Then use him."

Fiona blinked, confused. "What?"

"Play into it. If he's not who he says he is, let him think you don't know. Get more information out of him. Play along and see where it takes you."

"I don't know ..."

"What has playing it safe ever gotten you? You're already in deep with this. Why not see it through to the end? What's the worst that could happen?"

Fiona chewed her lip, her thoughts racing. The idea of continuing to engage with imposter Henry made her nervous, but there was a part of her—the journalist, the investigator—that couldn't help but be intrigued by the possibility of finally getting answers.

"I guess ... I could ask him to meet me again. Maybe see if he'll slip up."

Denise's eyes lit up. "Exactly! When's the next time you can see him?"

Fiona hesitated. "There's the art festival tonight. I suppose I could text him and see if he wants to go with me."

"Perfect," Denise said, clapping her hands together. "It's public, so you'll be safe. And that's the perfect place to ask questions without him being able to cause a scene."

Fiona's chest tightened with apprehension. The idea of spending the evening with the imposter Henry made her skin crawl. But Denise was right. If he had been the one who'd broken into the museum, maybe she could suss that out of him. And a public event like the art festival meant she wouldn't be alone with him—there would be crowds, security, witnesses if anything went wrong.

She glanced down at her phone, her fingers tightening around it. "Claire's going to lose her mind when she sees me with him."

"Claire's not your boss," Denise said, smirking. "You're an adult. You can handle this."

Fiona nodded slowly, steeling herself. Claire would be furious, there was no question about that. Her sister had warned her repeatedly about continuing to engage with Henry. But this felt different—this wasn't naivety or trust. This was deliberate, a calculated risk to uncover the truth.

"Okay. I'll text him."

"That's the spirit! Just play it cool and let him think he's still got the upper hand."

Fiona opened her phone, pulling up Henry's last message. Her hands trembled slightly as she typed: *Hey, I was wondering—are you free tonight? The art festival sounds like fun, and I could use some company.*

She hit send before she could second-guess herself, the message disappearing with a soft whoosh. The seconds ticked by, feeling like hours as she waited for a response.

Her phone buzzed almost immediately, the screen lighting up with a reply.

That sounds great. What time should I pick you up?

Fiona's heart jumped, her nerves coiling tighter. There was no turning back now.

Denise leaned over, catching the look on Fiona's face. "He said yes?"

Fiona nodded, her fingers tightening around her phone. "Yep. He's in."

Denise grinned. "Get ready to do some digging."

Fiona forced a small smile, but her chest felt heavy. As she typed out her response—suggesting they meet at the festival entrance at seven—she tried to ignore the warning bells ringing in her mind.

Mia, who had been quiet during most of the exchange, finally spoke up. "Just be careful, Fi. If this guy isn't who he says he is, you don't know what he's capable of."

"I'll be fine," Fiona assured her, though the words felt hollow. "It's a public event. What's the worst that could happen?"

"Just keep your phone handy," Mia advised. "And maybe let us know if you need an emergency extraction. We can be your backup plan."

"Thanks," Fiona said, genuinely touched by her friend's concern. "I'll keep that in mind."

As Denise and Mia returned to their desks, Fiona stared at her phone, the exchange with Henry still on the screen. Part of her wanted to cancel, to retreat to the safety of avoidance and distance. But a stronger part—the part that had been unsatisfied with fluff pieces, that had pushed to investigate Dolores Bates in the first place—knew that this might be her only chance to get answers.

She glanced at the invitation to the regatta, still sitting on her desk. Everything was connected somehow—Dolores, Sarah Mercer, the imposter Henry, the vandalized painting. Tonight might be her chance to start untangling those connections.

As she turned back to her computer, attempting to focus on the blank document that was supposed to become her article, Fiona couldn't shake the feeling that she was walking into something far more complicated than she had initially realized. But it was too late to back out now. The wheels were already in motion.

chapter
thirty

THE SAVANNAH ART MUSEUM was alive with energy. Guests in cocktail attire wandered through the softly lit galleries, their murmurs blending with the classical music performed by a string quartet near the entrance. Fiona stood by the large marble staircase, her champagne flute already half-empty. Her fingers toyed with the stem of the glass as her eyes drifted toward the main doors.

Her chest tightened when he walked in. Even from across the room, Henry exuded the charm and confidence that had initially drawn her in. He was effortlessly polished in a tailored suit, his tie loosened as though he hadn't quite decided if he wanted to look professional or approachable. The corners of his mouth lifted in an easy smile as he greeted a passing waiter, and Fiona felt a pang of frustration at herself.

Get a grip, Fiona. He's an imposter. A liar. Don't let him charm you again.

Clenching her jaw, she straightened, preparing herself. Before she could step forward to greet him, someone grabbed her elbow.

"Please don't tell me that's who I think it is," Claire hissed, her voice low and sharp.

Fiona winced and turned to face her sister. "Don't be mad."

"Mad?" Claire whispered. "Fiona, what possible reason could you have for inviting him here?"

Fiona glanced toward Henry, who was scanning the room,

undoubtedly searching for her. The elegant crowd parted occasionally, offering glimpses of him as he moved through the space with practiced ease. She turned back to Claire. "Because clearly, he doesn't think I know he's an imposter. This is my chance to find out more—play along, see what else he lets slip."

Claire's grip tightened on Fiona's arm. "This is reckless. You're putting yourself in danger."

"I can handle it," Fiona said, her tone firm. "I'm an adult, Claire. And it's a public place. There are people everywhere."

Claire opened her mouth to argue, but before she could, Henry's stride brought him within earshot. Claire let go of Fiona's arm, plastering a tight-lipped smile on her face just as Henry reached them.

"Fiona," Henry said warmly, his voice rich and confident. "There you are. And who's this lovely lady?"

"This is my sister, Claire," Fiona said, forcing a bright smile. "Claire, this is Henry."

Claire extended a hand, her grip firm and professional. "Nice to meet you."

Henry returned the handshake, his smile unwavering. "Likewise. Fiona's mentioned you—she said you're the brilliant lawyer in the family."

"Guilty as charged," Claire said lightly, though her sharp eyes didn't waver. She held the handshake a moment longer than necessary before adding, "You know, I don't think I've seen you at any of the bar association meetings. Do you practice here in Savannah?"

Henry's smile didn't falter, but there was a faint flicker of something in his eyes. He released her hand and smoothed his tie. "Oh, no, I'm not really one for social events like that. Too much small talk and not enough time for the real work, you know?"

"I suppose that's fair." Claire tilted her head, her expression unreadable. "It's a small world, though. I usually know most of the attorneys around here."

Henry chuckled, a practiced, effortless sound. "I tend to keep my head down. Too many late nights at the office to be out mingling."

"Understandable. Well, it's nice to finally meet you." She stepped back, giving Fiona a pointed look. "You two enjoy yourselves. I'll catch up with you later."

Fiona watched as Claire walked off, her shoulders stiff. She turned back to Henry, who was studying her curiously.

"Everything okay?" he asked.

"Of course," Fiona said, taking a sip of her champagne. "Shall we take a look around?"

Henry smiled and gestured for her to lead the way. They strolled through the galleries, the soft light highlighting the vibrant colors of the paintings and the polished sheen of the sculptures. Fiona tried to focus on the art, but her mind was a storm of questions.

The museum's high ceilings and marble floors amplified the sounds of conversation and laughter, creating a pleasant hum that filled the spaces between their words. Couples and small groups gathered around exhibits, their hushed discussions occasionally punctuated by exclamations of admiration or surprise. In another room, a curator was giving a talk to a small, attentive audience.

After a long moment, Henry said, "You surprised me."

Fiona glanced at him. "How so?"

"I didn't think I'd hear from you again," he admitted. "You'd gone quiet. I wasn't sure if I'd done something to put you off."

Fiona forced a casual laugh. "No, nothing like that. I just took an impromptu trip with my sister. A little break from everything."

"Where'd you go?" he asked, his tone light but curious.

Fiona hesitated. She was about to tell him the truth but thought better of it. "Just up the coast," she said vaguely, taking another sip of her champagne.

Henry frowned, quickly masking it with a smile. "I'm glad you reached out. I missed your company."

Fiona's nerves tightened, but she still smiled faintly. "It's good to see you, too."

They stopped in front of a painting, a striking landscape of marshland at sunset, its golden hues capturing the ethereal quality of coastal Georgia. Fiona seized the opportunity. "Did you hear about the break-in here?"

"Of course," Henry said, his expression neutral. "It was all over town."

"It was a Sarah Mercer painting," Fiona whispered, watching his reaction as her grip tightened around the champagne flute. "The thief ripped open the back of the frame and ran off with an envelope. Do you know anything about that?"

Henry raised an eyebrow, his expression calm. "No, I don't. Why do you ask?"

"I thought maybe it could help with my article."

"I wish I could help, but I'm afraid I don't know anything about it."

Fiona's chest constricted. He was so composed, so convincing—but wasn't that his specialty? She studied his face, searching for any hint of deception, any crack in his carefully constructed demeanor. His eyes met hers steadily, betraying nothing.

They moved to the next room, where the string quartet's music filtered softly through the air. Henry shifted the conversation. "Speaking of the article, did you receive Dolores' formal invitation to the regatta?"

Fiona glanced at him. "I did."

"Good. It starts next week, with some socials ahead of the races. I hope you're planning to attend. I'd be happy to drive you out to the site."

Fiona hesitated, her guard snapping back into place. "Actually, I'll probably go out there with my sister."

Henry's smile faltered, his jaw tightening almost imperceptibly. "Of course. That makes sense."

The moment stretched between them, weighted with unspoken questions. Around them, the museum continued its elegant flow of patrons and conversation, oblivious to the tension brewing beneath their polite exchange.

Before he could ask her anything else, another couple approached, introducing themselves and making small talk. Fiona used the distraction to her advantage, keeping the conversation light for the rest of the evening. She found herself playing a careful game, balancing the need to appear normal with her determination to probe for information.

As they wandered through the remaining exhibits, Fiona noticed Claire watching them from across the room, her expression a mix of concern and disapproval. Fiona gave her a subtle nod, silently reassuring her that everything was under control, even as her own doubts gnawed at her.

By the time Fiona said goodbye, her nerves were frayed. They stood beneath the museum's grand entrance, the night air cool against her skin after the warmth of the crowded galleries.

"Can I give you a ride home?" Henry asked, his voice soft as they stood by the museum's entrance.

Fiona shook her head quickly. "Thanks, but I'm helping Claire with cleanup. I'll see you another time."

Henry nodded, though his eyes lingered on her for a moment longer than she liked. "Goodnight, Fiona."

As he walked away, Fiona exhaled deeply, her pulse racing. She watched him disappear into the night, his silhouette fading as he reached the parking lot. Her instincts screamed at her that there was more to Henry's story than he let on. But for now, all she could do was wait—and watch.

chapter
thirty-one

FIONA CRADLED her phone between her ear and shoulder as she unlocked the door to her apartment. Claire's sharp tone rang through the receiver, her words as cutting as ever.

"I still can't believe you invited him. What were you thinking? He is not who he says he is, and you're waltzing through a museum with him like you're on a date."

"I wasn't 'waltzing,' Claire," Fiona snapped, pushing the door open and stepping inside. She kicked the door closed behind her with more force than necessary. "I was trying to get information. Isn't that what I'm supposed to do? Find out the truth?"

Claire sighed on the other end of the line. "There are safer ways to do that. Ways that don't involve spending an evening with a man who's clearly been lying to you since the moment you met him."

Fiona dropped her bag onto the couch, sighing as she leaned against the door to kick off her heels. "Can we not have this argument again? Please? My feet hurt, I'm exhausted, and—" She winced as she tugged off the second shoe. "And I swear these damn heels are a torture device."

Claire's tone softened slightly. "You should've worn flats."

"Yeah, thanks," Fiona muttered, tossing the heels aside.

The apartment was quiet, the streetlights casting long shadows across her living room floor. She could hear the distant hum of traffic outside, a reminder of the city that never truly slept. After the bustle of the art museum, the stillness felt almost eerie.

As she bent down to pick up her bag, something else caught her eye —a white envelope, its corner peeking out from beneath the door. She froze, her pulse quickening. "Claire, hang on a second."

"What's wrong?" Claire asked, her voice sharpening again.

"There's an envelope." Fiona crouched to pick it up. The paper was slightly crumpled, as though it had been hastily shoved under the door. She straightened, holding it up. "It looks like someone slid it under my door."

"Fi, don't open it," Claire said firmly. "Not until we know—"

"Too late." Fiona had already torn it open, curiosity and dread clawing at her in equal measure. She pulled out a stack of papers and unfolded them, her breath catching as she read the first page.

"What is it?"

Fiona's voice was barely above a whisper. "It looks like a marriage license."

Claire paused. "For whom?"

Fiona scanned the document, her eyes widening as she read the names aloud. "Sarah Mercer ... and Charles Bates."

"That's impossible. Charles was already married to Dolores. How could he have married Sarah too?"

Fiona shook her head, flipping through the papers with trembling hands. "I don't know, but—there's ... a divorce agreement here too."

"Between Charles and Dolores?"

"Yes." Fiona looked at it. Was it the same one that she'd seen in Henry's office? Without looking at the photographs she took, she wouldn't know.

"Is it signed?"

Fiona nodded, even though Claire couldn't see her. "Yes, it's signed. By both of them. It looks official." She scanned the text, her eyes racing over the legal jargon until something caught her attention. Her breath hitched. "Oh my God. If this ever came out, Dolores would lose everything. The entire Wesley estate would go to Sarah's son, Samuel."

"Are you sure that's what it says?" Claire asked, her voice laced with disbelief. "Read me the exact language."

Fiona flipped back to the page with the terms of the agreement, her hands trembling slightly as she skimmed the dense legal text.

"Okay," she said, swallowing hard. "'In the absence of additional heirs of Charles Bates, the entirety of the Wesley estate shall pass to Anthony Bates and remain under the control of his legal guardian until he reaches the age of majority.'"

Claire exhaled sharply. "So ... if Charles had no other heirs, the estate would stay with Dolores and Anthony."

Fiona nodded. "Which means if Sarah and Samuel were out of the picture, everything would eventually return to Dolores and Anthony."

A heavy silence filled the room, broken only by the faint ticking of the clock on her wall. Fiona paced across the apartment, the documents still clutched in her hand, the weight of the implications bearing down on her with each step.

"And this is signed? By both of them?"

"Yes," Fiona whispered, her voice trembling. "Charles and Dolores both signed it. There's a notary stamp, too."

Claire let out a low whistle. "So if this is real—and I'm not saying it is—then Dolores had every reason to want Sarah and Samuel gone. But why would Dolores agree to something like this in the first place? Giving Charles a claim to the estate if there were other heirs?"

Fiona flipped through the pages, desperate for more answers. The paper felt cool against her fingertips, the weight of history and potential scandal tangible in her hands. "Maybe she thought it wouldn't matter. Maybe she assumed Charles would never have another child. Or maybe ..." She hesitated, her voice growing softer. "Maybe Sarah threatened to go public. Savannah's all about reputation. That could be a pretty big blow to the Wesley reputation. Maybe this was Dolores' way of trying to control the situation."

"And if anyone found out about this? About the agreement—about Samuel?"

Fiona's throat felt tight. "This would've destroyed her. She wouldn't just lose the money—she'd lose everything. Her reputation, her standing in society, her entire life."

Claire's voice dropped, cold and calculating. "So if Sarah had leverage like this ... Dolores had every motive to make her disappear. And if she knew about Samuel—"

Fiona inhaled sharply. "He would've been the rightful heir. Not Anthony. If Charles had acknowledged him, the Wesley fortune would've gone to Sarah's son."

"That would've made Samuel a target, too," Claire said grimly.

Fiona sank onto the couch, her mind racing.

Motive.

Dolores had motive.

"Fiona." Claire's sharp tone pulled her back to the moment. "This feels wrong. Someone's trying to mess with you."

Fiona frowned. "What do you mean?"

"Think about it—this just happened to show up at your door? After everything else? After you started digging into the Bates family and Sarah Mercer? This is way too convenient."

Fiona shook her head, the envelope still clutched in her hand. "What if it's not? What if this is what the thief took from the museum? What if this is why the painting was vandalized?"

"And what if it's fake?" Claire countered. "You don't know if any of this is real, Fi. You can't just take it at face value."

Fiona's grip on the papers tightened. "Then how do we figure it out? We can't just sit on this."

"Turn it over to the authorities," Claire said, her voice firm. "This isn't your job. You're not a detective. Let the police handle it."

Fiona's jaw clenched. "I'm a journalist, Claire. This is my job. If this is real, then it's the key to everything."

Her voice dropped to a whisper as she stared at the documents, years of secrets and lies condensed into a few sheets of paper. "Dolores killed Sarah," she said, fully convinced now. "And now ... I finally know why."

"Then let the police investigate that. You can't confront her on this. It's reckless, and you don't have all the facts."

"I'm not waiting around for someone else to take care of this," Fiona snapped. "I'm confronting Dolores at the regatta. I'm done chasing ghosts."

"Fiona—"

"I'll talk to you later," Fiona said, ending the call abruptly.

She tossed the phone onto the couch and leaned forward, her head in her hands. Guilt prickled at the edges of her thoughts—Claire was just trying to protect her. But Fiona couldn't let this go. Playing it safe wouldn't get her to the truth.

The silence of her apartment pressed in around her, the only sound the distant hum of traffic and the soft rustling of papers as she gathered them into a neat stack. Each sheet represented another piece of the puzzle, another reason for Dolores to have wanted Sarah gone. The evidence was mounting, the story taking shape in a way that Fiona couldn't ignore.

Her fingers hovered over the papers before she made her decision. She snapped a photo of the marriage license and divorce agreement and sent it to Henry. *Imposter Henry,* she corrected herself. She typed out a message.

New development. Any thoughts?

The response came quickly. *Wait until we can go over it together at the regatta.*

Fiona's jaw tightened, frustration bubbling up. *Why does everyone want me to wait?* she thought bitterly. *Wait for the police, wait for the regatta, wait for the answers to just fall into my lap.*

She set the phone down and stared at the envelope still sitting on the coffee table. The room was too quiet, the shadows stretching too far. She couldn't shake the feeling that someone was watching, waiting for her next move.

But whoever they were, they'd underestimated her resolve.

chapter
thirty-two

THE LUNCHEON BUZZED with the sound of Savannah's elite mingling under a pristine white tent. The salty breeze rolling off the water brought a welcome relief from the summer heat, rustling the edges of the linen tablecloths and the skirts of the well-dressed guests. The lawn surrounding the estate was impeccable, every blade of grass trimmed to perfection, with clusters of hydrangeas lining the edges of the property. Waiters in crisp uniforms navigated the crowd, balancing trays of champagne and hors d'oeuvres that looked more like art than food.

Fiona adjusted the strap of her dress as she stepped farther into the tent, her heels clicking softly against the tiled flooring that had been laid out over the grass. She scanned the room, noting familiar faces from the Savannah social circuit—faces she usually avoided. But today, she wasn't here to avoid anyone. Today, she was here for answers.

Imposter Henry stood further inside, already ingratiating himself with a group of older men near the champagne bar. His laugh carried across the space, warm and easy, slipping effortlessly into the conversation like he had belonged there all along. The men laughed with him, engaged, captivated, as if they had known him for years rather than mere minutes.

Fiona knew exactly how that felt.

Her eyes flickered over him, taking in the perfect fit of his tailored blazer, the relaxed way he carried himself, the way his smile—damn that smile—reached his eyes just enough to feel real. He exuded effortless confidence, the kind that didn't have to try too hard but still managed to command attention.

And she hated that it still affected her.

Even now, knowing what she knew—that his name wasn't Henry Caldwell, that he had spent weeks lying to her, manipulating her, using her to further whatever twisted plan he had—even knowing all of that, she still felt the pull.

It was maddening.

Her breath hitched when he turned slightly, just enough for his gaze to brush over her. He held it there for half a second too long, and even though she wanted to turn away, ignore him, pretend like she didn't feel anything at all—she didn't.

She couldn't.

Damn it, Fiona. Get a grip.

She squared her shoulders, inhaling deeply as she forced herself to snap out of it.

This man is a liar.

You're not here to fall for his act—you're here to figure out who he really is.

But it wasn't that easy. When he turned toward her, his blue eyes catching the light just so, she was reminded of why she'd fallen for his charm in the first place. It wasn't just his looks, but the way he could make you feel like the only person in the room, even in a sea of people. She quickly looked away, focusing instead on the nearest tray of champagne.

Henry finished his conversation and returned to her side. "You doing okay?"

"Fine," she said, taking a sip of the champagne. The bubbles danced against her tongue, but they did little to ease the tension in her chest.

Deciding to cut straight to the point, she kept her voice low. "So, about those documents I sent you—"

Henry's expression didn't change, but he waved his hand dismissively. "We'll have time to go over those later. This isn't the place."

"But they're critical for the article," Fiona pressed, her frustration bubbling beneath the surface. "If they're real, they could change everything."

"And they will," he replied, his voice still calm and measured. "But let's not get ahead of ourselves, okay? Let's enjoy the luncheon. There's no rush."

Fiona's fingers tightened around the stem of her glass. *No rush?* she thought, frustration prickling at her. *If he wants this article written so badly, why does he keep avoiding the most important details?*

She was about to press him further when a man in his early fifties, dressed in a slightly rumpled blazer, approached them with a broad smile. His cheeks were flushed, likely from a bit too much champagne, and there was a glint of recognition in his eyes as he looked at Henry.

"Well, I'll be," the man said, clapping Henry on the shoulder with a little too much enthusiasm. "Haven't seen you since the old sailing days. How's life treating you?"

Henry froze for a fraction of a second, his easy smile faltering before he quickly recovered. "It's been good," he said, his tone smooth but slightly clipped. "Busy, you know how it is."

"Sailing days?" Fiona asked, glancing between the two of them.

"Oh, yeah," the man said with a laugh, completely ignoring her as he turned back to Henry. "You still get out on the water? Or did all that time behind a desk ruin you?"

Henry's chuckle sounded forced. "I haven't had much time for it, unfortunately. Busy schedule."

"Shame. You were a natural out there. Fastest crew in the regatta back in the day. I'd give anything to see that kind of teamwork again."

Henry stepped back slightly, his posture stiffening. "It was good to see you. Excuse us, won't you?"

Without waiting for a response, Henry placed a hand lightly on Fiona's back and steered her away from the man, his grip just firm enough to suggest he wasn't in the mood for questions.

Fiona looked up at him as they walked, her curiosity bubbling over. "What was that about?"

Henry shrugged, his smile returning but not quite reaching his eyes. "Clearly someone who's had too much to drink."

"He seemed to know you pretty well."

"People say a lot of things after a few glasses of champagne. I wouldn't read too much into it."

Fiona bit the inside of her cheek, her mind drifting to the photo she'd seen at the coffee shop on Tybee Island. *It looked so much like him,* she thought. *The same smile, the same posture.*

She was about to push further when the energy in the room shifted. A wave of murmurs rippled through the crowd, drawing Fiona's attention to the entrance of the tent.

Dolores Bates had arrived.

She was dressed in a flawless white suit that matched the tent's pristine decor, her pearl necklace catching the light as she moved. Her hat was wide-brimmed and elegant, her gloves spotless. She carried herself with the confidence of someone who had been at the center of Savannah society for decades, and despite the whispers trailing behind her, she seemed unbothered.

Fiona glanced at Henry, expecting him to stay by her side. But the moment Dolores entered, he stiffened and turned to her.

"Excuse me for a moment."

"Wait—" Fiona started, but Henry didn't even turn back. He strode off toward the far end of the tent, his steps quick and purposeful, disappearing into the throng of guests.

Fiona frowned, her chest tightening with frustration. She flicked her gaze back to the entrance of the tent just in time to see Dolores making her way inside.

The whispers around Fiona grew louder as the socialites near her exchanged glances.

"She's got nerve showing up here," one of them muttered, her voice laced with disdain.

"I heard she's only here because her name's still on the donor list," another replied, smirking.

"Imagine walking in like that after everything. You'd think she'd stay in that big house of hers and let us forget about her for once."

The comments grated on Fiona's nerves, but they also fueled her determination. *I'm not going to let her intimidate me,* she thought. *If Dolores knows something, I'm going to find out what it is.*

She handed her glass to a passing waiter and made her way toward

Dolores. As she approached, she rehearsed what she wanted to say, trying to keep her tone neutral and her emotions in check.

"Mrs. Bates," Fiona greeted.

Dolores turned slowly, her expression as composed as ever. Up close, her presence was even more formidable. "Ms. Stevens," she said coolly. "I wasn't expecting to see you here."

Fiona hesitated, taking a deep breath. "I was invited," she said firmly. "By Henry Caldwell."

Dolores' eyes narrowed slightly, but her expression didn't waver. "Henry invited you?"

"Yes," Fiona said, watching her carefully. "I was just speaking with him a moment ago. Surely you saw him. He was standing right here."

Dolores' lips pressed into a thin line, a flicker of discomfort crossing her face. "I don't know what you're talking about. And I certainly didn't authorize any invitation on my behalf."

"Are you saying you didn't send the formal invitation to the regatta either?"

Dolores tilted her head slightly, her gaze cold. "That's correct. And given the circumstances, Ms. Stevens, I must ask you to leave. You're not welcome here."

"I'm here to tell the truth, Mrs. Bates. Surely you understand the importance of that."

"The truth, Ms. Stevens, is often subjective. I suggest you consider that carefully before making any further moves."

Fiona hesitated before speaking again, her tone sharper than before. "Some truths are harder to bury than others. Especially when they're written down."

Dolores' smile faltered just slightly, her eyes narrowing as she studied Fiona's face. The crack in her composure was brief, but it was there— enough to make Fiona's chest tighten with the rush of adrenaline.

"I don't know what you're insinuating," Dolores said, her voice icy now. "But if you're looking for trouble, you'll find it."

The warning was clear, but Fiona held her ground. "I'm just looking for answers. If there's nothing to hide, then there's nothing to worry about."

Fiona stared at the woman, her heart pounding. But before she could press her further, Dolores turned and walked away, her movements as smooth and deliberate as ever.

Fiona stood there a moment, her mind racing.

But, with the weight of the room's stares pressing down on her, Fiona had no choice but to leave. Turning toward the exit, her pulse racing, she pushed through the doors into the fresh air outside.

chapter
thirty-three

FIONA SAT in the driver's seat of her car, the door still ajar as she stared out at the sprawling estate. Her hands gripped the steering wheel tightly, her knuckles white against the black leather. The words Dolores had spoken were still ringing in her ears, sharp and pointed. *You're not welcome here.*

She exhaled slowly, leaning back against the seat. The warm air filtered through the open window, but it did little to calm her nerves. The luncheon had been a disaster—at least as far as her plans to confront Dolores were concerned. The woman had shut her down with the practiced ease of someone who had been silencing opposition for decades.

Fiona reached for her bag on the passenger seat, fishing out her phone. She should call Claire, let her know what happened, maybe even admit that her sister had been right to warn her about confronting Dolores directly. The thought left a bitter taste in her mouth.

As she unlocked her phone, the screen reflected the brilliant blue of the sky above. Such a beautiful day for such an ugly encounter. She glanced around at the other cars in the parking area—sleek luxury vehicles that probably cost more than she made in a year. The kind of cars that belonged to people who could afford to pay their way out of trouble.

She wasn't sure what her next move was supposed to be. But as she reached for the ignition, something caught her eye. Movement near the side of the building.

Fiona froze, her hand hovering over the key. Through the gaps between the parked cars, she saw Dolores Bates striding purposefully toward the side of the estate. Even from this distance, her posture was rigid, her steps quick and deliberate. The white suit she wore stood out starkly against the green of the manicured lawn, making her easy to track as she moved with surprising speed for a woman her age.

Fiona's heart jumped, and she leaned forward, squinting to see where Dolores was going. That's when she spotted him.

Henry.

He was standing near a small gravel path that disappeared behind the building, his hands in his pockets. When Dolores approached, he took a step back, his shoulders stiffening as she closed the distance between them. Even from her vantage point, Fiona could see the tension in his stance, the way he seemed to brace himself for whatever storm was coming.

Fiona's pulse quickened.

She ducked lower in her seat, instinctively not wanting to be seen. The parking area was partially secluded by a row of hedges, giving her some cover while still allowing her to observe the unfolding drama. Her reporter's instincts kicked in—this was a moment she needed to capture.

The confrontation happened so quickly, it almost didn't feel real. Dolores said something, her voice sharp, but Fiona couldn't make out the words. Henry responded, his tone lower but equally heated. The body language between them was unmistakable—this was no friendly chat.

Fiona reached for her phone instinctively, her hands trembling as she swiped to the camera and hit record. She zoomed in on the scene, steadying her grip as best she could. The two of them were arguing now, their gestures growing more animated with each passing second.

Dolores pointed a finger at Henry, her gloved hand jabbing at him. Henry stepped forward, closing the gap between them, his face set in a hard line. Whatever they were saying, it wasn't friendly. Fiona strained to hear their words, but the distance and the gentle rustle of the breeze through the nearby trees made it impossible to catch anything more than the occasional raised voice.

Fiona's mind raced as she continued to film. *What are they arguing about? Is this all some scam they're in on together?* She zoomed in further, trying to capture their expressions, any clue that might help her piece together this bizarre puzzle.

The sun cast long shadows across the gravel path as the confrontation intensified. Dolores' hat shifted slightly as she shook her head emphatically, clearly disagreeing with whatever Henry was saying. Her perfect composure from the luncheon had cracked, revealing something raw and authentic underneath—something Fiona had never seen in the carefully curated public image Dolores presented to the world.

Henry raised his hands in a gesture of frustration, then turned on his heel and started walking away. Dolores called after him, her voice ringing out across the quiet evening air. Henry didn't stop.

He strode quickly to a sleek black car parked near the edge of the lot. Fiona watched as he yanked open the driver's door and slid inside. The engine roared to life, and within seconds, the car was speeding down the gravel driveway, kicking up a cloud of dust as it disappeared onto the main road.

Fiona lowered her phone, her heart pounding against her ribs. She glanced at the screen to make sure the video had recorded properly, then looked back at the now-empty spot where Henry's car had been. The dust was still settling on the gravel, the only evidence that he had been there at all.

Had anyone else witnessed the exchange? She scanned the area quickly, but the other guests seemed to be contained within the tent, oblivious to the drama that had just unfolded. The wait staff moved between tables with practiced efficiency, and the soft strains of classical music drifted across the lawn, creating an eerie contrast to the tension she had just witnessed.

Her eyes drifted to Dolores, who was still standing on the gravel path, her back to Fiona. The older woman stood perfectly still for a moment, her shoulders rising and falling as if she were trying to calm herself. Then, with the same poise she had carried into the luncheon,

Dolores adjusted her hat and walked back toward the tent, smoothing her white suit as if nothing had happened.

Fiona let out a shaky breath, reaching for the small notepad she kept in her glove compartment. She flipped it open, grabbing the pen tucked inside, and scribbled down Henry's license plate number before it slipped from her memory. *G9L-7249.*

She stared at the note for a moment, her thoughts spinning. *What just happened?* The interaction she had just witnessed contradicted everything she thought she knew. If Dolores and Henry were working together, why would they argue so intensely? And if they weren't working together, what was their connection?

Fiona replayed the video, studying their body language, the way they moved around each other like combatants in a ring. There was history there—something deeper than a professional relationship. Something personal.

She leaned back in her seat, gripping the phone tightly. She had proof now—proof that Henry and Dolores knew each other and that their connection wasn't as professional or distant as either of them had implied. But what did it mean?

The weight of the afternoon settled over her as she replayed the scene in her mind. Dolores' sharp gestures, Henry's tense posture, the way he had stormed off without a second glance. Whatever they were hiding, it was big enough to cause a public confrontation.

Fiona started her car, the engine humming to life beneath her. She would need to follow up on this—track down Henry's car using the license plate, maybe even find out who he really was once and for all. The imposter had played his part well, but the facade was beginning to crack.

As she pulled out of the parking area, Fiona glanced back at the tent one last time. The luncheon continued, the guests mingling, laughing, completely unaware of the drama that had just unfolded beyond their view. Savannah's elite, carrying on as they always had, while secrets simmered just beneath the surface.

Fiona's fingers tightened around the steering wheel as she glanced back at the tent. *You're closer than you think,* she told herself. *Don't let them scare you off now.*

THE HOTEL ROOM was small but clean, the kind of generic space designed to be just comfortable enough to forget you weren't at home. She could have driven back to Savannah each night—technically, it wasn't that far—but she'd opted to stay here instead, in the same hotel as the other regatta guests. Maybe it was convenience, or maybe it was the nagging feeling that if she left, she'd miss something.

Now, as she perched on the edge of the neatly made bed, she wasn't sure it had been the right choice.

The lamp on the nightstand cast a pale glow over the room, the artificial warmth doing little to soothe the restlessness coiling in her chest. A faint hum of chatter from the hallway filtered through the thin walls, voices rising and falling in casual conversation—other guests laughing, drinking, slipping into their rooms with the easy satisfaction of people who belonged here.

Fiona ignored it, her focus entirely on her phone as it rang in her ear.

When Claire finally answered, her voice crisp and suspicious, Fiona let out a shaky breath. "Claire, I need a favor. A big one."

"Oh, no," Claire said immediately, the warning clear in her tone. "What happened now?"

Fiona closed her eyes, pinching the bridge of her nose. "Look, I just need you to help me find out who owns a car."

"What?" Claire's voice sharpened. "Are you seriously asking me to misuse public resources for something like this?"

Fiona winced. "Okay, when you say it like that, it sounds bad."

"Because it is bad," Claire shot back. "License plate searches aren't for fishing expeditions. They're for law enforcement, not nosy journalists with a death wish!"

"Please, Claire," Fiona begged, leaning forward, her elbow resting on her knee. "You know I wouldn't ask if it wasn't important. I just—" Her voice cracked slightly, and she took a deep breath, trying to steady herself. "I saw something today. Something big. And I need to know who this man really is."

Claire sighed, the sound crackling through the speaker. "Fiona, you know how many ethical lines this crosses? Not to mention, legal ones?"

"Yes, I know," Fiona said quickly. "But you always figure out a way to justify things when you know they're the right call."

"That's not a compliment."

"Claire, come on," Fiona pressed, her voice softer now. "You've bent rules for worse reasons. Please, just this once. I'm asking you as your sister. You know I wouldn't do this if it wasn't important."

There was a long pause, and Fiona could practically hear Claire thinking, her lawyer brain weighing the risks and consequences.

Finally, Claire sighed again, more resigned this time. "Detective Lawson owes me," she said begrudgingly. "I'll ask her. But if she finds out this is for you and not some official case, she's going to kill me. And then I'll kill you."

"Thank you," Fiona said, relief washing over her. "I promise I'll owe you big for this."

"You already do," Claire muttered. "Now, tell me what happened. Why do you need this?"

Fiona leaned back against the headboard, staring at the textured ceiling as she recounted the day. Her words tumbled out in a rush, her tone bitter and anxious. "Dolores told me to leave the luncheon. She was cold, defensive, and clearly evasive about everything. And Henry—" She stopped, catching herself. "The imposter Henry disappeared the moment she showed up. But then I saw them outside, arguing. They know each other, Claire."

"Whoa, whoa, whoa," Claire cut in, her voice sharp. "What do you mean, they were arguing? Who was arguing?"

Fiona groaned, pressing her hand to her forehead. "Dolores told me to leave, right? She practically ordered me out like she was queen of the luncheon or something. She said she didn't authorize any invitation for me and acted like I had no right to be there."

"Which tracks, given the lawsuit," Claire muttered. "Go on."

"So Henry—imposter Henry—was with me at the luncheon. But as soon as Dolores walked in, he got all weird. He made up some excuse and walked off without even letting me finish my sentence. And then, when I was sitting in my car, I saw them."

Claire's tone sharpened. "Who's them?"

"Dolores and Henry," Fiona said, her voice rising slightly. "They were outside, off to the side of the building. I saw them arguing—like, really arguing. Dolores was pointing her finger at him, and he was getting defensive. It wasn't just some casual conversation. They clearly know each other, Claire."

There was a pause on the other end of the line before Claire spoke again, her voice more cautious now. "You're absolutely sure it was him?"

"Yes," Fiona said firmly. "I saw his face, Claire. It was definitely him."

"And they were arguing? About what?"

"I don't know," Fiona admitted, frustration creeping into her voice. "I was too far away to hear what they were saying. But they looked angry —Dolores especially. She was doing that thing she does where she gets all stiff and points at people like she's trying to pin them to the ground with her glare."

Claire let out a low whistle. "That's not nothing. But how do you know they weren't just ... I don't know, disagreeing about something mundane? Could it have been business-related?"

"Claire, he left without even saying goodbye to me, then stormed off in his car. And Dolores? She walked back into the tent like nothing happened. That wasn't mundane. It was heated." Fiona sat up straighter, gripping the phone tightly. "They know each other, and they're hiding something."

Claire was quiet for a moment. "So what did you do?"

"I filmed it."

"You what?"

"I recorded the whole thing. They were yelling. It wasn't subtle. And then he sped off in a car, so I got his plate number."

"And now you want me to violate about six different laws to find out who he is?"

"Exactly," Fiona said, ignoring her sister's sarcasm.

Claire groaned softly, but her frustration was tinged with worry. "Fiona, don't you think this is ... I don't know, a little too convenient? Dolores and this guy clearly know each other, right? She's suing you, but he's the one encouraging you to write this story?"

Fiona froze, the words hitting her like a splash of cold water. "What are you saying?"

"I'm saying," Claire continued, her voice growing more insistent, "what if they're working together? Think about it. She sues you to scare you off. He swoops in pretending to be on your side, and meanwhile, they're playing both ends against the middle."

Fiona's grip on the phone tightened as her mind raced. "But why? What would they gain from that?"

"That's the part I don't know. Maybe it's a way to control what you write, to manipulate the narrative. Or maybe they're trying to discredit you completely—set you up to publish something that blows up in your face."

Fiona swallowed hard, her pulse quickening. "But if that's true, then why would he push so hard for me to write the article? If he's working with Dolores, wouldn't he want me to back off?"

Claire's tone dropped, low and serious. "Unless the goal is to get you to write exactly what they want. Maybe he's feeding you just enough information to steer you in a direction that benefits them—or hurts someone else."

Fiona stared at the blank wall in front of her, her thoughts spiraling. "You think this is a setup?"

"I don't know," Claire admitted. "But the whole thing stinks. Dolores knows this guy, Fiona. The man who's pretending to be her lawyer—and who's been in your apartment, by the way—isn't some random nobody. He's got an angle, and I don't like it."

Fiona's voice trembled. "What if he's not working with her? What if they're on opposite sides, and that's why they were arguing?"

"Maybe." Claire hesitated. "But even then, it's dangerous. If they're at odds, you're caught in the middle. And if they're working together, you're the pawn. Either way, you're the one who gets hurt."

The room seemed to close in around Fiona, the silence pressing down on her. "I can't just walk away from this, Claire. I've come too far."

Claire groaned softly. "Okay, so what now? Are you coming back to Savannah?"

"No," Fiona said firmly. "I'm staying here. The races are starting soon, and I need to see this through."

"You were disinvited, though," Claire said sharply. "Are you trying to get yourself banned from the whole event?"

"It's a public event. Dolores doesn't own it and can't stop me from showing up. And even if she could, I'm not going to let her scare me off."

Claire sighed, the sound long and tired. "Just promise me you'll be careful, okay? Stay in public places, don't go wandering off with anyone, and please don't provoke anyone into a fight."

"Got it," Fiona said, though she didn't miss the skeptical edge in her sister's voice.

"I'll call Lawson," Claire said. "But don't do anything reckless until I get back to you. I mean it, Fiona—nothing."

"Fine," Fiona said, though her tone lacked conviction.

"Fiona."

"I promise."

"Good. Watch your back, okay?"

"You too," Fiona said, smiling faintly.

They ended the call, and Fiona set her phone down on the nightstand, staring at it for a moment. The room felt quiet, and the shadows cast by the single lamp seemed to stretch longer than they should.

She leaned back against the pillows, her thoughts swirling. Henry, Dolores, Sarah Mercer, Samuel ... The pieces of the puzzle were there, but they refused to fit together.

Her chest tightened with frustration. She was so close to the truth, but every step forward seemed to reveal three more questions.

"Nothing reckless," she muttered to herself, echoing Claire's words. But even as she said it, she knew she wouldn't be able to sit still for long.

chapter
thirty-five

THE ONSHORE WIND carried the briny scent of the ocean as Fiona stood on the sidelines of the regatta, the excitement around her almost palpable. The first of the thirteen races was underway, the sleek white sails of the competing boats cutting through the waves with precision. Cheers erupted from the crowd gathered on the shoreline, their voices carried by the breeze as they urged their favorites forward.

Fiona squinted against the glare of the sun, her attention shifting between the boats on the water and the faces around her. The event was a spectacle of tradition and wealth, every detail polished to perfection, from the uniformed staff handing out champagne to the meticulously dressed spectators. Yet, despite the vibrant energy, Fiona's mind was elsewhere—caught in the complicated web of lies and half-truths surrounding Sarah Mercer, Dolores Bates, and, most frustratingly, Imposter Henry.

She tightened her grip on her phone, resisting the urge to text Claire again. She'd promised to wait for her sister to call back with the results of the license plate search, but the anticipation was wearing on her patience.

The sails snapped taut against the wind as the boats cut through the waves, their hulls skimming across the water with practiced precision. The ocean glinted under the midday sun, each crest catching the light.

Fiona stood at the edge of the spectator area, her fingers wrapped around the metal railing as she watched the race unfold.

The competition was intense. Two boats were neck and neck, their crews moving in perfect synchronization as they adjusted the sails and leaned hard into the turns. The sound of ropes cracking and sails flapping carried across the water, mingling with the cheers and shouts from the crowd. It was the kind of raw, adrenaline-fueled spectacle that made you hold your breath without realizing it.

A smaller boat trailing behind made a bold move, cutting sharply across the wake of the leaders in a desperate bid to gain ground. The maneuver earned a ripple of gasps and murmurs from the crowd around Fiona. She couldn't help but lean forward, her pulse quickening as the trailing crew fought to close the gap.

The lead boat's crew was relentless, however, their every move calculated and deliberate. Fiona caught glimpses of their concentrated faces through her binoculars, the captain barking orders while the crew scrambled to execute. It was the kind of unity and determination that spoke of years of practice—and privilege.

"Looks like the Mariner has this one in the bag," someone nearby murmured, and Fiona glanced over to see an older man with a weathered face and a pair of binoculars slung around his neck. He didn't look particularly invested, more like someone observing for the sake of it.

Fiona returned her gaze to the water just as the lead boat began to pull away, its sails catching a perfect gust of wind that sent it gliding effortlessly ahead. The other crews pushed harder, but the distance was undeniable. The winning boat soared across the finish line moments later, its sails catching the golden afternoon light as the crowd erupted into cheers.

As the cheers began to subside and the crowd started to disperse, her phone buzzed in her pocket. She snatched it out, her pulse quickening when she saw Claire's name on the screen.

"Claire," Fiona said breathlessly as she answered, stepping away from the crowd for some semblance of privacy.

"Fiona," Claire said, her tone unreadable. "I got the information you wanted."

Fiona's heart thudded in her chest. "And?"

Claire took a breath, her voice steady but weighted. "The car is registered to a Samuel Mercer."

Fiona froze.

For a moment, she couldn't breathe. It was as if the air had been sucked out of her lungs, leaving only that name—repeating, circling, growing louder in her mind.

Samuel Mercer.

Sarah Mercer's son.

Fiona's fingers tightened around the phone, her knuckles white. The revelation thundered through her, drowning out everything else.

It was him.

The man she had trusted.

The man she had spent nights unraveling mysteries with, sharing drinks, sharing secrets—The man she had let into her home.

"It makes sense now," Fiona murmured, her voice barely above a whisper, but the words felt too small for what was crashing down around her.

Because Henry Caldwell wasn't Henry Caldwell.

He was Samuel Mercer.

And everything—everything—had been a lie.

"What does?" Claire asked, her voice tinged with concern.

Fiona turned, staring out at the horizon where the boats were being towed back to the docks. "Henry—he's not Henry. He's Samuel. Sarah Mercer's son. That's why he's been so focused on this article, on exposing Dolores. He's trying to avenge his mother."

There was a long pause on the other end of the line. "Fiona, are you sure about this?"

"Yes," Fiona said firmly. "It all fits. The way he's been pushing me to write the story, the way he avoided questions about his past, even the way Dolores reacted to him. They know each other, Claire. He's Sarah's son."

"If that's true, then this just got a whole lot more complicated. You need to tread carefully. This isn't some exposé anymore—it's personal for him. And that makes it dangerous."

"I know."

"Are you coming back to Savannah yet?"

Fiona hesitated, her gaze drifting back toward the shoreline, where the crowd had gathered to congratulate the winning crew. Dolores stood at the center of the commotion, her pristine white suit and wide-brimmed hat making her impossible to miss. She was handing out a ribbon to the captain of the winning boat, her smile poised and practiced, the very image of composure.

Fiona felt a rush of indignation as she watched Dolores exchange polite words with the sailors and guests around her, nodding and gesturing as though she hadn't a care in the world. Beneath the polished facade, Fiona knew there were secrets—secrets Dolores had fought hard to keep buried.

"I can't leave yet," Fiona said firmly, gripping her phone tightly. "I need to see this through. Dolores is right there, acting like nothing's wrong. I need to talk to her."

Claire's voice rose sharply. "No. You can't just confront her out of the blue. She's already made it clear she doesn't want you there."

"Dolores knows what really happened to Sarah Mercer—I'm sure of it."

Claire groaned, her voice heavy with exasperation. "Just a few days ago, you were telling me how intimidating Dolores is—how you felt threatened by her. Do I need to remind you about the vase she threw? You said it made you feel like she was capable of anything."

Fiona hesitated. The memory of Dolores' outburst flickered through her mind—the shattering sound of porcelain, the fury in the woman's eyes. For a moment, doubt crept in, her earlier fear bubbling to the surface. But then she forced herself to stand straighter, her jaw tightening.

"I did feel that way," Fiona admitted. "But things have changed. Or maybe I've just found my courage."

"Courage?" Claire shot back, her tone edged with disbelief. "Fiona, this isn't about courage. This is about knowing when to pick your battles—and knowing who you're dealing with. Dolores might be dangerous, especially if she's hiding something as serious as this. You don't need to put yourself directly in her crosshairs."

"I'll be careful," Fiona promised, but the flutter of nerves in her belly betrayed her unease. "I just ... I can't let this go, Claire. If she knows something about Sarah Mercer, I have to find out. I can't walk away from this now."

Claire sighed, the sound weary and resigned. "Fine. Just promise me you'll stay public, stay safe, and call me the moment anything feels off."

"I promise," Fiona said, though the determination in her voice was far stronger than the hesitation she felt. She ended the call before Claire could argue further, slipping her phone into her pocket and glancing back toward the awards area.

Dolores was still there, standing on the makeshift podium and handing ribbons to the winning crew. Her expression was as composed and polished as ever, her movements deliberate and poised as she posed for photos with the sailors and exchanged pleasantries with the event organizers. To anyone else, she looked like the picture of grace and sophistication. But to Fiona, she was a woman harboring secrets—a woman who might hold the key to everything.

Fiona waited, her heart pounding as the ceremony wound down. Guests began to trickle away, mingling by the refreshment tables or making their way back toward the hotel. Dolores lingered for a few moments, speaking quietly with one of the event staff, before finally stepping off the podium and heading toward the path that led back to the hotel.

Fiona watched as Dolores walked away, her white suit almost glowing in the fading afternoon light. She hesitated for a moment, glancing around to make sure no one was paying attention to her, then slipped into the crowd, keeping a safe distance behind Dolores.

The path was quiet, the sound of Dolores' heels clicking softly against the pavement carrying through the still air. Fiona kept her foot-steps light, her movements careful as she followed. She stayed far enough back to avoid suspicion, ducking behind a hedge when Dolores glanced over her shoulder.

Dolores reached the hotel entrance and stepped inside, her pace unhurried. Fiona paused just outside, her breath coming in shallow bursts. She waited a beat, giving Dolores enough time to move through the lobby, before pushing the door open and slipping in behind her.

The hotel lobby was quiet, the faint hum of the air conditioning the only sound. Fiona spotted Dolores crossing the marble floor toward the elevator bank, her posture still ramrod straight. She ducked behind a potted plant as Dolores pressed the button, her face impassive as she waited for the elevator to arrive.

When the doors opened, Dolores stepped inside and disappeared from view. Fiona watched the numbers rise above and then stop at what was likely Dolores' floor. She hesitated, her resolve wavering as she glanced at the elevator panel. Her instincts urged her to turn back, to leave this confrontation for another time, but the memory of Sarah Mercer's name on the marriage license pushed her forward.

The next elevator arrived with a soft chime, and Fiona stepped inside, pressing the button for the same floor. As the doors closed, her reflection stared back at her in the mirrored walls, her wide eyes betraying the mix of fear and determination within her.

When the elevator reached Dolores' floor, Fiona stepped out, her footsteps muffled against the plush carpet. She spotted Dolores at the end of the hallway, her white suit a beacon against the dimly lit corridor. Dolores moved with purpose as she retrieved her key and unlocked the door to her room with a practiced motion.

Fiona hesitated, watching as Dolores began to enter her room. The moment stretched before her like a precipice, and she knew once crossed, there would be no going back. In that suspended moment, all her doubts and fears coalesced, then dissolved into a singular, crystal-clear certainty. She had come too far to turn back now.

As Dolores pushed the door open and began to step inside, Fiona moved. Her heels sank into the carpet as she hurried forward, her hand shooting out to catch the edge of the door just as Dolores began to swing it shut.

The older woman turned sharply, her eyes narrowing as she took in Fiona's face. For a moment, they simply stared at each other, the tension between them palpable.

"I think we should talk," Fiona said, her voice steady despite the rapid beating of her heart.

Dolores' lips pressed into a thin line, and for the first time, a flicker of uncertainty crossed her composed features.

chapter
thirty-six

DOLORES BATES FROZE, her hand gripping the edge of the door as she turned to face Fiona Stevens. The younger woman stood in the doorway, her expression a mix of determination and apprehension. The faint hum of the hotel's hallway lights seemed deafening in the silence.

Dolores felt a wave of unease wash over her, though she kept her face carefully composed. Years of social graces, of mastering the art of performance, had taught her how to keep the cracks hidden. But inside, her thoughts raced like turbulent waters. Not now. Not here. She tightened her grip on the door, her hand betraying the slightest tremor.

"Ms. Stevens," Dolores said smoothly, her voice a practiced blend of politeness and authority. "It's late. Surely this can wait until tomorrow."

"It can't," Fiona said firmly, her hand still on the door, her voice steady despite the rush of adrenaline coursing through her. "I know you've been keeping secrets, Dolores. And I think it's time you told the truth."

Dolores stiffened, her sharp gaze narrowing as she studied Fiona's face. "What exactly is it you think you know?"

Fiona leaned forward, lowering her voice, but not her intensity. "I know about Samuel Mercer. I know about Sarah. I know that whatever happened back then isn't what you've led everyone to believe. And I'm giving you the chance to come clean—to me—before I write about it in the paper."

Dolores' polished exterior wavered for the briefest moment. She quickly recovered, her lips pressing into a thin line. "You think you can intimidate me?"

"This isn't intimidation. This is me trying to give you a chance. You have an opportunity to tell your side of the story before the world finds out another version without you. I'm offering you that courtesy. But make no mistake, Mrs. Bates—I will get to the truth, with or without your help."

Dolores' pulse quickened painfully. She hesitated. *She knows more than she should. How? How much has she pieced together already? What has Samuel told her?*

"I don't know what you think you've uncovered," Dolores said finally, her voice even but edged with unease. "But you're treading into dangerous territory."

"That's a risk I'm willing to take." Fiona didn't flinch, her gaze steady as she met Dolores' sharp glare. "The question is, are you willing to take that risk? If you don't tell me your side of the story, someone else will—and you won't have any control over how it's told."

Dolores' jaw tightened, and for a moment, the two women stood in tense silence. The weight of Fiona's words pressed heavily on Dolores' consciousness, her mind racing as she calculated her next move. *She's bluffing,* Dolores told herself. *She doesn't have enough to bury me ... does she?*

But Fiona's expression remained resolute, her hand still braced against the door. Dolores' composure faltered slightly, and she stepped back, her hand gripping the edge of the doorframe. *Damn her persistence.*

Dolores exhaled slowly, her mind filled with the burden of secrets that had haunted her for years. She glanced down the hallway, ensuring no one was lingering nearby, then stepped aside, pulling the door open wider.

"Fine," she said, her voice clipped. "You've got your chance. Come in."

Fiona hesitated, but quickly stepped inside before Dolores could change her mind.

The room was elegant yet impersonal, with neutral tones and minimalist decor. The curtains were drawn tightly, leaving the space dim despite the warm light from the bedside lamp. A single suitcase rested neatly in the corner, and the bed looked untouched, as though Dolores hadn't truly relaxed here at all.

Dolores closed the door with a soft click, her back to Fiona for a moment as she gathered herself. The pressure of Fiona's presence weighed on her like a physical burden. She wasn't ready for this confrontation—not tonight, not ever—but it seemed the choice had been taken from her.

"Take a seat," Dolores said, gesturing to the small sitting area near the window. She moved to the armchair opposite the loveseat, her movements stiff, and perched on the edge as though prepared to defend herself at any moment.

Fiona sat down slowly, her notebook already in her lap, pen in hand. She leaned forward slightly, her posture determined but not overtly aggressive. "Let's start with Samuel Mercer."

Dolores tensed visibly, her breath catching. Samuel. Always Samuel. The name was like a specter, following her wherever she went, no matter how hard she tried to outrun it.

"What about him?" Dolores asked carefully, her voice tinged with bitterness.

"Who is he?" Fiona pressed, her eyes narrowing. "And don't give me half-truths. I know he's connected to Sarah Mercer—and to you."

Dolores felt her composure wavering, but she forced herself to remain calm. "I don't know what you mean," she said, but the words felt hollow even as she spoke them.

"Don't lie to me, Mrs. Bates. I know he's been posing as your lawyer, Henry Caldwell. Did you know he was doing that?"

Dolores blinked, the revelation landing like a physical blow. Henry Caldwell? The pieces clicked into place, and the implications settled over her. She shook her head slowly, her voice quieter this time. "No. I didn't know."

Fiona crossed her arms. "But you do know him."

Dolores hesitated, her fingers gripping the armrests of the chair. "Yes. I know him. He's been ... after me for quite some time now."

"Why?"

Dolores exhaled shakily, leaning back in the chair. For a moment, she looked out the window, her reflection faintly visible in the glass. She barely recognized herself anymore. The past few years had carved deep lines into her face that no amount of powder or foundation could hide. The loss of Anthony, her precious boy, had hollowed her out in ways she didn't know were possible.

Dolores finally spoke, her voice barely above a whisper. "Because he blames me."

"Blames you for what?"

"For everything." Dolores turned back to her, her gaze steady but weary. "For his mother. For his life. For the lies she told."

Fiona frowned, pulling something from her bag and unfolding it. "And what about this?" she asked, holding out a sheet of paper.

Dolores stared at it for a moment before taking it. Her breath caught as she recognized the forged divorce agreement, the bold scrawl of Charles' name at the bottom sending a ripple of anger through her.

"Where did you get this?" Dolores demanded, her sharp gaze flicking back to Fiona.

Fiona hesitated, then exhaled, choosing honesty. "It showed up at my apartment."

Fiona watched as she shook her head and then muttered, "The museum break in, the painting, it must have been him."

"Who?" Fiona asked, but Dolores was clearly lost in her own thoughts. They sat in silence for a minute before Dolores finally spoke again.

"This," she said, her voice unsteady as she grasped the paper, "is a lie."

"How so?"

Dolores' fingers tightened on the edges of the document, her grip almost trembling. Her voice, when she finally spoke, was thick with resentment, old wounds bleeding through.

"Sarah Mercer forged this," she said, her words clipped and sharp. "She thought it would convince Charles to leave me. Knew that he wouldn't if he thought his lifestyle would be impacted. He'd gotten used to the Wesley money."

"So, Sarah lied to him?"

Dolores nodded. "She wanted it all—for herself and for her son. She thought she could rewrite history with a pen."

Fiona felt a cold discomfort as she absorbed Dolores' words.

"And Charles believed her?" she asked, her voice softer now, hesitant —uncertain whether she truly wanted to hear the answer.

Dolores hesitated, her throat tightening. "For a time, yes," she admitted. "Sarah was ... persuasive. Manipulative. She knew how to play to his ego, to his vices." She exhaled, her gaze flickering toward the window as if she could see the past playing out before her. "But eventually, he saw the truth."

Fiona studied her, watching the way Dolores' mask faltered just slightly, just enough to see the years of exhaustion beneath it.

She had been fighting for so long—not just against Savannah's gossip mill, not just to preserve her name, but against a woman who had tried to take everything from her.

"And Samuel Mercer? How does he fit into all of this?"

Dolores' breath hitched. She placed the paper carefully on the coffee table, as though it might shatter like glass. "Samuel Mercer is the bastard child of Sarah and Charles' affair. He's been like a ghost haunting me ever since he was born. First through his mother's schemes, and now through his own."

The room fell into a tense silence, broken only by the faint hum of the air conditioning. Fiona stared at Dolores, her expression unreadable.

"And Sarah? What happened to her?"

Dolores' gaze flicked back to the window, her reflection staring back at her like a shadow. Her hands gripped the armrests of the chair. The burden of decades-old secrets pressed heavily upon her, each one a weight she had carried alone for too long. The truth, no matter how deeply she had buried it, was clawing its way to the surface.

"Sarah Mercer," Dolores began, her voice distant as if recalling a long-forgotten dream, "was determined to have what I had, no matter the cost. She didn't just want Charles—she wanted my life, my status, my security." Her fingertips traced invisible patterns on the armrest. "When the forgery failed to convince Charles to leave me completely, she became desperate. Reckless."

Fiona leaned forward, pen poised above her notebook. "What do you mean by reckless?"

Dolores exhaled slowly, her shoulders sagging ever so slightly. "You're not going to let this go, are you?"

"No," said Fiona. "I'm not."

The room fell into silence, the faint hum of the air conditioning the only sound. Dolores felt the weight of her past pressing down upon her, a burden she had carried alone for too long. There was no running from this anymore.

Finally, she said quietly. "You want the truth? Then you'll have it. But don't say I didn't warn you.

chapter
thirty-seven

THE ROOM BUZZED with quiet murmurs and the clinking of champagne flutes, the atmosphere alive with the hum of admiration and polite conversation. The art gallery was bathed in soft, golden light that illuminated the vibrant canvases lining the walls. Dolores Bates stood near the center of the room, her arm tucked through Charles' as they moved from one painting to the next. She wore an elegant navy dress that clung perfectly to her figure, the pearls at her neck a quiet nod to her old-money roots. But despite her polished appearance, she couldn't shake the nagging tension.

"Marvelous, isn't it?" Charles said, his voice smooth as he gestured toward a large, abstract painting of marshlands.

Dolores forced a smile, nodding. "It's striking," she replied, though her attention wasn't on the painting. She had noticed the way Charles' gaze kept drifting across the room, his eyes following someone else.

Dolores turned her head subtly, her discomfort rising when her suspicions were confirmed. Sarah Mercer stood by the far wall, surrounded by a small cluster of admirers. She was young, barely in her mid-twenties, with soft auburn hair that fell in loose waves over her shoulders. Her dress, a deep green that made her eyes shine, was far too modern and daring for the conservative Savannah crowd, but it didn't seem to bother her in the slightest.

She was laughing at something one of the men beside her had said, her expression open and inviting. Her hands moved animatedly as she spoke, and Dolores noticed the smudges of paint still lingering on her fingers.

"Excuse me for a moment," Charles said.

Dolores' grip on his arm tightened reflexively. "Where are you going?"

"To meet her," Charles replied, his tone casual as though it were the most natural thing in the world.

Dolores' breath caught, but she quickly masked her discomfort. "I don't think that's necessary. We're here to admire the art, not the artists."

Charles turned to her, a faint smirk on his lips. "Dolores, don't be ridiculous. She's the star of the evening. It would be rude not to introduce ourselves."

Before she could protest further, he slipped his arm free of hers and strode toward Sarah. Dolores stood frozen, her hand trembling as she gripped her clutch bag.

She watched Charles approach Sarah, his charm already on full display. The other woman looked up at him, her eyes lighting up as he said something that made her laugh. Dolores felt a wave of unease, a sour taste filling her mouth. This is nothing, she told herself. He's just being polite. Nothing more.

But the way Charles lingered, the way he leaned in closer than necessary, made her insides clench with worry.

The gossip started the very next day.

Dolores sat in the breakfast room of their estate, the morning sun streaming through the windows as she skimmed the day's paper. The column in the society section caught her eye immediately, her pulse quickening as she read the thinly veiled insinuations.

A certain up-and-coming painter caught the attention of one of Savannah's most prominent businessmen at the opening of her new gallery show. The two were seen deep in conversation long after the champagne had stopped flowing. Could this be the start of a new artistic collaboration—or something more?

Dolores' hands trembled as she set the paper down, the words burning in her mind. She looked up just as Charles strolled into the room, freshly shaven and humming softly to himself.

"You made the papers again," she said evenly, her voice betraying none of the anger simmering beneath the surface.

Charles arched a brow as he poured himself a cup of coffee. "What are they saying this time?"

"Apparently, you're quite taken with Sarah Mercer."

Charles froze, the coffee pot hovering over his cup for a moment before he set it down. He met her gaze, his expression unreadable. "It's nonsense."

"Is it?" Dolores challenged, her hands gripping the edge of the table. "Because it didn't look like nonsense."

"Don't blow this out of proportion," Charles said, his tone dismissive, as he turned to pour himself a glass of brandy from the sideboard. The clink of glass against crystal was unnervingly calm.

"Blow it out of proportion? Do you know how humiliating it is to open the paper and see them speculating about my husband and some girl barely out of art school?"

Charles' hand stilled on the decanter, but he didn't turn around. "Maybe if you weren't so uptight all the time, they'd have less to speculate about."

Dolores' breath caught, the jab hitting harder than she'd expected. "What is that supposed to mean?"

Charles turned slowly, his expression cold and unreadable. "It means that maybe if you paid a little more attention to your husband instead of constantly hovering over Anthony, I wouldn't feel the need to look elsewhere."

"You're blaming me?" she said, her voice rising. "Charles, I just gave birth to your son! Do you have any idea what that's done to me physically? The complications—"

"Here we go again," Charles interrupted, his voice growing louder. He set the glass of brandy down harder than necessary, the liquid sloshing over the rim. "You use that as an excuse for everything. The complications, the recovery, the doctors—how long is that going to be your crutch, Dolores?"

"It's not a crutch!" Dolores snapped, tears stinging her eyes. "It's the reality of what I've been through. What we've been through. But instead of supporting me, you're running off to flirt with a painter while I'm trying to heal and raise our child!"

Charles' jaw tightened, his hands curling into fists at his sides. "And what about me, Dolores? You think I don't have needs? You think it's easy for me to come home every night to a cold bed while you make excuses?"

Dolores flinched at his words, a lump forming in her throat. "I'm doing the best I can," she said softly. "But it's not enough for you, is it? It never is."

Charles' face twisted with frustration. He grabbed the small porcelain vase from the sideboard and hurled it across the room. It shattered against the wall, the sound reverberating through the house like an explosion.

Dolores gasped, stepping back as her hand flew to her chest. Her heart raced as she stared at the shards of porcelain scattered across the floor.

Charles pointed a finger at her, his voice low and seething. "Maybe you should take a good, long look in the mirror, Dolores. Maybe then you'll understand why this marriage is falling apart."

The words hung in the air, heavy and venomous. Dolores remained silent, too stunned to respond. Charles let out a sharp exhale, grabbed his coat from the back of a chair, and stormed out of the room, slamming the door behind him.

Sinking into the nearby chair, tears streamed down her face, but she bit her lip to keep from sobbing out loud. She couldn't fall apart. Not now. Not while Anthony needed her.

As she sat there in the quiet, the weight of her situation bore down on her heavily. She'd always known Charles had a temper, but this morning had been different. His words had cut deeper than ever before, and Dolores couldn't help but feel like whatever they used to have was beyond repairing now.

The nursery was dimly lit, the soft glow of the lamp casting a warm circle over the rocking chair where Dolores sat. Anthony's tiny chest rose and fell rhythmically as he slept, his small hand resting against her collarbone. The faint scent of baby powder hung in the air, a comforting contrast to the storm of emotions within her.

She stared at the curtains, barely seeing them. Charles had left in a rage, slamming the front door so hard it'd rattled the windows. Now she was alone, the silence of the house amplifying every creak and groan of the old wood beneath her bones.

Dolores glanced down at Anthony, her heart aching. "It's just you and me, sweetheart," she whispered, pressing a soft kiss to his forehead. "**But** we're going to be okay. I promise."

Leaning forward to place him gently in the crib, she tucked the small blanket around him with trembling hands. She lingered for a moment, brushing her fingers lightly over his cheek before forcing herself to straighten. You can't break now, she told herself. Not in front of him.

Just as she turned to leave the nursery, the front door slammed again. The sound reverberated through the house, louder than before. Her body stiffened. Heavy, uneven footsteps followed, accompanied by the distinct clinking of glass.

"Dolores!" Charles' voice bellowed through the halls, slurred and angry.

Her breath caught, and she instinctively stepped back into the shadows of the nursery.

"Dolores!" he shouted again, the sound growing louder as he stomped down the hallway.

She swallowed hard, her mind racing. Steeling herself, she stepped out of the nursery, closing the door behind her to protect Anthony from the chaos about to unfold.

"I'm here, Charles," she said, her voice trembling but steady enough to carry down the hallway.

Charles appeared at the other end, his shirt untucked, his tie dangling loosely around his neck. His eyes were bloodshot, and his gait unsteady, but the fury radiating from him was unmistakable.

"You've got a lot of nerve. Talking to me like that. Like I'm the problem in this marriage."

Dolores tried to keep her voice calm. "You've been drinking. We can talk about this in the morning."

"No," he snapped, his voice rising. "We're talking about it now."

"Charles, please. You'll wake Anthony."

"Anthony!" he spat, his words dripping with bitterness. "That's all I ever hear about these days. Anthony this, Anthony that. What about me, Dolores? Or have you forgotten you have a husband?"

"I haven't forgotten. But you don't make it easy, Charles. Do you think it's been simple for me? After what happened with the birth—"

"More excuses. You've been using that for months. 'Oh, poor Dolores, she can't possibly be a wife because she's too busy being a martyr!'"

"That's not fair," Dolores shot back, her voice cracking. "You don't know what it's been like for me—how hard it's been to recover, to try and take care of our son while you're out drinking and—"

"Shut up," Charles growled, closing the distance between them in a few quick strides. Before she could move, he grabbed a handful of her hair, yanking her toward him.

"Charles, stop!" she cried, her hands flying up to claw at his wrist.

"You think you can talk to me like that?" he hissed, his face inches from hers. The smell of whiskey on his breath made her recoil.

"Let go of me!"

He dragged her down the hallway, his movements erratic and fueled by anger. Stumbling into the bedroom, he released her with a shove that sent her crashing into the nightstand.

"Charles!" she gasped, clutching her arm where she'd hit the corner of the wood.

"Maybe if you acted like a wife for once, I wouldn't have to go looking elsewhere," he snarled, his eyes wild.

Dolores' chest heaved, tears streaming down her face. "Don't do this, Charles."

"What's the matter?" he sneered, his tone mocking. "You're always full of excuses. Too tired. Too fragile. Too busy with the baby. Well, I'm done with excuses."

Dolores' heart raced as he reached for her, his hand brushing her arm. She pulled away quickly, her voice trembling as she said, "Don't touch me."

Charles' face twisted with frustration. "I'm your husband," he snapped, his voice rising. "You don't get to tell me no."

"Stop!" Dolores shouted, her voice breaking. "You're scaring me!"

Her words seemed to pierce through his drunken haze for a moment, but then his expression darkened. He reached out again, but this time Dolores twisted away, bumping into the nightstand. The small candle perched there wobbled precariously before tipping over, the flame catching the edge of the window curtains.

They both froze for a heartbeat, the sudden burst of heat and light shocking them into silence.

"Charles!" Dolores screamed, her voice frantic.

Charles blinked, his drunken mind struggling to catch up. "Get out," he muttered, stumbling toward the door.

Dolores didn't wait. She bolted from the room, her bare feet pounding against the hardwood as she raced back to the nursery. Smoke was already curling down the hallway, and the acrid smell made her cough as she pushed open the door.

Anthony was still sleeping soundly, oblivious to the chaos. Dolores scooped him up, clutching him tightly as she ran for the stairs. Her heart pounded as she burst through the front door and into the cool night air, gasping for breath.

She turned back toward the house, the flames visible through the upstairs windows. The fire was spreading fast, and panic swelled within her.

"Charles!" she screamed, her voice cracking.

She expected him to follow, but instead, the sound of tires screeching cut through the night. Dolores spun around just in time to see his car tearing down the driveway, the taillights disappearing into the darkness.

Her knees buckled, and she sank to the ground, clutching Anthony as tears streamed down her face. She didn't know whether to feel relieved or terrified.

All she knew was that Charles was gone, and she was left standing in the ashes of what they once had.

chapter
thirty-eight

THE YEAR that followed the fire was one of whispers and absence. Charles didn't return to the house—not in any real sense. He stayed away most nights, and when he did come home, it was only to gather a few things before disappearing again. Dolores had stopped asking where he went; the answer was always the same, even if he didn't speak it aloud.

The gossip columns were relentless. Every week brought a new piece, a new insinuation about Charles Bates and Sarah Mercer. They speculated about private dinners, and secret rendezvous. Eventually, the rumors took a sharper turn.

Sources suggest the young painter has been seen shopping for baby clothes. Could a little one be on the way?

Dolores felt ill as she read the words. No longer subscribing to the paper, the whispers still found her, carried by society women eager to dissect every scandal in Savannah. She hated the pity in their eyes, the thinly veiled schadenfreude in their voices as they offered their condolences for a marriage that had clearly fallen apart.

Anthony was her only solace. Two now, he toddled around the house with an energy that left her breathless. His laughter was the only thing that broke through the fog of her days, and she clung to it like a lifeline.

But even Anthony couldn't shield her from the storm that came crashing down one rainy afternoon.

The first hint of trouble was the sound of tires on the gravel driveway, followed by the hard squeak of brakes.

Dolores was in the nursery, folding a stack of Anthony's clothes while he played with a set of wooden blocks on the floor. She froze when she heard the car door slam, her heart leaping into her throat.

"Stay here, sweetheart," she said softly, kneeling to kiss Anthony on the forehead. He babbled something in response, too focused on his blocks to notice the tension in her voice.

Dolores descended the stairs slowly, her hand gripping the banister as the front door swung open. Charles strode in, shaking rain from his coat, his face set in a hard line.

"What are you doing here?" Dolores asked, her voice steady but cold.

Charles didn't answer right away. Closing the door with a sharp click, he turned to face her, his eyes darker than she remembered. The months had not been kind to him. He looked worn, his face drawn and his hair streaked with more gray than before. But there was still that fire in his gaze—the fire that always seemed to burn hottest when directed at her.

"We need to talk."

Dolores crossed her arms, keeping her distance. "What about?"

Charles exhaled, running a hand through his damp hair. "I want a divorce."

The words landed like a blow, even though she'd expected them. Dolores' jaw tightened, but she kept her voice calm. "No."

Charles' brow furrowed, his lips curling into a bitter smile. "No? That's not how this works, Dolores."

"You made vows. You have a family. You don't just get to walk away because you've decided you want something new."

"It's not about 'something new,'" he snapped. "It's about Sarah. She's pregnant, Dolores. I need to marry her before the baby is born."

The room tilted for a moment, and Dolores gripped the back of a chair to steady herself. "You got her pregnant?" she whispered, her voice trembling with disbelief.

"Yes," Charles said, his tone unapologetic. "And I won't have my child born a bastard. One way or another, I'm going to get my divorce from you."

Dolores straightened, her hands trembling but her gaze unflinching. "No," she repeated. "I won't let you humiliate me—or Anthony. You're not walking away from this family just to play house with Sarah Mercer."

"This isn't about you, it's about me!" he shouted, his voice echoing through the house.

Dolores flinched, but she didn't back down. "It's always about you, Charles. Your needs, your desires, your whims. You don't care who you hurt as long as you get what you want."

"Enough!" he roared, grabbing a porcelain figurine from the mantle and hurling it across the room. It shattered against the wall, pieces scattering across the floor.

Dolores stumbled back, her heart racing as he turned toward the side table, knocking over a vase of flowers with a sweeping motion.

"You're not listening to me!" he shouted, his face contorted with anger. "I'm leaving, Dolores."

The sound of Anthony's voice calling for her drifted down the stairs, breaking through the tension. Dolores' breath hitched, panic setting in.

"Charles, stop," she said, her voice trembling. "You're scaring him."

Charles froze for a moment, his chest heaving as he stared at her. Then he ran a hand over his face, muttering under his breath.

Dolores took the opportunity to step around him, her movements quick but measured. "Stay here," she said firmly, but she doubted he was listening.

She climbed the stairs two at a time, her heart pounding as she reached the nursery. Anthony looked up at her with wide, curious eyes, his blocks scattered around him.

"Mama?" he asked softly.

"It's okay, sweetheart," she whispered, scooping him into her arms. She pressed a kiss to his forehead, breathing in his familiar scent to steady herself. "We're okay."

The sound of something else breaking downstairs made her flinch. She cradled Anthony tightly, backing into the corner of the room as tears welled in her eyes. She wanted to scream, to cry, to fight back—but all she could think about was keeping Anthony safe.

The shouting eventually stopped, and the front door slammed shut. Dolores crept to the window, peeking through the curtains just in time to see Charles getting into his car. The engine roared to life, and he sped down the driveway without a backward glance.

Her legs gave out, and she sank to the floor, clutching Anthony as he squirmed in her arms. She kissed the top of his head, tears streaming down her face.

"You don't deserve this, my love," she whispered. "You don't deserve any of this."

But deep down, a voice in her head whispered a bitter truth: neither did she.

The news came quietly, whispered in hushed tones at the corner bakery, in the society columns that Dolores had stopped reading months ago but could never fully escape. Sarah Mercer gave birth. A boy. Samuel.

Dolores clenched her fists at the breakfast table, her knuckles turning white as she stared at the plate in front of her. The eggs and toast sat untouched, her appetite gone at the thought of that woman—a woman who had already destroyed her marriage—now staking a claim to her future.

The staff kept their heads down, carefully avoiding eye contact.

"Samuel Mercer," she muttered under her breath, the name tasting bitter. The fork clattered loudly against the china as she stood abruptly, the chair scraping against the floor.

Dolores' world had been upended in ways she hadn't thought possible. Charles had stayed away even longer after the birth, his visits to the house becoming nearly nonexistent. Every moment felt like an agonizing reminder of the cracks that had shattered her life.

But it wasn't until the evening Sarah Mercer showed up on her doorstep that Dolores realized just how much further she could be pushed.

The knock came just as the house had settled into its nightly quiet.

Anthony had been tucked into his crib hours ago, his soft breathing the only sound in the nursery. Dolores had spent the evening reading in the parlor, but she couldn't remember a single word from the pages of the novel.

When she opened the door and saw Sarah Mercer standing there, reality seemed to shift beneath her feet. Sarah was dressed simply, her auburn hair pulled back into a loose knot. But her eyes were sharp, her expression unyielding. She held a folder in one hand, clutching it tightly as though it were a weapon.

"Good evening, Dolores," Sarah said, her voice calm but carrying an unmistakable edge.

Dolores didn't move. Her fingers tightened around the doorframe. "What are you doing here?"

Sarah smiled faintly, but there was no warmth in it. She stepped past Dolores, uninvited, into the foyer. "We need to talk."

Dolores closed the door slowly, tension rising within her. She turned to face Sarah, who was already making herself at home in the parlor, setting the folder down on the coffee table.

"You're bold, I'll give you that," Dolores said, her tone sharp. "But you have no business being here."

Sarah tilted her head, her smirk widening. "On the contrary. I have every reason to be here." She opened the folder and pulled out a document, holding it up for Dolores to see.

Dolores felt unsteady as she recognized the format.

"This," Sarah said, her voice dripping with satisfaction, "is a copy of a divorce agreement. Signed by you, I might add."

Dolores stepped forward, her eyes narrowing. "That's impossible. I never signed anything."

"Of course you didn't," Sarah said with a shrug, her tone mockingly casual. "But you'd be surprised how easy it is to create something that looks like you did. And the original is tucked away somewhere safe— just in case we need it."

Dolores felt her pulse pounding in her ears, her vision narrowing on Sarah's smug face. "You forged my signature?"

Sarah's expression didn't falter. "I did what I had to do. Charles and I want to be together, Dolores. And with this, we can ensure that happens. The Wesley estate will go to Samuel, to support him. And everyone will know that he is Charles' true heir."

Dolores laughed bitterly, her hands trembling. "You think you can just waltz in here, wave some fake documents around, and take everything? You've already ruined my marriage, Sarah. What more could you possibly want from me?"

Sarah's eyes gleamed with something dangerous. "I want what's due to us. You can either agree to this and walk away quietly, or we'll file this, and your reputation will be in shreds. Charles will back me, testifying that you did indeed sign this, and the court will believe us. You'll lose everything, Dolores."

Dolores' breath hitched, but she forced herself to stay calm. Inside, rage bubbleddangerously close to the surface. "You're delusional if you think I'm going to roll over and let you take what's mine."

Their voices had risen, and the tension in the room was thick when a soft sound broke through the noise."Mama?"

Dolores froze, her heart dropping as she turned to see Anthony standing in the doorway, clutching his favorite blanket. His big brown eyes were wide with confusion, his curls tousled from sleep.

Sarah's gaze shifted to him, and something in her expression changed. Her smile twisted into something darker, more sinister.

"So that's the heir," Sarah said softly, taking a step toward Anthony.

Dolores' body moved instinctively, placing herself between Sarah and her son. "Leave him out of this," she said, her voice trembling.

Sarah ignored her, her focus locked on Anthony. "He's an obstacle, you know. Even if I get you out of the way, the law says some of the inheritance will still go to him. Unless ..."

Dolores froze, her mind reeling as the weight of Sarah's threat settled over her heavily. The air seemed to thicken around her, her breath catching in her throat. She can't mean that, Dolores thought, but the dark glint in Sarah's eyes told her otherwise.

Sarah stepped closer to Anthony, her movements slow and deliberate. Her gaze flicked toward the little boy, who stood clutching his blanket by the doorway, his wide eyes darting between the two women.

"Don't," Dolores said sharply, her voice rising. "Don't you dare finish that sentence." She moved to block Sarah's path, her body taut with adrenaline.

Sarah tilted her head, her smile twisted and predatory. "You've already lost Charles. You've lost your marriage. Do you really think clinging to this house and your son will save you? You're finished, Dolores. You just don't know it yet."

"Get out," Dolores hissed, her hands trembling at her sides. "Get out of my house, now."

Sarah ignored her, her focus shifting entirely to Anthony. "Such a sweet boy," she said, her voice soft but laced with something that made Dolores' skin crawl. "He looks so much like Charles. But he's not my son. And that's the problem, isn't it?"

"Stay away from him!" Dolores snapped, her voice breaking.

But Sarah didn't stay away. She lunged.

"Anthony, run!" Dolores screamed, her voice cracking as panic surged through her.

The little boy froze, his small hands clutching the blanket so tightly that his knuckles turned white. His lip quivered, and tears welled in his big, innocent eyes. "Mama?" he whimpered, his voice shaking.

Sarah's hands reached out, her fingers clawing toward Anthony as if to grab him, to snatch him away.

Dolores' body moved before her mind caught up, her hands shooting out to grab Sarah's arm. "I said stay away from him!" she shouted, her voice raw with fear and fury.

Anthony stumbled backward, his blanket falling to the floor as tears streamed down his cheeks. "Go to your room, Anthony!" Dolores's grip tightened on Sarah's arm as the two women struggled. "Lock the door!"

Anthony hesitated, his tiny hands trembling, but the chaos in the room spurred him into action. Darting down the hallway, his sobs echoed as he disappeared into the nursery and slammed the door shut.

Dolores turned back to Sarah, her heart hammering in her chest. The woman was like a wild animal, her eyes crazed and her movements erratic. She clawed at Dolores, her nails raking across her arms, leaving angry red welts in their wake.

"You think you can stop me?" Sarah hissed, her voice venomous. "You think you can win?"

"You're insane!" Dolores shouted, her voice shaking as she shoved Sarah back toward the sofa.

"You'll regret this!" Sarah shrieked, her voice breaking into a high-pitched wail. She lunged again, her hands outstretched, her face twisted with fury.

Dolores stumbled, her foot catching on the edge of the rug. She fell back against the end table, into the sofa, her hand knocking over a lamp that clattered to the floor. Her breath came in shallow bursts as Sarah loomed over her, a predator ready to strike.

Her hand landed on a pillow, soft and yielding beneath her fingers. Without thinking, she grabbed it and swung it upward. A combination of the shock and impact knocked Sarah down and Dolores climbed on top of her before pressing the pillow against her face as she struggled to rise.

"You won't touch my son," Dolores growled, her voice trembling with rage and fear.

Sarah thrashed beneath her, her muffled screams tearing through the quiet of the room. Her arms flailed wildly, her nails scraping against Dolores' wrists and forearms, but Dolores didn't let go. Her mind was blank, her focus singular. Protect Anthony.

Tears streamed down her face as the fight drained from Sarah's body, her movements slowing, then ceasing altogether. Dolores staggered back, the pillow slipping from her grasp and falling to the floor with a dull thud.

The room was silent now, save for Dolores' ragged breathing. Staring at Sarah's lifeless form, her chest heaved as the realization of what she'd done crashed over her.

"Oh my God," she whispered, her knees buckling. She sank to the floor, her hands trembling violently. "What have I done?"

The sound of hurried footsteps broke through her haze. Dolores turned to see Margaret, one of the house staff, standing in the doorway. Her face was pale, her eyes wide as she took in the scene.

Margaret didn't speak at first, her gaze shifting between Dolores and Sarah. Then, with surprising composure, she stepped forward, kneeling beside Dolores and placing a hand on her shoulder.

"I saw everything," Margaret said firmly, her voice steady. "You did the right thing, Mrs. Bates. You protected your son."

Dolores shook her head, her tears falling freely now. "I didn't mean to ... I didn't want to ..."

Margaret gripped her shoulder tighter, her tone resolute. "Listen to me. She was going to hurt Anthony. You had no choice. You did what any mother would do."

Dolores stared at her, her mind spinning. "What do I do now?"

Margaret straightened, her expression hardening with resolve. "We'll clean this up," she said softly. "No one will ever know what happened here tonight."

chapter
thirty-nine

DOLORES SAT STIFFLY in the chair by the hotel room window, her hands clasped tightly in her lap. The glow of the bedside lamp streaked across her face, accentuating the lines etched by years of secrets, losses, and the weight of choices she could never undo. Fiona Stevens sat across from her on the edge of the bed, her notebook forgotten in her lap. The silence between them was heavy, filled with the gravity of everything Dolores had just revealed.

For the first time in years, Dolores felt naked—stripped of her defenses, her carefully crafted image crumbling. She had always known this day would come, but now that it was here, the weight of her own words threatened to crush her. The weight of decades pressed down, making each breath feel labored, each second stretched thin with tension.

"I lied," Dolores said finally, her voice low and strained. She didn't dare meet Fiona's gaze, instead focusing on the pattern of the carpet beneath her feet. "I've lied for years. Not just to protect myself but to protect my family—to shield my name, Anthony's name, from scandal."

Fiona leaned forward, her posture tense but attentive. "You made people think you killed Sarah Mercer in cold blood. Out of some crime of passion."

Dolores' lips pressed into a thin line. "I didn't make them think it, Ms. Stevens. I just didn't correct them." Voice trembling, she straightened her back, forcing herself to continue. "The truth is, Sarah's death wasn't about jealousy or rage. It was about Anthony. It was about protecting my son."

Her breathing quickened at the memory, the raw fear that had gripped her as Sarah lunged for her baby. The scene played in her mind as vividly as if it had happened yesterday. "I didn't plan it. I didn't want it to happen. But when she came after Anthony ..." Dolores shook her head, her voice breaking. "I didn't have a choice."

The shadows in the room seemed to deepen around them, matching the darkness of the confession. Outside the window, the distant sounds of the hotel grounds filtered through—a faint reminder of a world that continued to turn, oblivious to the secrets being unearthed in this room.

Fiona remained quiet for a moment, her brow furrowed. "And Charles?"

Dolores let out a bitter laugh, though it lacked any humor. "Charles ..." She looked up finally, meeting Fiona's eyes. "He didn't even know about Sarah's death at first. When he did come back, months later, it was to demand answers. He wanted to know why Sarah had vanished, why I wouldn't agree to the divorce. I told him she'd left Savannah—run off, abandoned her plans with him. He didn't believe me."

"What happened after that?" Fiona asked, her voice quiet.

Dolores exhaled shakily, her grip on the chair tightening. "We fought. It was the worst argument we ever had. He accused me of ruining his life, of destroying his chance to start over with her and their child. He was furious—he screamed, threw things." Her gaze dropped, her voice lowering to a whisper. "And then he collapsed. His heart gave out right there in the parlor. I ... I watched him die."

The room seemed to grow colder with her words. A shiver ran down Dolores' spine as she recalled that night—how still Charles had become, how the fury in his eyes had faded to emptiness. The silence that followed had been deafening, broken only by the ticking of the grandfather clock in the hallway, marking seconds that stretched into minutes, into hours.

Fiona's sharp intake of breath filled the silent room. "And you didn't tell anyone?"

"I couldn't," Dolores said, her voice rising. "Do you know what they would've done to me if they'd known the truth?" Her fingers clutched at the armrest, knuckles white with tension. Years of fear and self-preservation had hardened into instinct, each decision building upon the last until there was no going back.

"So you let the rumors grow," Fiona said. "You let people think ..."

"I let them think whatever they wanted. It was easier that way. Safer." Her tone was clipped, defensive—the voice of a woman who had spent decades justifying her actions to herself.

For a moment, the room fell silent again. Fiona stared at Dolores, her expression a mix of pity and apprehension. Dolores felt a pang of shame but refused to let it show. The soft hum of the air conditioning filled the void between them, a mundane counterpoint to the weight of confession.

"But now, it's clear that Samuel is the one pulling the strings," Dolores continued, her voice steadier. "He knows the rumors about his mother's disappearance. He's been using you to expose me as a murderer —so he can claim the Wesley inheritance for himself."

Fiona's eyes narrowed. "How does he know about the rumors? About Sarah?"

"I don't know. But he's smart. He's been digging for years, piecing things together. And with Anthony gone ..." Her voice faltered at the mention of her son, the wound still raw. "He thinks he can take everything else from me."

She paused, remembering Anthony's funeral—the sea of black-clad mourners, the hushed whispers, the weight of the casket being lowered into the ground. Her world had ended that day, yet somehow she had continued to exist, to move through the motions of living.

"That's why he's been pushing me to write the article." Fiona frowned, leaning back. "To destroy your reputation and solidify his claim."

Dolores nodded grimly. "He's playing the long game. And if he succeeds, he'll have everything I fought to protect—my name, my legacy, and the estate."

The lamp flickered briefly, casting dancing shadows across the walls. Outside, clouds had begun to gather, promising rain. The faint rumble of thunder in the distance seemed to underscore the gravity of their conversation.

Fiona was quiet for a moment, her expression contemplative. Her fingers tapped lightly against her knee, a subtle gesture of thought. Finally, she sat up straight, her notebook sliding off her lap and onto the floor with a soft thud. "Then we stop him."

Dolores blinked. "We?"

"Yes," Fiona said firmly. "We. If he's using me to manipulate the narrative, I can turn the tables. We can confront him, force him to slip up—publicly."

Dolores frowned, her fingers tightening around the armrest of her chair. "And why would you want to help me?" she asked, her tone sharp but laced with genuine curiosity. "You've spent weeks trying to expose me, digging into my past, ready to write a story that could ruin me. What's changed?"

Fiona met her gaze, unflinching. "When I decided to write this article, I thought you were the villain of this story. The rumors, the whispers—they painted you as this cold, calculating woman who'd stop at nothing to get what she wanted. And for a while, I believed that. In fact, it's what motivated me to want to write a piece on you in the first place."

Dolores flinched slightly but said nothing. She'd heard the whispers, seen the sideways glances at social events. For years, she'd cultivated an image of untouchable elegance—a shield that kept people at a distance, that prevented them from looking too closely.

"But now I see the truth. How much you've lost. Anthony, your reputation, your peace of mind—this isn't the life of a villain. This is the life of a woman who's been backed into a corner, trying to protect what little she has left."

Dolores' breath hitched, and she quickly masked it with a small cough. Her hand rose to smooth an invisible wrinkle from her skirt, a habitual gesture that betrayed her discomfort. "And that's enough to make you want to help me?"

"It's more than that," Fiona said. She shifted on the bed, determination evident in the set of her shoulders. She wasn't just chasing another story—this was something bigger.

"I've spent my entire career writing about the surface-level things—

society events, high-profile scandals, pieces that entertain but don't really matter. Followed Savannah's whispers, reported on the people who thrive on them, but I've never had the chance to do something real. Something that actually means something."

Exhaling, her fingers curled against the fabric of her dress. The clock on the nightstand ticked steadily, measuring the weight of her decision. "But this ... this is different. If Samuel gets away with this, if he ruins you and takes everything you've fought for, then I'm just as guilty as he is for letting it happen."

Her voice hardened, conviction no longer tempered. The dim light caught the determination in her eyes, turning them to amber. "I don't want to be part of his scheme, Dolores. I want to stop him."

Dolores studied her, searching her face for any sign of dishonesty. But all she saw was determination. For decades, she had trusted no one —had carried her burdens alone, had fought her battles in isolation. The possibility of an ally was almost foreign to her.

Slowly, she nodded, though her voice remained cautious. "And what about your article? You're still going to write it, aren't you?"

"Maybe," Fiona said. "But if I do, it'll be the truth—not the story Samuel's trying to manipulate me into telling. And if you're honest with me, I'll make sure your side of the story is heard."

Dolores exhaled slowly, leaning back in her chair. She didn't entirely trust Fiona—how could she? But there was something about her that felt... real. Perhaps for the first time in years, Dolores felt like she wasn't entirely alone.

Finally, Dolores said, "Fine."

chapter
forty

FIONA SAT cross-legged on the floor of her hotel room, papers, notebooks, and her laptop spread out around her in a chaotic sprawl. The late afternoon sun slanted through the partially drawn curtains, casting long shadows across her makeshift workspace. Staring at her phone, debating whether to make the call, her fingers hovered over Claire's name, hesitating.

What if she thinks I'm crazy? What if she tells me to drop it?

She shook her head, dismissing the doubts. She couldn't do this alone—not anymore. Taking a deep breath, she tapped her sister's name and brought the phone to her ear.

The line rang twice before Claire's voice came through, crisp and slightly weary. "Fi? What's going on?"

Fiona exhaled sharply, her words tumbling out in a rush. "I need your help. It's about Dolores and Samuel Mercer. Things have escalated —like, a lot."

"Slow down," Claire said, her tone firm but patient. "You're talking too fast. Start from the beginning."

Fiona stood and began pacing the small room, the carpet soft beneath her bare feet. Her reflection in the mirror caught her eye—hair disheveled, eyes tired but bright with determination. She looked like someone on the edge of something momentous.

"Okay, so you know I've been looking into Dolores Bates, right?

Trying to figure out what's really going on with her and all these rumors about Sarah Mercer's disappearance?"

"Yes? And?"

"It turns out Samuel Mercer, Sarah's son, is the imposter Henry Caldwell. He's been orchestrating this entire thing to take down Dolores and claim the Wesley inheritance for himself. He's been using me to write the story that'll expose her as a murderer."

"Wait," Claire interrupted, her voice sharpening with concern. "Samuel Mercer is Sarah Mercer's son? And he's been pretending to be Dolores' lawyer? Fiona, that's not just manipulative—it's criminal."

"It gets worse. Dolores told me that Samuel was the one who broke into the art museum."

"She what?" Claire's voice sharpened.

"Yeah," Fiona said, running a hand through her hair. Pausing at the window, she looked out at the pristine grounds of the hotel. The regatta festivities continued below, oblivious to the storm brewing behind the scenes. "Well, she didn't say it so much as mumbled it, but I put two and two together."

Claire let out a low whistle. "And you're sure about all this? You trust Dolores now?"

Fiona hesitated, leaning against the edge of the bed. The mattress sank slightly beneath her weight as she considered her answer. Trust was a complicated thing—especially when it came to someone like Dolores Bates, a woman who had spent decades crafting her public image.

"I don't know if trust is the right word. But everything she's told me lines up. And honestly, Claire, I don't think she's lying. Not about this."

There was a pause on the other end of the line. Fiona could almost picture her sister—brow furrowed, pacing in her own methodical way as she processed the information.

Then Claire said, "Alright. What do you need from me?"

."Backup. I need you to use your connections in law enforcement to investigate Samuel. He's been impersonating Henry Caldwell, black-mailing Dolores, and now he's tied to the museum break-in. There has to be enough there to at least bring him in for questioning."

"That is a bit of a longshot," Claire said, her tone cautious. "I can't just make the police arrest someone on a whim."

"Dammit, it's not a whim!" Fiona said quickly, her voice rising with urgency. She moved to her desk, rifling through the papers there—notes, interviews, timelines she'd meticulously assembled over the past weeks. "This guy is dangerous. He's manipulative, resourceful, and he's been playing all of us. If we don't stop him, he's going to ruin Dolores—and me."

Claire sighed, and Fiona could almost picture her rubbing her temples. "Let me think. Lawson still owes me a favor or two. I can talk to her and see what she can do."

"Thank you." The relief in Fiona's voice was palpable. She sank into the desk chair, her shoulders relaxing slightly.

"But if Lawson does get involved, this is going to get messy. You need to be sure about this."

Fiona glanced at her laptop, where the document she'd been working on glowed softly on the screen. Months of investigation, countless interviews, and now a truth that was stranger than any fiction. "I wouldn't be asking if I wasn't."

"Fine. I'll call Lawson. But what's your plan in the meantime?"

"I'm going to confront him."

Claire's voice shot up. "That's a terrible idea."

"It'll be at the regatta dinner," Fiona said quickly, her words rushing out to counter Claire's objection. The regatta dinner—a sea of Savannah's elite dressed in their finest, sipping champagne and exchanging pleasantries. The perfect stage for a confrontation. "I'm not stupid, Claire. It's a public event. There will be witnesses everywhere."

"Not stupid?" Claire let out a sharp, humorless laugh. "Do you hear yourself? You're planning to confront a man who you said yourself is dangerous, and your grand plan is to corner him at a dinner?"

Fiona sighed, pressing her fingers to her temples. The beginnings of a headache pulsed behind her eyes. "It's public enough that he can't try anything reckless, and with so many people around, I can control the narrative. He won't want to make a scene."

Claire was silent for a moment, and Fiona could practically feel her sister's frustration simmering through the phone. When she spoke again, her voice was measured but tense.

"You're betting everything on the assumption that he'll play nice because of the setting. What if he doesn't? What if he calls your bluff or turns the tables on you?"

"I'll handle it," Fiona said firmly, though she could feel her voice wobble slightly. She stood and moved to the window again, watching the boat crews bringing their vessels back to dock. The sun was beginning to set, casting a golden glow over the water. "I've been careful. I know what I'm doing."

"Do you?" Claire snapped. "Because this sounds less like a plan and more like you throwing yourself into the lion's den without backup. You don't know what he's capable of."

Fiona's grip on the phone tightened, her frustration bubbling over. "That's why I'm asking for your help. I need you there. You're the only one who can keep this from spiraling out of control."

Claire groaned again, and this time, it sounded like she was pacing. "So let me get this straight. You want me to show up at the regatta dinner, watch you bait this guy, and ... what? Sit there and hope nothing goes wrong?"

"No," Fiona said, her voice softening. She turned away from the window, her reflection pale against the darkening glass. "I need you to help me make sure nothing goes wrong. I need someone I can trust to have my back."

"And what exactly do you expect me to do if it does go wrong? Am I supposed to tackle him? Call the cops? Drag you out of there before you make things worse?"

Fiona hesitated, feeling the weight of her request. It was a lot to ask, even of Claire. "You'll know what to do. You always do. I just ... I can't do this alone, Claire. Please."

There was a heavy silence on the line, the kind that felt like it stretched for hours. The air conditioning hummed softly in the background, filling the void. Finally, Claire spoke, her voice quieter but still firm. "You really think this is the best way to handle this?"

"Yes," Fiona said, the word leaving her lips before she could second-guess it. She glanced at the scattered notes on the floor, each piece a fragment of the truth she'd been chasing. "I need to confront him, Claire. I need to get the truth."

Claire sighed heavily. "You are reckless, stubborn, and sometimes you drive me absolutely insane."

"But?" Fiona prompted, holding her breath.

"But," Claire said reluctantly, "if this is what you've decided to do, then I'll be there. Someone has to make sure you don't get yourself killed."

Fiona exhaled, the tension in her shoulders easing just slightly. "Thank you, Claire. I mean it."

"Don't make me regret it," Claire said, her tone sharper than her words. "And Fi?"

"Yeah?"

"This isn't just a game. If you start something you can't finish, call me. Don't try to be a hero."

"I won't," Fiona promised, but the flutter of apprehension told her it was a promise she might not be able to keep.

After ending the call, Fiona sat cross-legged on the floor again, her laptop humming softly in front of her. The open document glowed on the screen, the blinking cursor taunting her with its emptiness. She exhaled deeply, running a hand through her hair before placing her fingers on the keyboard.

For a moment, she hesitated, her thoughts swirling. The story she was about to write would change everything—not just for Dolores, but for herself. It would put her at the center of a storm, one she wasn't entirely sure she was prepared for. But she couldn't back down now.

Her fingers began to move, slowly at first, then faster as the words poured out. The tap-tap-tap of the keys filled the quiet room, a rhythm that matched her racing thoughts. Pausing occasionally, rereading what she'd written, her mind raced as she considered every angle.

Outside, the sky darkened to deep blue, then black. The hotel lights came on, casting a warm glow over the grounds. Inside, Fiona continued to write, fueled by determination and a need for justice.

By the time she finished, her shoulders ached from hunching over the keyboard, and her eyes burned from staring at the screen. Leaning back, she let out a shaky breath as she skimmed the article one last time.

It was done.

She opened her email and typed a message to Jacobs, her fingers trembling slightly as she attached the document. The subject line read: Final Draft—Hold for Approval.

In the body of the email, she wrote:

Jacobs, Here's the completed article. Do not publish this until I give you explicit permission. I'll let you know when it's time. Thanks for trusting me with this.

Her finger hovered over the send button, her pulse quickening. This was it—the moment she set the wheels in motion. In the quiet of her hotel room, with only the soft glow of the laptop illuminating her face, Fiona Stevens made her decision. Taking a deep breath, she clicked it.

chapter
forty-one

FIONA SAT on the edge of the hotel room bed, her heart racing as she listened to Dolores make the call. The older woman's voice was steady, sharp, and commanding, every word calculated. Fiona couldn't help but admire how composed Dolores sounded, despite the tension simmering just beneath the surface.

"I've given it some thought," Dolores said into the phone, her tone clipped. "And you're right, Samuel. Fighting this won't do anyone any good. I've decided it's time to end it."

Fiona glanced at Dolores, trying to gauge her mood, but the woman's expression was unreadable. Dolores gestured for Fiona to remain quiet, pacing slowly near the window as she continued.

"No," Dolores said firmly. "Fiona has already left. She's gone back to Savannah. I'll handle this myself."

Fiona felt a flicker of satisfaction. The lie was well-delivered, and Samuel would have no reason to suspect otherwise—at least not yet.

Dolores paused, listening to whatever Samuel was saying on the other end of the line. "Good," she said finally. "Then I'll see you tonight at the regatta dinner. We can discuss the terms in person."

The call ended with a sharp click, and Dolores exhaled deeply, turning back to Fiona.

"That should do it," Dolores said, her voice low. She sank into the chair by the desk, her composed exterior cracking slightly as she rubbed her temples.

Fiona leaned forward, her elbows resting on her knees. "Do you think he'll come?"

"Samuel can't resist the thought of winning. He'll show up expecting to gloat." She looked at Fiona, her expression hardening. "And when he does, we'll be ready."

The afternoon light filtered through the partially drawn curtains, casting the room in a subdued glow. Outside, the final preparations for the regatta dinner were underway, staff moving with practiced efficiency as they arranged tables and decorations on the hotel's terrace overlooking the water.

Fiona hesitated, studying Dolores for a moment. Beneath the steely exterior, she could see the cracks—the weariness etched into the woman's face, the weight of years of secrets and guilt pressing on her shoulders. She shifted in her chair, her voice softer now. "When did he show up? Samuel, I mean. When did he first come into your life?"

Dolores' lips pressed into a thin line, her gaze drifting toward the window. "Not long after Anthony's trial ended," she said quietly. "It was subtle at first—letters, phone calls, strange accusations. I thought it was just a disgruntled stranger, someone with nothing better to do than throw stones at the Bates name. But then ..." She paused, exhaling sharply. "He showed up in person. He made it clear who he was and what he wanted."

Fiona frowned, leaning forward slightly. "And you've been dealing with him ever since?"

Dolores nodded. "For years now, he's been like a shadow, hovering just out of reach but always there. At first, I thought I could handle it. Pay him off, make him go away quietly. But Samuel is not the type to be satisfied with silence. He thrives on chaos. And then, with Anthony's death, everything escalated."

She paused, her fingers tightening on the armrest. "I think he saw an opportunity. When the Chronicle announced it was doing a feature on my house for the Tour, he must have seen the article—or heard about it through the social grapevine. He knew I would refer you to my lawyer, just as I always do. And he found another angle. Inserted himself.

Pretended to be someone he wasn't so he could get close to you. Use you."

Fiona sat back slowly, the weight of that realization settling heavily within her. The careful manipulation, the calculated planning—it was more than just opportunism. It was methodical, patient, and frighteningly personal.

Dolores' voice softened, barely above a whisper. "And the truth is, I've felt the weight of it all—the guilt. I took his mother from him. I robbed him of that, and no one should have to endure losing a parent, especially like that."

Fiona felt a wave of empathy at the rawness in Dolores' voice. She reached out instinctively, placing a hand on Dolores' arm. "You were defending your son's life—any mother would have done the same."

Dolores looked at her, her sharp eyes softening just slightly. "That's easy to say now, but it doesn't change the fact that he grew up without her. And whatever Sarah was, she was still his mother. He's spent his whole life hating me for it."

"And maybe he has," Fiona admitted. "But his hatred doesn't justify what he's doing now. You can't carry that burden, Dolores. You've already carried too much."

The distant sound of boats returning to harbor drifted through the window, a reminder of the world continuing outside their fragile alliance. The evening would bring the confrontation they'd been planning, but for now, in this quiet moment, there was only truth between them.

Dolores' lips trembled, and for a moment, she looked away, composing herself. "Anthony wasn't perfect, you know," she said after a long pause, her voice quieter now. "He made mistakes. He got involved with people he shouldn't have—people who manipulated him, twisted him. That Elizabeth—or Meredith—whatever name she was going by then... she saw his weaknesses and exploited them."

Fiona nodded slowly, remembering the details her sister had uncovered about Meredith, the woman who had masterminded so much destruction in Anthony's life. "She preyed on him. That wasn't his fault."

Dolores' voice cracked as she continued, her words weighted with years of guilt. "He was always different after everything that happened with Charles. He was just a toddler, but the strain of it all left a mark. He withdrew, became more reserved. I thought I could fix it—I sent him away for therapy, hoping it would help. But it didn't. If anything, it made him feel more isolated."

Fiona listened intently, absorbing every word. The carefully crafted image of Dolores Bates was crumbling before her eyes, revealing not the cold socialite of Savannah legend, but a mother who had fought desperately to protect her child—and, in her own mind, failed.

"And then he came out." Dolores continued, her hands trembling. "Told me he was gay. I didn't react badly—not like you'd hear in some stories—but I was so afraid for him. In a town like Savannah, where every move is scrutinized, where the gossip spreads faster than wildfire... it wasn't easy for him. People whispered, pointed. Even those I thought were friends suddenly became distant."

Dolores let out a bitter laugh, her tone laced with self-reproach. "And I blamed myself for that, too. If I had protected him better—if I'd shielded him from all the ugliness in this world—maybe he wouldn't have felt like an outsider his whole life."

"Dolores," Fiona said, "you can't control how other people act. You did the best you could."

"Did I?" Dolores shook her head, her lips pressing into a thin line. "Because it feels like I failed him at every turn. When the gossip got too loud, I focused more on silencing it than helping him feel like he belonged." She paused, exhaling shakily. "That's why I trusted your sister with his appeal. Claire never seemed to be swayed by the noise. She had this ... steadiness about her, like the gossip didn't even touch her."

Fiona's eyebrows rose slightly. "Claire's definitely tough when it comes to Savannah's rumor mill. She's had her fair share of battles with it."

"That's why I thought she was the right person for Anthony," Dolores said. "And she was. She gave him a second chance."

The setting sun cast a warm glow across Dolores' face, softening the harsh lines of worry that had been etched there by decades of struggle. For a moment, Fiona could see glimpses of the younger woman she must have been—determined, fiercely protective, and ultimately vulnerable in ways few people had ever been allowed to witness.

Dolores' voice faltered, her hands tightening on the armrests of the chair. "But even then, I couldn't save him from himself. The moment he was free, he ran right back to Meredith. The woman who had framed him in the first place. I begged him not to—pleaded with him—but he wouldn't listen. He thought she loved him. He thought he could fix things with her."

A distant seagull cried out, its call mournful against the backdrop of their conversation. Dolores seemed to fold into herself, the memory visibly weighing on her.

"And it killed him. That decision, that blind faith in her ... it killed him."

Fiona's throat tightened, her own emotions threatening to spill over. She reached out again, this time holding Dolores' trembling hands in hers. "No one deserves what happened to Anthony," she said firmly. "But you didn't fail him, Dolores. You fought for him in ways most people wouldn't. You did everything you could to give him a chance— even if he couldn't see it."

Dolores let out a shaky breath, her tears spilling over as she nodded. "I just don't want to lose what little I have left."

"You won't," Fiona said, her voice steady with conviction. She squeezed Dolores' hands gently, the gesture bridging years of misunderstanding and judgment. "We're not going to let him win."

chapter
forty-two

THE REGATTA DINNER was a spectacle of wealth and tradition. It was held in an expansive open-air pavilion overlooking the shimmering water, the golden hues of the setting sun casting a warm glow over the crowd. Large white drapes hung from the ceiling beams, swaying gently in the breeze, while twinkling string lights wrapped around wooden columns illuminated the space in a soft, romantic glow. Tables were arranged in perfect rows, adorned with elegant floral centerpieces of hydrangeas and roses, their colors complementing the rich navy and white table linens.

The clink of champagne glasses and the hum of polite laughter filled the air, blending with the occasional sound of waves lapping against the docks in the distance. Waitstaff moved seamlessly between the guests, balancing trays of hors d'oeuvres and cocktails with practiced grace.

Fiona sat at a table near the edge of the pavilion with Dolores, her hand wrapped tightly around the stem of a champagne flute. The bubbling liquid inside remained untouched. She glanced at Dolores, who looked as poised as ever in an ivory silk blouse and tailored navy slacks, her composure masking the storm Fiona knew was brewing beneath the surface.

As Fiona scanned the room, she caught the subtle glances from nearby tables—the whispered comments passed behind hands, the quick looks darting toward Dolores before shifting away. It was the familiar hum of Savannah's rumor mill, a machine that never stopped churning. Sitting next to Dolores, Fiona felt the weight of it for the first time. To be on the other side of the whispers, to know they were dissecting every movement, every gesture—it was suffocating. And yet, Dolores sat unflinching, her spine straight, her expression calm.

Fiona realized how much poise it took to sit under that kind of scrutiny and not engage, not lash out, not crack under the pressure. She'd seen women crumble after a single scandal in Savannah, their reputations shredded in days. But Dolores had endured this for decades, holding her head high while the town picked her apart. There was strength in that, Fiona realized—a quiet, formidable strength that she couldn't help but admire.

"He'll show," Dolores said quietly, her voice steady. She didn't turn her head but kept her gaze fixed on the entrance.

Fiona exhaled, feeling a wave of tension and anticipation. "And if he doesn't?"

"He will."

Before Fiona could respond, a ripple went through the crowd as someone entered the pavilion. Fiona turned her head sharply. And there he was—Samuel Mercer. He was dressed sharply in a tailored navy suit, his expression confident but guarded.

Stepping into the room, his eyes scanned the crowd. When they landed on Dolores and Fiona, his entire body stiffened. For a split second, his mask slipped, and Fiona caught the flicker of recognition—and alarm—that flashed across his face.

"He sees us," Fiona murmured.

"Yes, I know," Dolores said, her tone low.

Samuel started to turn, his movements deliberate but betraying his intent to slip away unnoticed.

"Samuel!" Dolores' voice rang out, smooth and commanding, cutting through the buzz of conversation like a knife.

He froze, his back still turned. His shoulders were taut with tension as he paused, clearly debating whether to keep walking or turn around.

After a moment, he slowly pivoted, his face composed once more. "Mrs. Bates," he said warmly, but Fiona didn't miss the edge to his smile. "Good evening."

Dolores rose gracefully, her expression unreadable. "So glad you could make it," she said. "Come, there's someone I'd like you to meet."

Fiona stood as Samuel's eyes flicked to her, his discomfort visible despite his efforts to mask it.

"Samuel, this is Fiona Stevens," Dolores said, her voice smooth as silk. "She's writing a feature on the regatta—and the Wesley legacy."

Fiona extended her hand, forcing a polite smile. "It's a pleasure to meet you."

Samuel hesitated for the briefest moment before taking her hand. "Likewise."

"I understand you're close with Mrs. Bates." Fiona tilted her head slightly, studying him. "She's spoken highly of you."

"Yes, we've known each other for some time. I try to assist her where I can."

Dolores gave a faint smile, her sharp gaze flicking between the two of them. Before she could speak further, a man approached, touching her lightly on the arm. "Dolores, would you mind joining us for a moment? We'd like your input on something."

"Of course," Dolores said smoothly. She turned to Samuel, her smile never wavering. "You'll excuse me for a moment?"

"Of course," Samuel said, his voice easy, but his eyes betrayed his unease.

Dolores walked away, her movements calm and measured. Fiona watched her go, the tension between herself and Samuel thickening as they were left alone.

"So," Fiona said lightly, turning back to him with a polite smile that didn't reach her eyes. "Your name is Samuel, and you and Mrs. Bates go way back?"

He chuckled softly, but the sound rang hollow. "She must be confused. I was just playing along to avoid embarrassing her. Same as you, clearly. You know how it is with older people—they can get mixed up about things."

"Really? Because Mrs. Bates seemed pretty confident when she introduced you. I mean, you must admit, it's a big leap from 'Henry Caldwell' to 'Samuel Mercer.' That's not exactly the kind of mix-up most people make."

Samuel hesitated for a fraction of a second, his polite smile freezing before he forced a laugh. "Like I said, Dolores has been under a lot of stress lately. The rumors, the drama—it's all taken a toll on her. You've seen it, I'm sure."

"Of course," Fiona said, her voice smooth but pointed. "But it's still strange, isn't it? I mean, for her to mistake her own lawyer for someone else entirely. That's not just a slip of the tongue, is it?"

Samuel's shoulders stiffened. He quickly took another sip of his drink. "You'd be surprised. Dolores has a lot on her plate these days. It's understandable that she might—"

"Confuse your entire identity? You know, when someone changes names so abruptly, it usually means they have something to hide."

Samuel's eyes darkened, his polite façade cracking for just a moment. "I'm not sure what you're implying, Ms. Stevens."

"I'm just trying to get the facts straight for my article. After all, accuracy is everything."

Samuel stared at her for a moment, his jaw tightening as he weighed his response.

"Ladies and gentlemen," a voice boomed over the microphone, interrupting their conversation. The crowd quieted as the event's host stepped up to the podium at the front of the pavilion. "Dinner is about to be served. Please take your seats and enjoy the evening!"

Samuel turned back to Fiona, his easy smile returning. "Excuse me for just a moment," he said smoothly. "I need to take care of something before dinner."

Without waiting for her response, he turned and walked quickly toward the exit of the pavilion, his movements tense.

Fiona's heart raced as she watched him disappear through the open doors. Glancing around the room she spotted Dolores, who had just finished speaking with the man who had pulled her aside. Fiona caught her eye and motioned subtly toward the door.

Dolores nodded, her expression hardening, her shoulders squared with purpose.

The two women moved quickly, weaving through the maze of tables and into the cool night air. The hum of the regatta dinner faded behind them, replaced by the distant sound of water lapping against the docks and the faint creak of boats rocking in their moorings. Fiona shivered as the salty breeze hit her skin and the tension rose within her.

Up ahead, Samuel's brisk pace carried him toward the edge of the event grounds, his figure disappearing briefly into the shadows cast by the dimly lit walkway. Fiona's pulse quickened as she picked up her pace, trying to keep him in sight.

"Where's he going?" Fiona whispered, her voice low but urgent.

"We're about to find out," Dolores replied, her tone steady.

Fiona's phone buzzed in her clutch, and she quickly pulled it out, glancing at the screen.

"Claire," she said quietly, answering the call.

"We're ready," Claire said, her voice tinged with urgency. "Lawson's got her team in place, but you need to move fast. Whatever you're planning, do it now. We can't afford to lose him."

Fiona's heart raced as she glanced at Dolores, who was still moving purposefully ahead, her focus locked on Samuel's retreating figure. "We're on it. I'll call you back when it's done."

"Don't hang up. Keep the line open, just in case."

Fiona hesitated, then nodded. "Fine," she said before lowering the phone and turning to Dolores.

"Here," Fiona said, pulling the small listening device from her clutch and handing it to Dolores. The tiny device felt almost weightless. Its significance was anything but. "Get him talking. Get him to implicate himself—about the museum, the blackmail, everything."

Dolores stopped briefly under a lamppost, the warm light catching the sharp angles of her face. She took the device, her fingers steady as she clipped it to the inside of her blouse. "I know what to do," she said, her voice low but firm.

Fiona swallowed hard, her pulse pounding. "Are you sure you can do this?"

Dolores looked at her, and for the first time, Fiona saw something unshakable in her eyes. A quiet strength, born of years of enduring and surviving. "Yes," Dolores said simply. "This ends tonight."

Fiona nodded. "I'll be close by," she said, before stepping back as Dolores squared her shoulders and strode forward with the confidence of a woman who had nothing left to lose.

chapter
forty-three

THE DOCKS WERE EERILY QUIET, save for the faint creak of wood and the occasional lap of water against the pilings. Dolores approached Samuel slowly, her heels clicking softly against the planks. She kept her head high and her posture steady as her heart pounded in her chest.

Samuel stood at the edge of the dock, his arms crossed tightly, his silhouette sharp against the faint glow of the water. He turned as she drew closer, his expression cold, but his eyes betrayed his suspicion.

"You lied to me," he said, his voice low and sharp.

Dolores stopped a few feet away, forcing her features into an expression of calm. "I needed to get you here."

"So what is this? A trap?" He took a step closer, his voice rising and lips curling into a sneer. "Or do you actually have the documents? Because that's the only reason I'm here, Dolores."

Dolores exhaled slowly, her hands trembling slightly, but she kept them hidden at her sides. "I have them," she said softly. "I'm ready to sign over everything to you—the Wesley estate, the inheritance, all of it. I just want this to end."

Samuel's expression darkened, his eyes narrowing. "Then where are they?"

"They're back at my hotel room. I just wanted to talk first."

"Bullshit," Samuel seethed. "I have nothing to say to you. You either hand them over now, or I take what I know and destroy you."

Dolores swallowed the lump in her throat before she took a small step forward, her gaze locked on his. "You'll get everything you want, Samuel. I just need you to listen to me first."

"Why would I do that? You've been lying and manipulating for decades, Dolores. You think I'll trust you now?"

Before she could respond, Samuel reached into his jacket and pulled out a gun. The metallic glint of the barrel caught the faint light from the nearby pier lamp, sending a shiver down Dolores' spine.

"You think you can stall me?" he growled, pointing the weapon at her. "Enough games. Hand over the documents now."

Dolores froze, her breath catching in her throat as she stared at the gun. Her pulse thundered in her ears, but she forced herself to stay calm. "Samuel, please," she said softly, her voice trembling but measured. "I'm not your enemy."

"Don't," Samuel hissed, stepping closer, his voice sharp and venomous. "Don't try to spin this. You've done nothing but take from me. This ends tonight."

Dolores swallowed hard, her throat tightening as fear and guilt tangled within her. She fought to steady her shaking hands.

"And what about you?" she asked. "You've been blackmailing me for the better part of a year now. You don't think that you've taken things from me, too?"

Samuel's grip on the gun didn't waver, his chest rising and falling with quick, shallow breaths. His entire body was tense, his fingers twitching as if he were barely holding himself back.

"All I did is try to take what's rightfully mine."

Dolores held his gaze, keeping her posture composed despite the tension coursing through her. "Is that why you broke into the museum? Why you tore apart that painting looking for something? Some proof that you could use against me?"

Samuel's face twisted with fury. "It was mine. The truth was buried, just like my mother. I was done waiting for someone else to dig it up, so I did it myself."

Dolores nodded slowly, as if she were genuinely considering his words. "And what exactly were you hoping to find?"

"The proof you've been hiding for decades. The divorce agreement that would have handed over the Wesley fortune to my mother and me. The proof that my father wanted to leave you." His jaw clenched, his voice dropping into something colder, sharper. "But that was never going to happen, was it? You made sure of that."

Dolores inhaled slowly, the weight of the moment pressing down on her like a stone. "And now you think blackmailing me, terrorizing me, will give you the justice you think you deserve?"

"It's not blackmail. It's balance. You stole my mother's life, and I'm taking yours in return. Piece by piece."

Dolores' hands curled at her sides, her nails biting into her palms. "That's not justice, Samuel. That's revenge. And it won't bring her back."

Samuel's expression flickered, his mouth twisting as if he wanted to argue, but something in his eyes darkened instead. He stepped closer, raising the gun slightly.

"I don't care what you call it," he said through gritted teeth.

Dolores took a shaky breath as the cold metal pressed against her chest. The barrel of the gun dug into the fabric of her blouse, pressing against her ribs, and she had to will herself not to recoil.

"Say it," Samuel whispered.

Dolores' throat felt like it was closing. "Say what?"

Samuel shoved the gun against her a little harder, his face mere inches from hers. "Say you killed my mother."

A sharp breath hitched in Dolores' throat. She could feel his rage, his grief, radiating off of him like a fever.

The weight of it all pressed down on her—the years of secrets, of hiding, of carrying the truth like a stone strapped to her chest. She had never spoken the words aloud, never dared to voice them. But this was it. The moment when everything came crashing down.

She inhaled, her voice barely above a whisper. "I killed her."

A heavy silence followed, save for the distant lapping of water against the dock.

Dolores knew the words were traveling beyond this moment, beyond this night. Knew that somewhere in the darkness, law enforcement was listening, recording, documenting the confession that would likely lead to her arrest. Claire, Fiona, Lawson—they had all heard it. The weight of the law, the inevitable consequence of speaking the truth after so many years of silence, loomed in the distance like a tidal wave rushing toward her.

And yet, she felt lighter.

For decades, she had buried this truth beneath carefully constructed walls, disguising it with composure, with wealth, with the unyielding armor of a woman who had survived too much to let it break her. But now, the secret was out, and with it came an unbearable relief.

Samuel's eyes widened slightly, as if he hadn't actually expected her to say it.

Dolores' next breath was steadier, her voice raw yet strong. "I killed Sarah Mercer."

The words tumbled out, and with them, a strange, crushing relief.

"I did it to protect my son. She would have killed him. I did what I had to do."

"That's your justification?" Samuel's hand trembled against the gun, his breath ragged. "You expect me to believe that?"

Dolores didn't flinch. "I don't expect anything from you," she said softly. "But it's the truth."

Samuel was shaking now, his fury barely contained. He took a step back, his gaze flicking over her face. Dolores could see his mind working, trying to process her confession, to find a way to twist it into something that made sense to him.

And then his eyes darted down—just slightly.

His breath caught.

Dolores saw the exact moment the realization hit him. His gaze locked on the barely visible outline of the small device clipped under her blouse, a tiny black wire peeking from the edge of her lapel.

His face drained of color.

His grip on the gun tightened.

"You're wearing a wire," he hissed, his voice trembling with rage.

Dolores opened her mouth, but before she could speak, Samuel took a staggering step back, shaking his head.

"You set me up," he whispered, then louder, "You set me up!"

His breath came faster now, erratic. He swung the gun wildly toward her, but then, as if realizing there were more people listening—police, maybe even the entire world—he became desperate.

His eyes flicked past her and his expression changed. Before Dolores could react, Samuel lunged—not at her, but behind her. A sharp gasp cut through the night.

Dolores turned, her heart sinking.

Fiona.

Why was she here? She should have stayed out of sight! And now, Samuel had her. His arm locked around Fiona's throat, yanking her backward, dragging her against his chest as he shoved the barrel of the gun under her jaw. Fiona's eyes widened in terror, her fingers clawed at his arm, but his grip was iron-tight.

"No!" Dolores roared, her own panic rising.

Samuel jerked Fiona back toward the docks, his breaths ragged. "Nobody moves, or she dies!" he barked.

Dolores took a slow step forward, hands raised. "Samuel, let her go."

Samuel's grip tightened, and Fiona let out a strangled noise, her feet barely scraping the wooden planks beneath them.

"I should shoot you both," he spat. "I should end this right now."

The docks were suddenly flooded with movement—officers emerging from the shadows, weapons drawn, voices cutting through the humid night.

"Drop the weapon!"

"Let her go, Mercer!"

Samuel's body stiffened, his pulse visible in the tension of his jaw. His grip on Fiona shook, his desperation a wildfire burning out of control. Dolores took another measured step closer, her heart hammering. "Samuel, listen to me," she said carefully, her voice low, steady. "You have nowhere left to run."

His hand trembled on the gun. Fiona held her breath. Dolores saw the moment he realized she was right. And the moment he decided he wasn't going to prison without a fight.

In a sudden, brutal motion, Samuel swung Fiona around, using her as a shield, his finger tightening on the trigger. The officers shouted warnings, but Dolores didn't hear them. She only saw the terror in Fiona's eyes. And in that split second, she knew—this could end in blood.

chapter
forty-four

FIONA CLIMBED into the backseat of the unmarked car, her pulse a frantic drumbeat in her ears as she pulled the door shut behind her. The moment the latch clicked, it felt as though she had sealed herself inside a pressure cooker.

The interior was dimly lit, shadows stretching across the leather seats, the only real glow coming from the dashboard and the faint green light of the radio equipment humming softly in the background. The static-filled silence made everything feel tense, expectant—as if the night itself was holding its breath.

Claire sat in the passenger seat, her arms folded tightly, her expression carved from stone. Fiona recognized that look instantly—the sharp jawline, the set of her shoulders, the way her fingers curled into the fabric of her coat as if bracing for impact. She had seen it a hundred times before, in courthouses, in late-night phone calls, in quiet moments when Claire was preparing for the worst but hoping for the best.

Detective Lawson was in the driver's seat, her fingers resting lightly on the receiver. She looked calm—too calm, in that way law enforcement officers often did when they knew something was about to go down but weren't letting on just how bad it could get.

Fiona pressed herself back against the seat, feeling like she was strapped into a rollercoaster that was inching toward the inevitable drop.

What were they waiting for?

A confession. A slip-up. Something that would seal the deal and give Lawson the green light to move in.

But what if Dolores didn't get it?

What if she had misjudged the entire situation?

She clenched her hands into fists, staring at the glowing numbers on the dashboard clock. The minutes felt like hours.

Fiona had spent her career chasing gossip, writing puff pieces that entertained more than they informed, following Savannah's social elite from one scandal to the next. But this was different.

This wasn't a neatly packaged society column, a whispered rumor she could spin into a headline. This wasn't controlled. She wasn't safely tucked behind her laptop, sifting through sources and cross-referencing facts from the comfort of her office.

This was real.

This was dangerous.

And no matter how much she tried to convince herself otherwise, there was no undoing it now.

She thought of Dolores out there alone, face to face with Samuel, knowing that he was unpredictable, knowing that he had already proven himself capable of manipulation, deceit—and worse. If he wasn't afraid to break into a museum, what else might he not be afraid to do?

Fiona swallowed hard, pressing her palms against her thighs.

She should have been relieved that Samuel was finally getting caught, that this was the moment where his web of lies would unravel. But instead, all she could think about was Dolores standing on that dock, looking more determined than she ever had before.

She wasn't just walking into a confrontation.

She was walking toward the past she had buried for decades.

And Fiona couldn't shake the feeling that she was about to lose her, too.

The static crackled softly, and Fiona swallowed hard. "Can you hear them?"

Lawson nodded, adjusting the dial. "It's coming through."

Fiona leaned forward, gripping the edge of Claire's seat as Dolores' voice drifted through the speakers.

"Samuel."

Even through the distortion of the feed, Fiona could hear the tension in Dolores' voice, the carefully measured calm masking a deep, unshakable storm.

"You lied to me," Samuel snapped back, his voice colder than she'd ever heard it before.

Fiona barely breathed, watching as Claire stiffened beside her.

"I needed to get you here," Dolores said smoothly, though Fiona could hear the slight tremor underneath.

Samuel let out a short, bitter laugh. "So what is this? A trap?" A beat of silence. "Or do you actually have the documents? Because that's the only reason I'm here, Dolores."

Claire shot Fiona a warning glance, as if to say Don't react, just listen. But Fiona felt a wave of anxiety, her pulse racing.

"I have them," Dolores said, her voice calm. "I'm ready to sign over everything to you—the Wesley estate, the inheritance, all of it. I just want this to end."

There was a pause on the feed, and Fiona could picture Samuel's calculating stare, the way his mind was likely dissecting every syllable, looking for a lie.

"Then where are they?" Samuel demanded.

"They're back at the hotel room," Dolores said smoothly. "I just wanted to talk first."

"Bullshit," Samuel seethed. "I have nothing to say to you. You either have the documents on you right now that you can hand over, or I walk until you can produce them."

Fiona bit her lip, her nails digging into the leather of the seat. Claire's hands were locked together, her fingers clenched tight.

And then—

A metallic click.

Fiona sucked in a sharp breath.

Samuel had drawn a gun.

"You think you can stall me?" Samuel growled. "Enough games. Hand over the documents now."

Claire swore under her breath, her fingers curling into fists.

Fiona turned to Lawson, whispering urgently, "Move in. He's armed."

But Lawson didn't respond, her grip firm on the receiver, her posture unchanging.

Fiona felt herself tense with disbelief. Why aren't they moving?

"Samuel, please," Dolores' voice wavered but didn't break. She was keeping him talking. "I'm not your enemy."

"Don't," Samuel hissed. "Don't try to spin this. You've done nothing but take from me—from my family. This ends tonight."

"And what about you? You've been blackmailing me for the better part of a year now. You don't think that you've taken things from me, too?"

"All I did is try to take what's rightfully mine," he seethed."

"Is that why you broke into the museum? Why you tore apart that painting looking for something—some proof that you could use against me?"

Fiona could barely breathe. This was it. The moment she'd been waiting for. That they all had.

"It was mine. The truth was buried, just like my mother. I was done waiting for someone else to dig it up, so I did it myself."

Fiona glanced between Claire and Lawson, the urgency mounting in her voice. "He just admitted to breaking into the museum—what more do you need? Move in!"

"Not yet," Lawson said, her voice unnervingly calm.

Fiona felt her blood turn cold. "Not yet?" she echoed. "Are you kidding me? What are you waiting for?"

Claire closed her eyes, exhaling.

The conversation between Dolores and Samuel continued coming through the speakers.

Fiona's mind reeled. "You're waiting for her." She turned back to Lawson, accusation lacing every word. "You set her up too."

Neither Lawson nor Claire spoke.

Fiona turned her gaze back to the radio as Dolores' voice cracked over the speakers.

"That's not justice, Samuel. That's revenge. And it won't bring her back."

Samuel's voice, tight with fury. "I don't care what you call it. I only care that it's happening."

A heavy pause.

Then Samuel's sharp, biting words. "Say you killed my mother."

Dolores' voice was barely above a whisper, but it rang loud and clear over the feed.

"I killed her."

Fiona sucked in a breath, her fingers going numb.

"I killed Sarah Mercer."

Claire exhaled beside her, her shoulders sagging.

Fiona was paralyzed. She couldn't move, couldn't breathe.

"I did it to protect my son," Dolores continued, her voice raw but steady. "She would have killed him. I did what I had to do."

Samuel let out a breath—somewhere between a laugh and a growl. "That's your justification? You expect me to believe that?"

Samuel's breath came heavier now. Fiona could almost picture him, standing there, gun trembling, his mind working through everything Dolores had just admitted.

Then, suddenly—

"You're wearing a wire."

Claire's head snapped toward Lawson, who immediately grabbed her radio.

"You set me up!" Samuel roared, his voice sending static through the receiver.

"Authorization to make an arrest of both suspects. Units, move in now," Lawson commanded. Fiona barely heard the officers responding.

Fiona turned her gaze on Lawson. "You're arresting Dolores?"

Lawson was already halfway out of the car, reaching for her holster. "She just confessed to murder. We don't have a choice."

"You do have a choice! She was protecting her child!" Fiona's heart pounded, her breath coming short and fast. "She trusted me with this!"

"It doesn't matter," Lawson said, her voice clipped as she slammed the car door shut. "She killed Sarah Mercer and covered it up. That makes it murder."

Fiona turned to Claire, desperate. "Claire, do something!"

Claire's expression was tight, her voice softer but unwavering. "This is how it has to be. You knew this was a possibility."

"No," Fiona whispered, shaking her head. "No, this isn't right."

Before she could think twice, she threw open the car door and sprinted toward the docks.

chapter
forty-five

FIONA BARELY HAD time to react before Samuel yanked her forward, his grip like iron around her wrist.

"Move," he snarled, shoving her ahead of him toward the dock.

The cold metal of the gun pressed into her back as he forced her forward. She stumbled, the wooden planks beneath her feet slick with salt spray, her mind racing.

Think, Fiona. Think.

She could hear the chaos behind them—officers shouting, orders being barked through the static of police radios. But none of them were close enough. Samuel was dragging her toward a small sailboat. He was going to take her with him. A surge of pure panic shot through her veins.

No.

Fiona planted her feet, throwing her weight back, trying to make herself a dead weight in his grip. But Samuel was stronger, desperate and running on adrenaline. He jerked her forward so hard she lost her balance, slamming into the side of the boat as he shoved her inside. He let slip the sole mooring line and jumped in after her as the wind blew the boat astern into the stream.

"Stay down," he ordered, his voice low, shaking with fury.

The next second, the boat lurched forward, catching the wind as

Samuel frantically hauled in the mainsheet and jerked the rudder. Fiona scrambled upright, but the gun was back on her in an instant.

"Don't even think about it," he hissed.

She stared at him, chest heaving, her mind scrambling for a way out. Then, movement caught her eye—another boat, gliding across the dark water. She turned her head just slightly, just enough to see Dolores at the helm, the moonlight catching the loose strands of her dark hair as she steered the boat with terrifying precision.

She wasn't alone.

Two officers were with her. Armed. Closing in.

Fiona swallowed hard, her heart slamming against her ribs.

Samuel hadn't seen them yet. He was too focused on the water ahead, on his escape. She had seconds—maybe less—before he realized they were being pursued. Fiona's eyes flickered back to him, her mind whirring. She needed to buy time.

"You're not getting away," she said, her voice surprisingly steady. "They're going to find you."

Samuel snorted, keeping one hand on the tiller while keeping the gun trained on her with the other. "I wouldn't be so sure about that."

Fiona's fingers curled into fists. "So what's the plan, Samuel? Sail off into the sunset? You really think you're going to disappear?"

His expression twisted, something dark flickering across his features. "I would have. If you'd just stayed out of it."

Fiona braced herself, keeping her voice level. "I didn't stay out of it because I wanted to know the truth. You should understand that—you were looking for it too."

Samuel let out a bitter laugh, shaking his head. "No, I wasn't. I knew the truth. I just wanted the world to hear it. To hear what she did."

The boat rocked beneath them as they cut through a small wake. In the distance, Fiona could make out the faint glow of coastal lights, a reminder of the world beyond this desperate moment. The cool night air carried the scent of salt and seaweed, mingling with the metallic tang of fear that seemed to cling to her skin.

"She didn't kill Sarah in cold blood," Fiona said firmly. "She was protecting her son."

Samuel's grip tightened on the gun. "You weren't there."

"No," Fiona admitted. "But I know what it's like to want the truth to matter. And I know what it's like when it doesn't change anything."

Samuel's jaw tensed. For a split second, she thought she saw something break behind his eyes. A flicker of the grief that had driven him all these years—the loss of a mother he barely knew, the weight of a lifetime wondering what might have been.

The slap of waves against another hull cut through the night.

Samuel's head snapped up, his whole body going rigid as he finally saw Dolores closing in. Fiona moved instantly, lunging forward and grabbing his wrist just as the boat slammed into theirs. Samuel stumbled back, cursing as the impact rocked them both. The gun went off, the sound shattering, so close to her. But the shot went wide, hitting the mast instead.

Fiona didn't waste the chance. She threw her full weight into him, knocking him off balance.

Another shot fired—then chaos.

She felt hands—strong, steady hands—grabbing her, pulling her back as officers leapt onto the boat, tackling Samuel to the deck. The boat rocked violently beneath them, water splashing over the sides as the struggle continued.

The gun skittered across the floorboards, vanishing into the darkness. Fiona gasped, blinking up into Dolores' face, her expression unreadable as she helped steady her. The two women watched in silence as Samuel was pinned down, his wrists locked in handcuffs, his shouts futilely lost in the wind. Somewhere was the distant hum of helicopter blades.

It was over.

Fiona's body trembled, exhaustion finally catching up with her. The adrenaline that had propelled her through the night began to ebb, leaving behind a bone-deep weariness that made her limbs feel like lead.

Dolores turned, her gaze sweeping toward the dock where a crowd had gathered. Dozens of people stood there, watching, whispering, their silhouettes frozen in the artificial glow of the helicopter's beam. Regatta attendees in formal attire stood alongside hotel staff and curious onlookers, all of them witnesses to the dramatic conclusion of a story decades in the making.

Fiona followed her gaze, knowing exactly what she was thinking.

Savannah's rumor mill is about to have a field day.

Then, to her surprise, Dolores let out a soft chuckle. "I imagine the rumors will be especially creative this time."

Fiona let out a breathless laugh, shaking her head. "No doubt."

For a moment, they just looked at each other, a strange understanding passing between them. The gentle rocking of the boat beneath them seemed to mirror the shifting ground of their relationship—once adversaries, now bound by something neither of them could have anticipated.

And for the first time in a long time, Fiona saw Dolores Bates as she truly was—not the cold, untouchable socialite Savannah gossiped about, not the controlled, poised woman hiding behind decades of secrets.

She saw the girl from the wedding photograph.

The woman who had fought for her son, who had lost everything, and who had still managed to survive.

Dolores' hair, loose and wild from the wind, whipped around her face, her sharp features softer in the moonlight. She looked free.

But the moment didn't last.

The officers stepped forward, their voices cutting through the wind.

"Dolores Bates," one of them said, pulling out a pair of handcuffs. "You are under arrest for the murder of Sarah Mercer."

Dolores nodded, not resisting. She straightened her shoulders and lifted her chin, the dignity that had carried her through decades of whispers and judgments evident in every line of her body.

As they reached for her wrists she asked, "Do either of you know how to sail? You can place the cuffs on me after I get us back to the dock. I assure you I won't run away. She didn't struggle, didn't fight, didn't beg for mercy. Simply sailed them back into the dock.

She had made her choice.

And despite the ache in Fiona's chest, despite the gnawing guilt in knowing she had played a part in this—this was the ending Dolores had chosen.

THE ROAD STRETCHED AHEAD of them, dark and winding, the distant glow of Savannah's city lights barely visible beyond the horizon. The city felt impossibly far away—as if the past few days had dragged her into another world entirely, one where reality twisted and unraveled, leaving only uncertainty behind.

Inside the car, the air was thick, weighted with everything they had left behind at the docks—Dolores being led away in handcuffs, Samuel fighting against his own arrest, the distant sound of water slapping against the hulls of sailboats.

It was over.

Fiona sat slumped in the passenger seat, her fingers absently tracing the seam of her dress, her mind running over and over through the events of the night. The sting of saltwater was still in her hair, the scent of the ocean still clinging to her skin. Having spent so long chasing the truth, unearthing the pieces that everyone had buried, that now, with it all laid bare, she didn't know what to do next.

Claire kept both hands on the wheel, her knuckles tight, her posture rigid. She wasn't speaking, but Fiona thought maybe her mind was still at the docks. It had been ever since they'd pulled away—since they had watched the police take Dolores, since they had seen the weight of an entire lifetime settle on her shoulders as she let it happen.

Claire broke the silence first. She said, her voice softer than usual, "I know you didn't want this."

Fiona sighed, locking her phone and setting it on the center console. "I know it wasn't your call. It was Lawson's. This was an opportunity to close the book on the Sarah Mercer case. It's been an open mystery for decades."

Fiona's voice felt distant, like she was reciting facts instead of processing them.

Because what was there left to process?

Dolores had confessed. She had known what would happen the moment she'd spoken the words.

Claire nodded. "I think so too." She hesitated before adding, "But it wasn't just about closing a case. You heard Dolores. She didn't fight it. She didn't deny it."

But what if Fiona had never gone digging? What if she had never written the article, never followed the trail that had led her straight to the truth? Would Dolores still be free? Would she still be out on the water, sailing beneath the moon, instead of in the back of a police car?

Fiona rubbed her hand over her face.

She wasn't sure she had done the right thing.

She had spent so much of her career convincing herself that the truth always mattered, that it had to come out no matter the cost.

But what if the cost was too high?

What if, for once, the world didn't deserve to know?

Swallowing against the lump in her throat, she looked out the window, watching as the trees blurred past, as the road stretched on and on, leading them back to Savannah—to a city that was waiting for its next piece of gossip.

She knew what tomorrow's headlines would be.

She had written them herself.

And yet, as she sat there replaying everything in her mind, she wondered if for the first time in her life, she had been wrong.

Fiona exhaled, rubbing her hands together as if trying to warm them. "Maybe she wouldn't have agreed to this if she knew it would end with her in handcuffs."

Claire gave her a knowing look, flicking her eyes toward Fiona before returning her attention to the road. "I don't think so."

Fiona turned her head toward her sister. "Why?"

Claire tightened her grip on the steering wheel. "Because she knew," she said simply. "She agreed to wear the wire. Admitted to killing Sarah. She could have denied it, could have tried to spin it in her favor, but she didn't."

Fiona frowned, staring at the blurred streaks of headlights passing in the opposite lane. "But why?" she asked, more to herself than to Claire. "Why now? After all these years of keeping it a secret, why admit to it when she knew the police were listening?"

Claire was quiet for a long moment before answering. "Because sometimes the truth just can't stay buried anymore."

Fiona pressed her lips together. "Do you think she wanted to be caught?"

"I don't know. But I think she wanted it out. Maybe she's just tired, Fi. Can you imagine carrying that for decades? Having to relive that over and over again? The guilt alone would be unbearable."

Fiona nodded slowly. She could imagine it. She had seen the weight of it in Dolores' eyes, in the way she carried herself in the final moments before her arrest.

"She looked ... relieved," Fiona said, her voice softer now. "Like she was free."

"That's probably because she is. No more running. No more secrets. In a way, it's over for her now."

Fiona glanced out the window, watching the blur of trees and road signs fly past. "And what about Samuel?" she asked. "What happens to him?"

Claire's mouth tightened. "He'll be charged with fraud, identity theft, breaking and entering, blackmail, and probably a few other things. The DA will want to make an example out of him."

"Do you think he'll try to spin it?"

"Oh, absolutely. He'll claim he was avenging his mother, that Dolores manipulated him, that he's the real victim. His lawyers will do everything they can to throw the focus back on her."

"And what happens to Dolores?"

Claire hesitated. "It depends. She confessed, but it was a decades-old crime. And the self-defense claim might hold up in court, especially if we can prove Sarah Mercer really did threaten Anthony."

"But she covered it up. That's what's going to get her."

"If she'd come forward when it happened, maybe things would be different. But lying about it for years? That's not going to do her any favors with a jury."

Fiona exhaled slowly. "So she's going to prison."

Claire kept her gaze on the road. "Most likely."

A lump formed in Fiona's throat. It was the outcome she should have expected, but it still didn't feel right. She could still see Dolores on the deck of that boat, her hair down, her eyes bright and free for the first time in decades.

She had done terrible things. She had kept secrets. She had manipulated, controlled, and deceived.

But she had also loved.

She had protected.

She had fought, in her own way, for what she believed was right.

And now, she had nothing left.

Fiona reached for her phone again, glancing at the email she had typed to Jacobs earlier. Her fingers hovered over the send button. Maybe she could play some small part in changing the woman's fate.

Go ahead and publish. ASAP. Big news is about to break. We need to be first.

She stared at it for a long moment, then pressed send.

The email disappeared into the ether, and with it, the story she had spent the last few weeks chasing.

Claire glanced over at her. "It's done?"

Fiona nodded. "Yeah. It's done."

Claire gave her a small, approving nod before turning back to the road.

A beat of silence passed.

And then, completely out of nowhere, Fiona blurted, "I slept with him."

Claire jerked the steering wheel slightly, eyes snapping to Fiona before fixing back on the road. "You what?"

Fiona groaned, rubbing a hand over her face. "Imposter Henry. Samuel. Whatever the hell we're calling him. I slept with him."

Claire gaped at her. "When—how—what?!"

Fiona waved a hand dismissively. "Back when I still thought he was Henry Caldwell. You know, before I realized he was a total fraud."

Claire's mouth opened, then shut again. Then, finally, she said, "You told me he spent the night. I assumed you meant, like, he just slept in the apartment."

"He slept alright," Fiona muttered, sinking lower in her seat.

Claire let out an incredulous laugh, shaking her head. "Jesus, Fiona. And you just now decided to tell me this?"

"It's been eating me alive, okay?" Fiona groaned. "It's completely against journalistic ethics to get involved with a source. And I did."

Claire tilted her head, considering. "Technically, he wasn't really a source. He wasn't even who he said he was."

Fiona turned her head toward her sister.

Claire smirked. "So, maybe you didn't cross any ethical boundaries after all."

Fiona let out a dry laugh. "That's definitely the takeaway here."

They both burst into laughter, the tension of the night cracking just enough to let a little relief through.

For a moment, it was just the two of them again—two sisters on the road home, sharing a secret, a moment of levity before the storm that was sure to come.

A YEAR HAD PASSED since the night at the regatta, and in that time, Savannah's infamous rumor mill had run itself ragged. The truth about Sarah Mercer's disappearance had finally been unearthed—her body recovered from its decades-long resting place and laid to rest in Tybee. The news had made headlines, speculation running wild as the city dissected every last detail.

But in the end, the anticipated trial of Dolores Bates had never come.

The prosecutor had ultimately decided not to pursue charges. The evidence, combined with Dolores' confession, painted a clear picture of self-defense. A woman backed into a corner, a mother protecting her child. The years she had spent keeping the secret had worked against her, yes, but they had also spoken to a truth that no jury would have been able to ignore—she had gained nothing from Sarah Mercer's death. She'd had no malicious intent, no grand plot for more wealth or power. Just a desperate act in a desperate moment.

With that decision, Dolores had walked free.

Samuel, on the other hand, hadn't been so fortunate. He'd been sentenced to a year in prison for impersonation, fraud, and obstruction of justice. Fiona had heard he'd just been released, though no one in Savannah seemed to know where he'd gone—or if he planned to return.

Now, Dolores sat across from Fiona in her sunlit garden, sipping tea as if the past year had been nothing more than a particularly long and exhausting social season. The flowers around them were in full bloom, vibrant petals swaying gently in the afternoon breeze. Fiona could hear the faint buzz of bees moving from blossom to blossom, the chirping of birds overhead. It was peaceful here, untouched by the scandal that had once consumed Savannah's high society.

And in a way Fiona had never seen before, Dolores Bates looked at ease—unburdened, as if the weight she had carried for decades had finally been set down.

Her hair, once always pinned into an elegant updo, was loose now, long and silver-streaked, shifting in the light breeze. It softened her sharp features, made her look more relaxed, more *herself*. The severity she had once carried in her posture had melted away, replaced by something lighter. Something easier.

Dolores watched the steam curl up from her teacup. "Do you know how many people have stopped me in the past year just to tell me that they were on my side all along?"

Fiona smirked, lifting her own cup. "Savannah's finest, always hedging their bets."

Dolores let out a dry chuckle, shaking her head. "It doesn't matter anymore." She set her teacup down on the saucer, her expression turning thoughtful. "I've made a decision."

Fiona arched a brow. "Oh?"

Dolores exhaled, as if she were finally releasing something that had been weighing her down for far too long. "I've had enough of Savannah's rumor mill. Enough of high society. Enough of this *life*—the kind where you have to perform every second of every day for people who will never truly accept you."

Fiona set her cup down, watching her carefully.

"I'm done," Dolores said simply. "I have no interest in returning to the social circles, the charity luncheons, the exhausting game that people like me are expected to play."

A slow smile crept across Fiona's lips. "What are you going to do instead?"

Dolores' eyes brightened with something new—excitement. Possibility. "I'm going to travel," she said, a quiet kind of wonder in her voice. "For the first time in my life, I have nowhere I have to be. No obligations, no events, no appearances to keep up. I can just *go*."

Fiona felt a warmth spread through her chest. "That sounds like a marvelous idea."

Dolores gave a small, knowing smile. "I think so, too."

A silence settled between them, the comfortable kind where words weren't needed. The garden around them buzzed with life, as if the earth itself was waking up from a long slumber.

Then, after a moment, Dolores reached into her cardigan pocket and pulled out a folded newspaper clipping. She placed it on the table between them, smoothing the edges with her fingertips.

It was a printout of Fiona's article. The one that had changed everything.

"I never properly thanked you for this."

Fiona blinked, surprised. "You don't have to thank me, Dolores."

"I do," she said firmly. "That article didn't just tell my side of the story—it *saved* me. It turned the tide when I needed it most. And I never thought, in a million years, that anyone would be on my side."

Fiona swallowed against the sudden tightness in her throat. "I didn't publish it to take sides. I published it because it was right."

Dolores studied her for a long moment, then nodded. "I suppose that's why I trusted you in the first place."

Fiona blinked, caught off guard. She let out a short laugh, tilting her head. "What? You never trusted me."

Dolores arched a brow, lips curving into something resembling amusement. "That's not true."

Fiona scoffed. "Oh, come on. You practically threatened to have me sued the first time we met. And then, did sue me!"

Dolores smirked. "Well, you *were* a nuisance."

Fiona gasped, hand to her chest in mock offense. "Excuse me?"

Dolores chuckled softly, shaking her head. "I trusted you, Fiona. You just didn't know it. I trusted you enough to agree to an interview. Do you have any idea how many journalists I've ignored over the years? How many people tried to get me to talk?"

Fiona paused, considering that. "I suppose I never really thought of it that way," she admitted.

Dolores smiled knowingly. "That's because you were still too busy chasing a *story*."

Fiona frowned. "And I'm not now?"

Dolores leaned back slightly, studying her. "No," she said simply. "Now, you're chasing what's right."

Fiona felt a prickle of something unfamiliar—a weight she hadn't noticed before *lifting*.

Because Dolores was right. She wasn't the same woman who had first walked into this, bright-eyed and eager to uncover Savannah's next big scandal. She wasn't just looking for *headlines* anymore. She had learned the difference between chasing a story and chasing the truth. And those were very different things.

Fiona smiled softly. "I guess that makes two of us, then."

"I suppose it does." Dolores lifted her tea cup in a slight toast, her gaze holding a quiet understanding. "You know," Dolores said after a moment, her voice lighter now, "I've always wanted to sail the coast. Just take a boat and go. No plans, no destination—just *water* and *wind* and the open world ahead."

Fiona let out a short laugh. "You say that like you're actually going to do it."

Dolores grinned. "How else would I travel the world?"

Fiona blinked. "You're serious?"

"Completely. I've already arranged for the boat. I leave in a few weeks."

Fiona shook her head in disbelief, but a smile pulled at her lips. "Of course you are."

Dolores just laughed, the sound rich and unburdened.

And as Fiona watched her, she saw it again. The woman in that photograph. The one who had existed before everything went wrong.

The girl who had once been free.

And now, finally, she was again.

epilogue

The Love of a Mother
by Fiona Stevens
Published in the *Savannah Chronicle*

FOR DECADES, the name Dolores Bates has been whispered across Savannah's drawing rooms, passed between porcelain teacups and behind closed doors. She has been called many things—a *socialite*, a *widow*, a *woman of influence*—but more often than not, she was called something else.

A murderer.

The disappearance of Sarah Mercer has haunted Savannah for nearly forty years. Her name became a local legend, a cautionary tale of what happens when someone crosses a woman like Dolores Bates. The rumors painted her as cold, calculating, ruthless. The kind of woman who could make someone disappear with a snap of her fingers.

The kind of woman who killed her husband.

But stories, much like people, are rarely that simple.

Dolores Bates did kill Sarah Mercer. That much is now undeniable, spoken aloud in her own voice, recorded for the world to hear. But the truth is far more complex than the whispers would have you believe.

Because Dolores Bates was also a mother.

A mother who'd spent years in a marriage to a man who degraded her, humiliated her, raised his fists in anger and walked away unscathed. A man who sought out other women, not in secrecy, but in public defiance of the vows he'd made to his own wife. A man who, in the end, cared more about his mistress than he did Dolores and the child they'd shared.

Sarah Mercer was not just Charles Bates' lover—she was the woman who told Dolores that her son, Anthony, was an obstacle. A problem to be dealt with.

It was then, on that fateful night, that Dolores Bates became a woman capable of killing.

She did not kill Sarah Mercer for revenge. Not out of jealousy, nor for power, nor for any of the salacious motives people had whispered about for years.

She did it for Anthony.

Because when you are a mother, you do not think—you act. When someone reaches for your child, you lunge at them. You fight. You protect. Even if it means becoming something else. Something darker.

For nearly four decades, Dolores buried the truth, choosing silence over spectacle, condemnation over explanation. She let the rumors grow like ivy, choking out any chance of redemption, because she had already lost everything that mattered.

Her son. Her family.

The life she had built.

And yet, despite what was taken from her, she survived. She held her head high. She lived in a city that dissected her every move, that *never* let her forget, and she refused to crumble beneath the weight of it.

This is the real story of Dolores Bates.

A woman who made impossible choices. A woman who, when pushed to the very edge, became something the world never expected her to be.

Not a *murderer*.

A mother protecting her child.

And now, after all this time, after all the years spent hiding in the shadows of her own past, she is free.

Not because the world forgave her.

Not because the law absolved her.

But because the truth has finally been spoken.

And sometimes, that's the only absolution we ever get.

So before we condemn her, before we cast the final judgment, we should ask ourselves one question—

What would you have done?

If you had spent years trapped in a marriage where your voice was dismissed, where your worth was measured only by the name you carried and the wealth you inherited—what would you have done?

If you had been forced to endure the humiliation of a husband who no longer cared for you, who paraded his infidelities in front of an entire city that thrived on gossip, who abandoned you and your child for another woman—what would you have done?

If that woman had walked into your home, into the space where you raised your son, and told you that he was an obstacle to *her* future, that he stood in the way of the life *she* wanted—what would you have done?

If you watched as she lunged for your child, saw the madness in her eyes, heard the sharp intake of your baby's frightened breath, felt his tiny fingers gripping your dress as he ran to hide—what would you have done?

If, in that split second, the only thing standing between your child and harm was *you*—what would you have done?

Would you have screamed for help, knowing there was no one to hear you?

Would you have attempted to reason with a woman who had already made up her mind?

Would you have stepped aside and allowed fate to decide who walked away?

Or would you have fought? Would you have used every ounce of strength in your body, every desperate breath, every trembling hand, every frantic thought—to protect your child at all costs?

Would you have done what Dolores Bates did?

We sit in judgment of people like her, the ones who make the impossible choices, the ones who stand at the edge of the abyss and take the irreversible step forward. But do we ever stop to wonder—if the moment had belonged to us, would we have done any differently?

Because when the world strips away the rumors, the money, the name, and the scandal, what remains is something far simpler.

A mother.

A child.

A single, desperate decision.

And, in the end, a truth that any parent would recognize.

Ready for another gripping thriller set in Savannah? Click below to get your copy of *Dead Air*, or continue to the next page for a sample.
https://a.co/d/4eYtxzS

Join the LT Ryan reader family & receive a free copy of the Alex Hayes story, *Trial by Fire*. Click the link below to get started:
https://ltryan.com/alex-hayes-newsletter-signup-1

dead air: prologue

The night was oppressively humid, typical for Savannah in August. Detective Erin Lawson leaned against her squad car, the metal still warm beneath her palm despite the late hour. She wiped sweat from her forehead with the back of her hand and checked her watch for the third time in as many minutes. Monica was late.

They had agreed to meet at the abandoned warehouse at 11 p.m. sharp. Monica had called earlier, her voice tight with excitement. "I've got something big on the Rafferty case. Meet me at the old paper mill warehouse tonight. Come alone."

That last part had raised flags, but Lawson trusted her partner's judgment. Monica Landry had been with the Savannah PD for eight years, two years longer than Lawson herself. They'd been partnered together for the last three years, and for the past eleven months, their relationship had evolved beyond the professional boundaries of the force—a fact they both kept carefully hidden.

Lawson's phone buzzed. A text from Monica: *Two minutes away. Get ready.*

Lawson shoved her phone back into her pocket and drew her service weapon, checking it quickly before returning it to her holster. The Rafferty investigation had been consuming their lives for months now—a drug trafficking operation that reached into the highest echelons of

Savannah society. They were close to a breakthrough. Monica had been working her connections, and it seemed she'd finally hit pay dirt.

She took a long drag from her cigarette, the ember glowing orange in the darkness. The nicotine did little to calm her frayed nerves. The distant thrum of an engine broke the night's stillness. Headlights flashed once, briefly illuminating the crumbling brick facade of the warehouse. Lawson recognized Monica's silver sedan as it pulled alongside her own unmarked cruiser.

"Thought you'd quit," Monica said, nodding at the cigarette as she opened the door.

Lawson flicked ash onto the pavement. "I quit quitting. What took you so long?" Lawson asked as Monica stepped out.

"Had to shake a tail," Monica replied, glancing nervously over her shoulder. Her usually immaculate dark hair was disheveled, and her olive complexion looked pale even in the moonlight.

"A tail? What's going on? Why are we meeting here, anyway?" Lawson asked.

"I think someone at the precinct is compromised."

Lawson frowned. "That's a serious accusation."

"I know. That's why I needed to see you alone," Monica said. "I think someone in the department is compromised. Someone high up."

Lawson frowned. "That's a serious accusation."

"I know it is." Monica's eyes darted around the darkness surrounding them. "I've been following the money on the Rafferty case. The deeper I dig, the more convinced I am that someone's protecting their operation from inside."

"You have proof?" Lawson asked, her pulse quickening.

Monica shook her head. "Not yet. But I have a source meeting me tonight. Says they have evidence—bank records, offshore accounts, the whole nine yards."

"Jesus," Lawson whispered. "When's this meeting?"

"Twenty minutes from now."

"Here? This place is—""Neutral ground," Monica interrupted. "My source picked it. Said it would be safe."

A flicker of unease crawled up Lawson's spine. "I don't like this, Mon. It feels off."

Monica reached out, her fingertips brushing against Lawson's wrist—the closest thing to public affection they ever allowed themselves. "Trust me, Erin. This is our chance to break this case wide open."

Lawson checked her watch again. "Fine. Twenty minutes. Then we take what we have to IA, with or without your source."

Monica nodded, then tensed suddenly, her eyes fixed on something behind Lawson. "Did you hear that?"

Lawson turned, hand instinctively moving to her holster. The warehouse loomed like a hulking beast, its windows black and empty. "Hear what?"

"I thought I heard—" Monica stopped, shaking her head. "Never mind. Probably just rats."

Lawson wasn't convinced. "Let's wait in my car."

They started toward the cruiser when a sharp crack split the air. Lawson felt something whiz past her ear, followed by the metallic ping of a bullet striking her car door.

"Get down!" she yelled, drawing her weapon and pushing Monica toward the ground. They scrambled behind the cruiser as two more shots rang out, shattering the driver's side window.

"My source," Monica gasped. "It must be a setup."

Lawson peered around the car's bumper, trying to locate the shooter in the darkness. Another shot, this one closer, striking the pavement inches from her foot. The muzzle flash gave away the position—second-floor window of the warehouse.

"I'm calling for backup," Lawson said, reaching for her radio.

"No time," Monica replied, her own weapon drawn now. "We need to move. That car won't shield us for long."

Lawson nodded grimly. "On three, we make for the loading dock entrance. One... two..."

Before she could say "three," Monica was on her feet, sprinting toward the warehouse. Lawson cursed under her breath and followed, keeping low as another shot kicked up dirt at her heels. The loading dock was thirty yards away, exposed ground with no cover.

Lawson stood but a brilliant white flood light suddenly blazed to life, mounted on the corner of the warehouse. The harsh beam swept across the lot, momentarily blinding her. She threw up her arm to shield her eyes, spots dancing in her vision.

In that blinding moment of vulnerability, a shot cracked through the night.

Lawson blinked desperately, trying to clear her vision. As the world came back into focus, she saw Monica standing exposed in the flood light's merciless glare, her body jerking backward. A dark stain blossomed across her white blouse, spreading with terrifying speed.

"Monica!" Lawson screamed, lunging forward as her partner crumpled to the ground.

A figure emerged from the shadows at the edge of the light—just a silhouette, featureless and dark. Before Lawson could aim, the shooter melted back into the darkness, footsteps fading as they fled into the night.

Lawson reached Monica's side, dropping to her knees beside her fallen partner. Blood soaked through her clothes, hot and slick against her hands as she pressed down on the wound. Monica's eyes were wide with shock, her breathing already shallow and labored.

"Monica!" Lawson screamed, abandoning all caution as she raced the remaining distance.

"I've got a 10-999! Officer down! Send help immediately!" Lawson shouted into her radio, fumbling with her good arm. "Warehouse district, old paper mill. Shots fired, officer down. Need immediate medical assistance!"

Monica's eyes fluttered weakly, her breathing shallow and rapid. Lawson pressed her hand against the wound in Monica's chest, feeling warm blood seep between her fingers.

"Stay with me, Mon," Lawson pleaded, tears blurring her vision. "Help is coming. Just stay with me."

"Monica?" Lawson's voice broke. "Monica!"

No response.

Lawson barely registered the approaching sirens, or the shouts of officers securing the perimeter. She remained kneeling beside Monica's body, her hand still futilely trying to stem the flow of blood from a heart that had already stopped beating.

Later, she would remember fragments of the aftermath. Someone

pulling her away. The paramedics working frantically. The pronounce-
ment of death at 11:47 p.m. Her supervisor, Captain Richardson,
arriving on scene, his face a mask of professional concern as he put a
comforting hand on her shoulder.

"We'll find who did this," he promised.

Lawson said nothing. Because she knew how corruption worked. It
devoured everything, even the truth. Especially the truth.

Monica's source would never be found. The investigation would hit
dead end after dead end until it was eventually shelved as an unsolved
tragedy.

As the ambulance doors closed on Monica's body, Lawson made a
silent vow. She would find justice for Monica, even if it took the rest of
her life. Even if it meant becoming someone she barely recognized.

Even if it meant becoming someone Monica would have hated.

The first drops of rain began to fall, washing away the blood on the
loading dock. But nothing would ever wash away the memory of this
night from Lawson's mind.

Or the guilt that would haunt her for years to come.

dead air: chapter 1

Lawson woke with a jolt, sweat-soaked sheets twisted around her limbs like restraints. Her heart hammered against her ribs as the nightmare faded, leaving behind the familiar taste of copper in her mouth. The clock on her nightstand read 3:17 AM. Another night, another failed attempt at decent sleep.

She ran her hands over her face, willing her pulse to slow. Five years since Monica's murder, but in her dreams, it always happened yesterday. The flood light, the gunshot, Monica falling, blood spreading across her white blouse—the details never dulled with time.

Her bedroom was stuffy, the ancient air conditioner struggling against Savannah's relentless August heat. She kicked off the sheets and reached for the half-empty whiskey bottle on her nightstand. A year ago, she might have poured a glass. Six months ago, she'd have skipped the glass entirely. Tonight, she just stared at it, fingers tracing the label.

She'd been sober for four months, two weeks, and three days. Her longest stretch since Monica died. The temptation gnawed at her like a physical hunger, but something kept her from unscrewing the cap. Maybe it was the memory of Richardson's thinly veiled threat last time she'd shown up to work hungover.

"You're more useful to the victims sober," he had said with that blunt honesty that still made Lawson wince.

She set the bottle back down. Tomorrow was another day of pretending she had her shit together.

Her phone vibrated on the nightstand, screen illuminating the dark room. Who the hell was texting at this hour? She grabbed it, squinting at the sudden brightness.

A message from Claire Stevens: *I think you're going to want to listen to this.*

Claire was a complicated figure in Lawson's life. They'd started out on opposite sides of the courtroom—Claire the sharp defense attorney who'd overturned Anthony Bates' conviction, Lawson the detective whose shoddy work had made it possible. That case should have made them enemies, but instead, it had forged an unexpected alliance, built on mutual respect if not quite friendship. Lawson had encouraged Claire to take a job on the DA's side after the dust had settled, seeing in the attorney a razor-sharp mind that could do real good on the right side of the law. Claire was still weighing her options, but they'd maintained a wary professional relationship in the meantime.

Beneath Claire's text, a link to something called "Dead Air" with a subtitle: *The 10-999 Tape.*

Lawson's blood ran cold. 10-999. Officer down.

Her finger hovered over the link. Whatever this was, it wouldn't be good. She took a deep breath and tapped the screen.

The podcast loaded, a crisp black and white logo appearing before a woman's voice filled the room.

Welcome to Dead Air. I'm Leah Blackwell, and this is the first episode of our new season: 'Silence in Savannah.'"

Lawson sat up straighter, every muscle tensing.

"Five years ago, Detective Monica Landry was murdered at the old paper mill warehouse on the eastern edge of Savannah. The case remains officially unsolved, with no arrests and no suspects named publicly. But tonight, we're going to hear something that's never been released."

There was a pause, then audio that made Lawson's stomach drop.

"I've got a 10-999! Officer down! Send help immediately!" Her own voice, raw with panic. *"Warehouse district, old paper mill. Shots fired, officer down. Need immediate medical assistance!"*

The sound of her own ragged breathing, muffled sobs as she frantically tried to stop Monica's bleeding.

"Stay with me, Mon. Help is coming. Just stay with me!"

Lawson felt the walls closing in. That call had never been released. It was sealed as part of an active investigation. How the hell did this podcaster get it?

"That was Detective Erin Lawson," the woman continued, "Monica Landry's partner, calling for help that would arrive too late. This recording has never been released to the public until now. Multiple sources within the Savannah PD have confirmed its authenticity."

The room began to spin. Lawson's chest tightened, her breathing becoming shallow and rapid. The familiar vise grip of panic squeezed her lungs. She fumbled for the whiskey bottle on her nightstand, fingers trembling as they closed around the smooth glass. Four months, two weeks, three days of sobriety hung in the balance as she unscrewed the cap, the sharp scent of bourbon filling her nostrils.

She held the bottle just inches from her lips, the amber liquid promising temporary relief from the memories flooding back. Monica's blood on her hands. The light fading from her eyes. The sound of her own voice, broken and desperate, pleading for help that came too late.

With a strangled curse, Lawson slammed the cap back on and threw the bottle across the room. It didn't break, just rolled across the hardwood floor, coming to rest against the wall like a silent accusation.

She bent forward, head between her knees, forcing herself to take deeper breaths as her heart hammered wildly against her ribs. Her hands balled into fists, nails digging into her palms until the pain helped anchor her back to reality.

"The official investigation concluded that an unknown assailant ambushed Detective Landry at the old paper mill warehouse, shot her twice in the chest, and escaped into the night without being identified. But there are troubling inconsistencies in this narrative."

The podcaster's voice took on a sharper edge.

"Why were two detectives meeting at an abandoned warehouse after hours? Why was Detective Lawson the only witness, conveniently unable to identify the shooter? And why, despite an extensive investigation, was no evidence ever found to identify who lured Detective Landry to her death that night?"

Lawson's breathing quickened.

"I'm heading to Savannah next week to investigate these questions and more. Someone knows the truth about what happened to Detective Monica Landry, and I intend to find it. Stay tuned to Dead Air, because this story is just getting started."

The podcast ended, leaving Lawson in silence broken only by her own harsh breathing. She sat motionless for several seconds before pulling up her browser, fingers trembling as she typed "Leah Blackwell Dead Air podcast" into the search bar.

Results flooded her screen. The podcast had over three million subscribers. Blackwell had started it while still in law school at Columbia, focusing on cold cases and suspected miscarriages of justice. Her investigations had led to the reopening of three cases and one exoneration. She'd won multiple awards and had recently signed a deal with Netflix.

Lawson clicked on an image. Leah Blackwell was younger than she'd expected—early thirties, with sharp features and intense eyes that seemed to see right through the camera. She looked like someone who wouldn't back down easily.

Scrolling further, she found what she was looking for: Blackwell's previous episodes. She'd covered cases from across the country, but none from Savannah. So why Monica's case? Why now?

The answer came in the form of a recent interview with Blackwell in a digital media magazine. The reporter had asked why she'd chosen Monica's case for her next investigation.

"I never choose my cases; they choose me," Blackwell had responded. "Someone reached out with compelling information suggesting Detective Landry's murder wasn't a random act of violence, but a targeted hit to silence her. When they sent me that radio call, I knew I had to look deeper."

Someone reached out? Someone with access to sealed evidence and a grudge? Someone who wanted the past dug up?

Lawson hurled her phone across the room. It hit the wall with a crack before dropping to the carpet. She stood, unable to stay in bed any longer, pacing like a caged animal, her breathing ragged.

Five years. Five goddamn years she'd spent trying to find Monica's killer, hitting wall after wall, dead end after dead end. Running up against the blue line that seemed to materialize whenever she got close to something significant. Richardson's warnings still echoed in her ears. "Let it go, Lawson. For your own good."

She'd never let it go, not really, but she'd learned to live with the open wound. To function despite it. To do her job while carrying the weight of that failure. All the while the wound festered just beneath the surface.

Now this Blackwell woman was going to rip it all open again, probing and prodding. And the worst part? It seemed like she suggesting Lawson had something to do with it.

Lawson picked up her phone, the screen now sporting a spiderweb of cracks. She pulled up Claire's number and typed a response.

Where did you find this?

The reply came almost immediately: *It's everywhere. Viral on TikTok.*

Of course it was. The public loved a juicy conspiracy, especially one involving corrupt cops. They'd eat this up with a spoon, regardless of the damage it might do to the department—or to the people who still mourned Monica.

You need to hear the rest of it, Claire texted. *She mentions files that went missing after Monica's death.*

The Rafferty case files. Monica had been certain someone inside the department was protecting the operation. She'd been killed before she could prove it. After her death, key documents had disappeared, including Monica's personal notes.

Lawson had tried to pursue it, convinced Monica's murder was connected, but the case had been reassigned. Six months later, the Rafferty investigation was quietly closed due to "insufficient evidence." Whenever Lawson brought it up, she was reminded that she was too close, too emotionally invested. Eventually, she'd been given a choice: drop it or turn in her badge.

She'd chosen to keep her badge, convinced she could do more good inside the system than out. But the guilt had eaten away at her, driving her deeper into the bottle with each passing year.

Now Blackwell was coming to town, ready to expose everything, with no idea of the danger she was putting herself in.

If someone had killed Monica to protect a secret, they wouldn't hesitate to kill again.

Lawson grabbed her gym bag from the closet and stuffed in a change of clothes. She needed to clear her head, and sitting in her apartment staring at the whiskey bottle wasn't going to help. The 24-hour gym downtown was usually empty this time of night. She could pound out her frustration on a punching bag, then shower and head straight to the precinct.

She had one week to prepare for Blackwell's arrival. One week to decide whether to help her uncover the truth—or to warn her away from a grave she was about to dig.

Neither option would bring Monica back. But at least one of them might keep this podcaster from joining her.

dead air: chapter 2

Lawson hunched over her desk, rubbing her temples as she stared at the stack of case files waiting for her review. She'd managed two hours at the gym, pushing her body to exhaustion in hopes of quieting her mind. It hadn't worked. The podcast, Monica's voice, the accusations—they followed her like shadows.

The desk outside her office remained empty. She'd gone through four partners in the five years since Monica's death, none lasting more than a year. The department had finally given up, letting her work solo. Most days she preferred it that way.

"Detective Lawson?"

The voice yanked her from her thoughts. A woman stood in her doorway—petite, with dark hair cut in a sharp bob that accentuated angular features. She wore a tailored navy blazer over a white t-shirt, designer jeans, and boots that probably cost more than Lawson's monthly rent. But it was her eyes that Lawson noticed most—calculating, intense, missing nothing.

"Leah Blackwell," the woman said, stepping into the office without waiting for an invitation. "Dead Air podcast."

Lawson's jaw clenched. "I know who you are."

"Good. That saves time." Blackwell dropped into the chair opposite Lawson's desk, crossing one leg over the other. "I wasn't sure you'd be familiar with my work."

"Please, make yourself comfortable," Lawson scowled sarcastically. "Who the hell let you in here anyways?" she muttered.

Leah just smiled, as if not picking up on the nuance, or more likely, ignoring it.

"Thought you weren't due in town until next week." Lawson leaned back, keeping her face neutral despite the adrenaline surging through her system.

Blackwell shrugged. "I like to get a feel for a place before I officially start digging. Meet the players, so to speak."

"And I'm a player?"

"You're the centerpiece." Blackwell pulled a sleek digital recorder from her bag and placed it on the desk between them. "I'd like to get your perspective on Monica Landry's murder. Ensure accuracy."

Lawson barked a laugh. "Right. Because accuracy is what you're after."

"It is, actually." Blackwell's expression remained calm, unfazed by Lawson's hostility. "I don't sensationalize. I investigate."

"By obtaining sealed evidence? Broadcasting a private radio call of the worst moment of my life?"

"I didn't steal that recording, Detective. It was given to me by someone who believes the truth deserves to be heard."

Lawson leaned forward. "And what 'truth' is that? That I couldn't save my partner? That the shooter got away? Trust me, I'm well aware."

Blackwell studied her for a moment. "I think you're smarter than that. You know there's more to this story."

"What I know is that you're exploiting a tragedy for clicks and subscribers."

"If that's what you believe, you haven't listened to my work." Blackwell reached for her phone. "Let me give you a preview of episode two. Maybe then you'll understand what I'm trying to do here."

Before Lawson could object, Blackwell tapped her screen and a voice filled the office—Blackwell's voice, calm and methodical.

"Following Detective Landry's death, her partner's career took a significant downturn. In the five years since the shooting, Detective Erin Lawson has been written up for excessive force three times, insubordination twice, and showing up to work intoxicated on multiple occasions. Sources within the department report that she's become increasingly isolated, obsessive about unsolved cases, and resistant to authority."

Blackwell paused the audio, watching Lawson's reaction.

"You forgot the public indecency citation," Lawson said flatly, masking her shock with sarcasm. Her disciplinary record was confidential, accessible only to department personnel.

"That was dropped," Blackwell replied without missing a beat. "But the night in the drunk tank wasn't."

Rage boiled up from Lawson's gut. "Where are you getting this?" she growled, the words scraping her throat raw.

Blackwell just smiled, a small, knowing curve of her lips that made Lawson want to flip the desk between them.

"I have multiple sources, Detective. People who believe it's time for the truth to come out." She stood, gathering her things. "I'll be in touch. If you change your mind about that interview, you have my card."

"I didn't get a card," Lawson said.

Blackwell looked surprised, then chuckled. She reached into her blazer pocket and placed a business card on the desk. "So you didn't," she said. "My mistake."

Without another word, she walked out, leaving Lawson alone with the lingering scent of expensive perfume and the bitter taste of exposure.

The moment the door closed, Lawson snatched her cracked phone and dialed Claire.

"This has to be illegal," she said when Claire answered, not bothering with a greeting. "She has my disciplinary record, Claire. My goddamn disciplinary record."

"Slow down," Claire replied, her voice maddeningly calm. "What happened?"

"Blackwell showed up at my office. Played me a preview of her next episode—all about what a disaster I've been since Monica died. She knows about the drunk tank, the write-ups, everything. Tell me that's not illegal."

There was a pause on the line. "It depends on how she got it," Claire said finally. "If someone inside the department leaked it to her—"

"Of course someone inside leaked it! These aren't public records!"

"Then it's possibly an issue for whoever leaked it, but not for her. She's protected under the First Amendment as a journalist, Erin. She's allowed to report on information she receives, even if it was obtained questionably by her source."

Lawson slammed her fist against the desk. "So what, she just gets to air all my dirty laundry? Turn me into some kind of suspect?"

"You don't have to participate," Claire said. "You can refuse to comment. But you can't stop the podcast. Not unless you can prove actual malice—that she's knowingly publishing false information with intent to harm you."

"She's coming after me, Claire." Lawson's voice dropped, the anger giving way to something more vulnerable. "She's going to try to pin Monica's death on me."

Claire was quiet for a moment. "If she's this prepared, she's not just a click-chaser," she said finally. "She has a goal. The question is, what?"

"To crucify me, apparently."

"Or maybe to find answers about a case that's been cold for five years." Claire's tone softened. "Look, I know this is hard. But antagonizing her will only make it worse. If you're worried about what she might say, maybe you should talk to her. Control the narrative."

Lawson stared at the business card on her desk. Crisp white cardstock with bold black lettering. Professional. Confident. Just like its owner.

"I gotta go, Claire."

"Erin—"

She ended the call, shoving her phone into her pocket. Her gaze fell on the bottom drawer of her desk—the one that held the bottle of bourbon she kept for emergencies. Her fingers twitched toward the handle.

No. She wasn't going to give Blackwell the satisfaction of driving her back to the bottle. She'd find another way to deal with this.

Lawson grabbed her jacket and keys. The Rafferty case files would have been archived by now, stored in the basement of the county records building. If Blackwell was digging into Monica's death, that was where she'd start too.

Time to see just how much the podcaster already knew.

———

Continue the story in *Dead Air*.
    Order yours here: https://a.co/d/4eYtxzS

savannah shadows series

Echos of Guilt
The Silence Before
Dead Air

also by l.t. ryan

Find All of L.T. Ryan's Books on Amazon Today!

The Jack Noble Series

The Recruit (free)

The First Deception (Prequel 1)

Noble Beginnings

A Deadly Distance

Ripple Effect (Bear Logan)

Thin Line

Noble Intentions

When Dead in Greece

Noble Retribution

Noble Betrayal

Never Go Home

Beyond Betrayal (Clarissa Abbot)

Noble Judgment

Never Cry Mercy

Deadline

End Game

Noble Ultimatum

Noble Legend

Noble Revenge

Never Look Back

Bear Logan Series

Ripple Effect

Blowback

Take Down

Deep State

Bear & Mandy Logan Series

Close to Home

Under the Surface

The Last Stop

Over the Edge

Between the Lies

Caught in the Web

Rachel Hatch Series

Drift

Downburst

Fever Burn

Smoke Signal

Firewalk

Whitewater

Aftershock

Whirlwind

Tsunami

Fastrope

Sidewinder

Mitch Tanner Series

The Depth of Darkness

Into The Darkness

Deliver Us From Darkness

Savannah Shadows Series

Echos of Guilt

The Silence Before

Dead Air

Cassie Quinn Series

Path of Bones

Whisper of Bones

Symphony of Bones

Etched in Shadow

Concealed in Shadow

Betrayed in Shadow

Born from Ashes

Return to Ashes

Blake Brier Series

Unmasked

Unleashed

Uncharted

Drawpoint

Contrail

Detachment

Clear

Quarry

Dalton Savage Series

Savage Grounds

Scorched Earth

Cold Sky

The Frost Killer

Crimson Moon

Maddie Castle Series

The Handler

Tracking Justice

Hunting Grounds

Vanished Trails

Smoldering Lies

Affliction Z Series

Affliction Z: Patient Zero

Affliction Z: Abandoned Hope

Affliction Z: Descended in Blood

Affliction Z : Fractured Part 1

Affliction Z: Fractured Part 2 (Coming Soon)

about the authors

L.T. RYAN is a *Wall Street Journal* and *USA Today* bestselling author, renowned for crafting pulse-pounding thrillers that keep readers on the edge of their seats. Known for creating gripping, character-driven stories, Ryan is the author of the *Jack Noble* series, the *Rachel Hatch* series, and more. With a knack for blending action, intrigue, and emotional depth, Ryan's books have captivated millions of fans worldwide.

Whether it's the shadowy world of covert operatives or the relentless pursuit of justice, Ryan's stories feature unforgettable characters and high-stakes plots that resonate with fans of Lee Child, Robert Ludlum, and Michael Connelly.

When not writing, Ryan enjoys crafting new ideas with coauthors, running a thriving publishing company, and connecting with readers. Discover the next story that will keep you turning pages late into the night.

Connect with L.T. Ryan
Sign up for his newsletter to hear the latest goings on and receive some free content
➜ https://ltryan.com/jack-noble-newsletter-signup-1

Join the private readers' group
➜ https://www.facebook.com/groups/1727449564174357

Instagram ➜ @ltryanauthor

Visit the website ➜ https://ltryan.com
Send an email ➜ contact@ltryan.com

—

LAURA CHASE is a corporate attorney-turned-author who brings her courtroom experience to the page in her gripping legal and psychological thrillers. Chase draws on her real-life experience to draw readers into the high-stakes world of courtroom drama and moral ambiguity.

After earning her JD, Chase clerked for a federal judge and thereafter transitioned to big law, where she honed her skills in high-pressure legal environments. Her passion for exploring the darker side of human nature and the gray areas of justice fuels her writing.

Chase lives with her husband, their two sons, a dog and a cat in Northern Florida. When she's not writing or working, she enjoys spending time with her family, traveling, and bingeing true crime shows.

Connect with Laura:

Sign up for her newsletter: www.laurachaseauthor.com/

Follow her on tiktok: @lawyerlaura

Send an email: info@laurachase.com

Made in United States
Cleveland, OH
06 May 2025

16722344R00174